ILLUSION OF SAFETY

ILLUSION OF SAFETY

A ROMANTIC SUSPENSE NOVEL

DISILLUSIONED BOOK 1

K INGRAHAM

ISBN (paperback): 979-8-9995757-2-2

www.kingrahamauthor.com

NOT CROSS   CRIME SCENE - DO NOT

A NOTE FROM THE AUTHOR

Everyone handles grief differently.

In **Illusion of Safety**, Clara is estranged from her family due to differing religious beliefs. When you have to cut someone out of your life—no matter the reason—the pain is real, and you handle that pain in whatever way gets you through the day. The way Clara deals with this particular grief is based upon my own experiences and may look very different from yours.

Similarly, everyone handles trauma differently. Two people can endure the same exact trauma, but they will never address or handle the trauma in the same way. Clara experiences significant trauma within these pages, and she handles it the best way she sees fit. It may look completely different from what you'd expect or what you've experienced. And that's okay.

Regarding cultural and investigative aspects of IOS:

Parts of my Filipino culture are weaved into this book. Some of that includes the way linking verbs are sometimes left out in Filipino English (e.g., "You need to eat" is "You eat!" and "Why did you do that?" is "Why you do that?"). If you notice that during particular scenes, know that it was intentional.

There's a heavy focus on the criminal investigation in this book. I'm not an FBI agent, nor do I have a background in law enforcement or forensics, but I've done my best to research aspects of the investigation because I wanted to be as realistic as possible. At the end of the day, this is a work of fiction—liberties have been taken, however intentional or unintentional. If you happen to have background knowledge in this area and notice something completely off the rails, you are welcome to let me know (truly–that's how I learn!) or simply pretend I've taken fictional liberties.

Happy reading!
xoxo, K. Ingraham

CONTENT WARNINGS

Illusion of Safety is a romantic suspense novel that contains dark and mature themes meant for those who are 18+. While it is not a dark romance, *Illusion of Safety* deals with heavy topics that may be triggering for some readers.

This book contains explicit language and explicit sexual content. Additional content and trigger warnings include: Parental loss (past, not depicted), graphic physical violence, sexual assault (fades to black, not on page); PTSD, panic attacks (on page), familial estrangement due to religious beliefs, references to childhood neglect, abduction, stalking

— ———— —

Your mental health takes precedence over everything. If you have any questions at all, would like more information about a specific trigger, or feel that I missed something, please reach out to me at: author@kingrahamauthor.com

PROLOGUE

DIES IRAE

MY HEAD THROBS.

It feels like a heroic feat just to open my eyes. I can't see. There's no light; no sliver of brightness to penetrate the black depths of my surroundings.

My chest feels heavy. There doesn't seem to be enough air, and I can feel the burn in my lungs with every inhale. Why is it so hard to breathe?

Where am I? Why can't I remember anything before right now?

Darkness overloads my senses; the taste and smell of loam envelop me. It's so strong, I have to fight back a gag. I can feel my heart racing against an invisible force, beating at what feels to be hundreds of miles per minute. I need to fight the panic long enough to think straight, but it's nearly impossible.

I take a small breath to steady myself and make a concerted effort to take stock of my body. Maybe I can figure out where I am.

Restraints.

Coarse, thick rope cuts into my wrists. The skin beneath the rough fibers feels raw. I attempt to break free from the bindings, pulling my wrists apart, but it only hurts more. Nothing I do loosens the rope—no matter how I maneuver my fingers and hands, it won't budge.

Abandoning thoughts of breaking free, I wiggle my legs. They're untied. I kick out, my feet colliding with something hard above me. Next to me. Beneath me.

Wood. The sound of my bare feet hitting the planks is unmistakable.

It's everywhere.

I'm trapped.

Heart quickening, I close my hands into a fist and pound whatever solid surface I can reach. The sound ricochets in the small space, causing me to wince. Dirt drifts down, settling on my face and making me cough, forcibly expelling what little breath I have left.

I still.

No, no, no.

This can't be happening.

How long have I been down here? How much time do I have left?

Memories flash. A cloth on my face. The distinct, sweet smell of chloroform. Rough hands bruising my arms. A sharp pinprick in my neck. Then, nothingness.

Oh, god. I can't breathe.

I know I should save my breath, but the panic doesn't abate; it only heightens to a fever pitch until I swear my heart will give out.

I just need someone to hear me.
So I scream.
Someone help me.
Please.

CHAPTER 1
MAVERICK
THE WALL

AUGUST 27TH, MINNEAPOLIS, MN

Six.

The number of photos pinned to the evidence board spanning an entire wall in my office.

Four.

The number of state lines our unsub has crossed to find his victims. He lures them into a false sense of safety, then holds them captive for weeks at a time only to bury them alive. Sadistic bastard.

Three.

The number of commonalities between the women. Living in a state with no family nearby, working in entry-level hospitality positions, and, of course, their strikingly similar appearances—dark hair, dark eyes, relatively small stature, and each objectively beautiful.

Zero.

The number of leads we have.

Leaning back against the corner of my desk, I scrub a hand down my face and stare blankly at the map. Red pins mark the location where each victim was found; white string connects them together, creating a spider web that taunts me.

Exhaustion and frustration wear me down. I don't remember the last time I slept more than a handful of hours, but there is no time. I need every waking moment to catch this son of a bitch.

The case was assigned to the FBI office in Minneapolis after the third victim—a 32-year-old single woman from Poplar Grove, Illinois—was found buried in the same manner as two others in St. Paul and Minnetonka. So far, the known locations appear to be anywhere from 60 to 380 miles from Minneapolis. What a fucking stretch.

To say narrowing down where he'll strike next has been a challenge would be a severe fucking understatement. I have feelers out in every damn police department in Minnesota and its surrounding states, but it's been five weeks since our unsub has been active.

He's been too quiet.

That's never a good sign, and we're running out of time. I can feel it.

Any day now, he could take his next victim, leaving me with one more face to haunt me in my sleep.

It's why I don't sleep.

As the Supervisory Special Agent for the FBI Minneapolis field office, the weight of catching this serial killer and giving some semblance of peace to the families is heavy. It's a mantle I'm not sure I want to bear much longer. I feel like a failure each time we pin something new to the evidence board.

For as long as the victims' families exist without closure, I'm letting them down. Just like I let *her* down.

Shaking my head to clear my thoughts, I push off my desk and stand in front of the photo of our last known victim.

"What else do we know about Sarah Rodriguez?" I aim the question at my team, the five agents seated around the conference table in the middle of my office.

"She was single, no current relationships of note. Her parents live in Sacramento, California and have been notified. They're on their way to Chelsea and should be there within the next few days." Arlo Grant, the rookie computer analyst, speaks as he sifts through the information he's compiled.

Sarah Rodriguez was abducted roughly two months ago and found buried just off a rural route in Chelsea, Iowa. She was reported missing by her boss when she didn't show up for her Sunday morning shift at Beans & Brew.

"Sarah was buried alive on a Friday." Spencer Anderson turns on the projector and deftly connects his laptop to the device, broadcasting a calendar and timeline of the victims so far. Spencer, a former Marine and the longest standing special agent on the team, has a knack for patterns. I can always count on him to find one, even when one may not exist. If there's a pattern to be found, Spencer will find it.

"Is this a pattern I'm sensing, Spencer?" Riley Morgan

shoots a smirk his way, already anticipating his presentation.

Spencer narrows his eyes in jest at Riley before turning his attention back to the screen. The timeline marks the days and times each victim was reported missing and later found. "So far, local precincts and county medical examiners estimate that all six victims were deceased for approximately three weeks before discovery. Coupled with the missing person's reports and dates they were last seen, our victims have all been abducted over the weekend. Likely on a Friday or Saturday."

"So, definitely a pattern."

Riley's saved from Spencer's comeback by the trill ringtone coming from the inside of my suit pocket. Lucky woman. She and Spencer love trading digs, and I could've used their entertainment to lighten my mood.

I hear Evie Baker and Jesse Hernandez, our resident forensic specialists, whisper to Riley—something about making sure Spencer doesn't make her coffee—as I answer my phone.

"Rhodes."

"It's Cruz." I'm instantly on alert, my body stiffening at the sound of Detective Jonathan Cruz's voice. Cruz has worked for the Rochester, Minnesota police department for decades, and he's been my contact for half of that. I'd trust him with my life. He wouldn't be calling unless he had critical information.

"Hold on, I'm putting you on speaker. I'm with the team." I turn the speaker on and place my phone down in front of me, pushing it to the middle of the table. "What do you know?"

"I need you in Rochester. You and the team."

"Rochester?" I parrot. It's not often I travel to Rochester unless it can't be helped; there's nothing I can do there that I can't do in Minneapolis.

"Rollins Orchard, Rhodes. We found a body. We think she was buried alive," Cruz's voice trails off as though there's more to the story.

I wait a few beats, then press further. "There's more. I can hear it in your voice, Cruz."

Silence greets my statement, so I lean forward and tap the phone screen to make sure we're still connected. "Cruz?"

"Yeah, there's more." His sigh is heavy, causing wary glances from everyone in the room. "There's been a missing person's report. A bartender was last seen about two weeks ago on August 16th. It was called in by her friend who's also a waitress at the bar. The original report never made it to my desk, but I happened to be in the front office when Tamara Martin—the missing woman's friend —came storming into the precinct. She had a picture with her."

In my periphery, I see the projector screen flash and glance that way. Spencer's marked the date on the calendar.

August 16th.

A Friday.

Fucking patterns.

"Don't leave us hanging, man. What about the picture?"

Jesse prods. Patience is not his strong suit, which is ironic considering he's in forensics.

"The missing woman, Clara Santos, appears to be a dead ringer for our Jane Doe. From what I've seen, they could be twins for how much they look alike."

I freeze. My hands grip the armrests of my chair so tightly that it sends pinpricks through my fingers, and I hear a creak in the plastic.

"We're on our way." As I say the words, the team silently packs up and heads out of my office. They know what to do.

Fucking hell.

I knew our unsub had been too quiet. But now there'll be two more photos to pin on that fucking evidence board. That's two more faces to haunt me when I close my eyes.

Seven.

Seven women, dead.

One missing, and the clock is ticking.

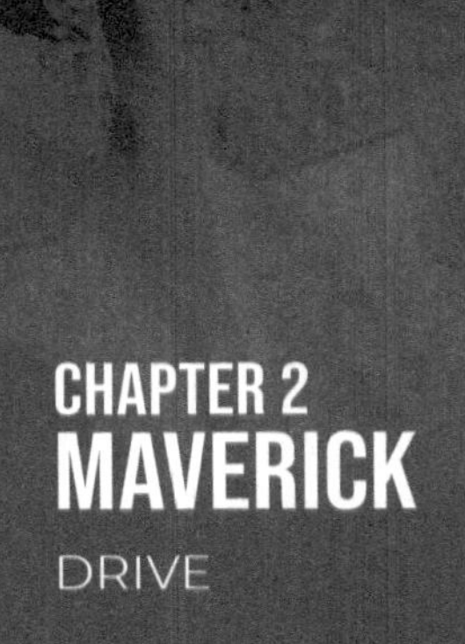

CHAPTER 2

MAVERICK

DRIVE

IT TAKES 1 hour and 30 minutes to get from Minneapolis to Rochester.

I made it in an hour.

Rollins Orchard is a sprawling property, spanning over 175 acres and peppered with trees, pumpkin and produce patches, and numerous outbuildings. Surprisingly, the orchard is only four or so miles away from downtown and has two official entry and exit points monitored by cameras.

The location Cruz gave me led to a slightly less developed area closer to the Silver Creek Reservoir. There are no cameras here, and the only lights come from perimeter lights Jesse and Evie requested Cruz's men set up.

Gravel crunches beneath my tires as the car rolls to a stop a safe distance away from the crime scene. Naturally, I beat the rest of my team here, and the FBI forensics van is still on the way. I step out of the vehicle and take a moment to scan the cordoned-off area from afar, letting the cool breeze calm my nerves.

The calm doesn't last long.

Though I don't need it, I unclip the flashlight from my belt as I walk toward the police tape. I spot Cruz standing on the edge, waiting for me.

Despite the gruesome crime scene, Cruz looks as put together as ever. It's 10 p.m., and this guy looks as though he just got ready for the day. I know him well enough to know that his put-together appearance doesn't match the rolling storm inside him. One of the perimeter lights draws attention to his dark brown eyes, which reflect the dread and anticipation I feel.

"What do you know?" I ask Cruz as I reach his side.

"You made it in record time, Rhodes. Break any laws on the way over?"

It's a rhetorical question, so I don't answer.

He glances at the ambulance on the outskirts of the scene, and I follow his gaze. Paramedics attend to an older gentleman, sitting on the edge of the open truck.

"Owner's brother was out surveying the area this afternoon and noticed a disturbance to the crop lines over there." He points his own flashlight to the hole in the center of the barricade. "Robert," Cruz continues with a chin nod in the ambulance's direction, "said the crop lines should've been undisturbed since this area isn't as developed. There's never really any foot traffic out this way, especially right now. Jane Doe must've not been buried deep enough, or the thunderstorms over the last few nights must've caused a run-off. He saw an anomaly in the soil, went over to check it out. Didn't take long for him to notice the coffin. Called it in right away, but he's pretty shaken up."

"The entire coffin was out?"

"No. Robert said the soil here is pretty uneven. If it's not leveled properly, it typically runs down toward the reservoir. Add in all the rain, and I guess the mud drifted down and uncovered some of it. That's what got his attention. The responding officers uncovered the rest."

I wince, thinking of the evidence that may have been trampled. Not that I don't trust his guys—I do—but when it comes to forensics and evidence collection, only two people have my complete confidence. And they're not here yet.

Donning latex gloves and disposable shoe covers, I duck under the police tape. I keep the flashlight aimed at the wet soil beneath my feet, following the print path from the responding officers to the grave.

I hear Cruz behind me. I don't need to see him to know he's minding the path just the same.

We stop at the edge of the burial site. The sight that greets me causes me to close my eyes involuntarily. My heart beats against my ribcage as I reopen them and gaze down at the coffin.

Jesus. Fuck.

This isn't the first time I've seen a victim buried in this manner, but the shock of seeing a lifeless body, face contorted in terror and hands bound by rope, never goes away.

I scan her hands and note the red, raw skin beneath the

bindings on her wrists. Her fingernails are all but gone, fingers bloodied by a feeble attempt to open the box. The scratch marks are evident on the inside of the lid.

God. What a fucking terrible way to die.

I avert my eyes from the body and scan the surrounding area. I'd bet the unsub was counting on the thunderstorms to cover up his tracks, but it didn't conceal everything.

About 2 yards away, I spot four small holes that don't belong in the field. I'm not able to get any closer without risking contamination, so I drop to my haunches and focus my flashlight on the indentations. They appear relatively small—maybe the size of a quarter—but deep enough that mud hasn't completely covered them up. They're not exactly equidistant: two circles are further apart than the other two, but the distinct shape of a rectangle is clear. My gut clenches at the familiarity.

"Cruz." I stand and call out, nodding for him to come over when his eyes meet mine. "See those?" I wave the flashlight over the circles.

"What would've made them?" He crouches down next to me, careful to not get any closer but still wanting to examine the oddity further.

"If this really is our unsub, those are the markings of a portable table. We think he sets it up and uses it to hold his tools or whatever-the-fuck the sick bastard uses."

At the rumbling sound of approaching vehicles, Cruz and I turn toward the makeshift parking lot. Arlo, Spencer, and Riley exit a black SUV just as the FBI crime scene van pulls into the space next to them, Jesse and Evie at the helm.

We watch as the team rounds the back of the van and begins to haul out the equipment. "Can you tell your officers to help them set up the additional arc lights? Agents Hernandez and Baker are about to light this place up." And knowing them, they're going to expand the main crime scene to roughly 200 feet from the grave in every direction.

Cruz simply nods and carefully treks back to the RPD officers to relay the information.

It only takes around ten minutes before this side of the orchard looks as bright as a movie set. Jesse and Evie walk over to meet me at the edge of the burial spot, followed closely by Cruz and the rest of our team, each of them decked out in gloves and shoe covers.

"Hey, Rhodes. I'm going to video the murder scene within the perimeter, then start on the photos," Evie informs as she checks the lenses on her camera. Both Evie and Jesse are highly trained forensic scientists, but Evie specializes in photographic evidence. She'll record the scene exactly as it is before taking pictures. When we make it to Rochester's FBI resident agency office and sift through her work, it'll look like we're still at the scene.

"As soon as that's done, I want to examine the victim's fingers more closely. My guess is she tore them up real good trying to escape, but if we're lucky, maybe she tore him up real good at some point, too." Jesse's role begins when Evie's ends. His specialty lies in collecting trace evidence, but he'll wait until Evie's wrapped up before he starts his ritual. He'll make sure he collects anything that may get lost once the victim is transported.

"Obviously, we'll have to wait for the medical examiner to determine the time of death, but it looks like the victim has been here for at least a week or two. Maybe even longer," Riley, our criminal investigator, says just as the Southern Minnesota Regional medical examiner approaches.

Sammie Jamison made waves in the medical community as one of the youngest medical examiners in the state. A year ago, her genius and achievement took over the news coverage, which is the only reason I recognize the woman walking toward us. She's definitely not what someone would expect to see when they think "medical examiner." Her blonde hair is mostly pink and thrown into a messy bun on the top of her head. Her brown eyes are slightly too big for her face, and the excitement of a new case is hard to miss.

She stops in front of the group, stepping her red sneakers into shoe covers and snapping on gloves. "Hi. I'm Sammie, SMR's medical examiner. Anything I need to know before I take a look at Jane Doe?"

"I'm Special Agent Rhodes. This is Detective Cruz with RPD, and Special Agents Baker, Hernandez, Morgan, Anderson, and Grant." As I introduce each of them, they offer Sammie a brief nod or a wave. "Special Agent Baker is just about to start on videos and photos."

"Perfect! I'll get caught up on the details while I wait, then watch her in action," she says before casting her eyes on Cruz. "Detective Cruz. Walk with me?"

As Cruz leaves to update Sammie, I turn toward Spencer. "Were you able to get the missing person's report from RPD?"

He nods. "I'm cross referencing the information with the missing reports from the other victims. Clara Santos was last seen at The Pour House on August 16th where she worked until 2 a.m. Arlo pulled the surveillance cameras."

"Yup," Arlo confirms. "I have the videos from The Pour House, both inside and outside. I also pulled external video from the surrounding shops and restaurants, including the ATM camera across the street. I'm going to sift through it all when I get back to the office."

I don't want to get my hopes up, especially after this shit show of a day. But it's hard not to. This is the first time we've been able to hit the ground running before a body shows up.

Well, another one, I think as I look toward the activity humming near the victim's grave.

There's still a chance we can save Clara, and I'm going to do everything in my power to find her.

I let the others down. I won't let her down, too.

CHAPTER 3

MAVERICK
TEARS OF GOLD

IT'S BEEN A LONG FUCKING night.

I help haul the last piece of equipment into the FBI forensics van before shutting the doors and knocking twice, letting the team inside know everything is secure. Evie and Jesse will return it to the resident agency office before they head to their FBI assigned rental for some well-deserved sleep.

That's exactly where I plan to go once I wrap up with the medical examiner. We could have driven back to Minneapolis to sleep in the comfort of our own beds, but it's three in the fucking morning, and not a single one of us wants to make the drive back. Especially since it looks as though we'll be taking up residence in Rochester for the foreseeable future.

The van pulls away and I turn toward the crime scene. Cruz and the rest of the RPD officers have just finished securing and closing it up. Sammie stands at the edge of the police tape, shifting impatiently on her feet. I get it—

she's tired. So am I.

Sammie waits until I'm directly in front of her before sharing her findings. "Based on the body's decomposition, I'd guesstimate Jane Doe has been deceased for at least three weeks. Preliminary cause of death is suffocation. She died slowly. Agent Hernandez collected evidence from her fingers and body, but I'll likely find more during the autopsy. I always do," she says confidently with a shrug before continuing, "I'll give her my full attention and should have something for you by tomorrow. You're welcome to stop by, but I'd wait. Don't wanna waste your time and all. I'll call you with anything I find."

I give her a nod and thank her quickly, then make the short trip back to my car.

Three weeks.

Just like the others.

With all my years in law enforcement, I've learned to trust my instincts. And my instincts tell me our missing person, Clara Santos, was taken by the same sick fuck we've been hunting.

The biggest lead we have so far is that there's still a chance Clara is alive. We're not three weeks behind this time, chasing ghosts and skeletons.

And I've already made the decision to give Clara Santos *my* full attention.

The rental house is quiet as I make my way towards the unfamiliar bedroom. I toe the door shut and drop my duffle bag next to it; I'm too fucking exhausted to bother with a shower.

I check my phone to make sure there's enough charge to last a few hours before I strip and climb into bed, tossing my phone onto the empty pillow case next to me. My body feels heavy like I'm submerged under water, and the second my eyes shut, sleep overtakes me.

What feels like minutes—*seconds*—later, I wake with a start, drenched in sweat. Though I can't recall the details of my nightmare, nor the faces that haunted it, the visceral unease that woke me lingers.

I grab my phone and look at the time. 6:30 a.m.

God. What I wouldn't give for a full night's sleep. There's only so much sleep deprivation my body can handle.

I head to the bathroom and splash some water on my face, hoping it'll ease the grittiness and burning of my eyes. The likelihood of going back to sleep is slim to none, so I might as well get some shit done while I can.

I opt for a quick shower to wash away the remnants of last night—both the crime scene and restless sleep. By the time I yank on a pair of pants, my phone vibrates and illuminates with Cruz's number. It looks like I'm not the only one having trouble sleeping.

"Rhodes."

"I had a feeling you'd be up," Cruz starts. His voice sounds groggy and heavy with sleep. He must've just woken up.

"Sounds like I'm the first thing on your mind, Cruz."

"Only because you're a pain in my ass. I wanted to catch

you before you made it back to Minneapolis. I have a meeting with Tamara Martin at The Pour House at 11 a.m. Her shift starts at noon, and she said she'd meet me there early."

"I haven't had coffee yet. Remind me: who's Tamara Martin?"

"The woman who filed the missing report on Clara Santos. Her friend and coworker."

"Shit. That's right. 11 a.m.?" I make my way into the bare bones kitchen and look at the time on the microwave. 7 a.m. "I'll meet you there. I'm headed to Minneapolis to pick up Juno."

"I bet he misses his daddy. He hardly leaves your side. You got the address?"

Ignoring his remark about Juno, I grunt an affirmative and hang up the phone.

The Pour House sits on the corner of Main Street's historic strip in the heart of downtown Rochester. It's an old brick building, and the only available parking is along the busy street. There's a shared parking garage across the way, nestled between a bank and coffee shop.

As I pull into a parking space, I take notice of the street lamps and lighting. I imagine it's a well-lit area at night, and I'm hoping Arlo is able to pull something from the cameras. I spot the ATM he mentioned, right in front of the bank with a direct view of The Pour House's entrance.

If there's a chance of catching Clara with the unsub,

Arlo will find it. It's 10:45 a.m., but there's no doubt in my mind that Arlo is still sleeping after having been up all night. I shoot him a text anyway and ask for any updates.

Cruz's unmarked SUV appears in the rearview, and I watch as he flawlessly parallel parks behind me. I pocket my phone and exit my vehicle, meeting him underneath the pub house's awning.

"Get Juno settled okay?" Cruz asks as he opens the door and heads inside, stopping at the hostess stand.

"Yeah. He's not particularly happy about the small space, but he'd be even worse if I left him home alone." Juno is a spoiled rotten German Shepherd—the only light in the darkness that is my life. He's been with me since our K-9 training days. Now he's five years old and a little over two feet, large enough to stir up trouble when he's mad at me for leaving him by himself. I don't even want to think about the damage he would've caused if I hadn't picked him up this morning.

Cruz laughs and shakes his head just as a waitress comes over.

"Table for two?"

"We're here to see Tamara," Cruz says as he removes his RPD badge and shows it to the lady.

Her eyes widen, but she nods quickly and leads us to a private booth in the back. "She said you'd be stopping by. It's about Clara, isn't it?"

"Did you work with Clara?" I ask as I slide into the circular booth. I pull my phone from my suit jacket and place it on the table, then lean back and position myself to take in the restaurant and entrance.

"Only sometimes. She usually worked the third shift, and I'm always on the first. We'd only work together for an hour or two if she came in early and our shifts overlapped, but that was rare. Would you like anything while you wait?"

"Coffee would be great," Cruz says while getting comfortable in the booth. He chose the last spot that gives him a full view of our surroundings, leaving Tamara with her back to the door when she arrives.

I signal that I'd like one as well, then turn my full attention on Cruz. "Tell me what you know. What happened when Clara was first reported missing?"

Cruz scrubs a hand down his face, swiping his trimmed beard a few times before letting out a sigh.

That's not a good sign.

"One of our rookies took Tamara's statement and filed the report. He made a few follow up attempts: visited her apartment and questioned the night manager who was working the night she went missing. Surveillance cams show Clara walking out those doors," Cruz nods his head toward the entrance, "at around two in the morning. She had her purse and phone with her. Officer Marquez reported no signs of foul play, and with Clara being 34, he assumed she left on her own accord."

"What about her cell phone records?"

Cruz shakes his head. "Marquez didn't request a warrant to ping her phone because he didn't think there was a reason. We attempted to trace it and triangulate her location after Tamara stormed into the precinct with Clara's photo. It's either dead or turned off, and the last location pinged was her apartment building at 2:30 a.m. that morning."

"Fuck."

"You can say that again. This whole thing is fucked. I don't know what would have happened if I hadn't walked into the precinct when I did. Clara's missing person's report should've hit my desk as soon as it was filed, but it didn't."

My response is cut off before it begins when another waitress approaches the table, our coffee mugs resting on a tray in her hand. A quick glance at her name tag tells me that this woman is Tamara. Clara's friend.

"Thank you for meeting me here," she says as she places our cups in front of us. She sets down small packets of cream and sugar, which Cruz and I both ignore, before sliding into the seat facing us.

"Thank you for meeting with us," Cruz replies with a voice softer and lower than his usual baritone. It's his attempt to appear non-threatening, but it makes me want to roll my eyes.

Tamara offers him a weak smile and a nod. "Clara and I used to talk every day. She doesn't have any family here… or at all, really. It doesn't feel right going this long without hearing her voice, you know?"

I dip my chin sympathetically. "What can you tell us about the last night you saw her?"

"God," she whispers. Tamara places her elbows on the table and leans her head forward, rubbing her temples and running her fingers through her dark, coily hair.

Her voice sounds pained, and the worry for her friend

is written all over her face. She's trying hard to keep the tears in, and I know from experience it's better to say nothing when someone is trying to keep from breaking down, so Cruz and I wait patiently while she takes a few deep, steadying breaths.

"It was a busy night. I mean, every Friday night is pretty busy, but it was really fucking busy. I remember thinking how I hadn't been able to take a break in hours. I usually have time to hang out at the bar when it's slow or while my tables are eating. Clara and I would always talk and laugh any chance we got. It helped the night pass by faster, you know?

"I never had a slow moment that night, though, and neither did Clara. Every time I went to the bar to collect orders, she was busy pouring drinks and talking with customers." Tamara looks down at the table with a blank stare.

"Was she talking to any customers more than others?" Cruz questions, a notepad laden with notes in front of him.

"Uhm… Well, I mean. Clara is the sweetest, and she was always talking to everyone when she was behind the bar. She was—" Tamara's voice hitches and she clears her throat, though it's still thick with emotion when she speaks again, "*is*—She *is* so easy to talk to. They say a bartender is like a therapist. People just sit there and share their stories while drinking. Some of the shit people told her was just unreal; they weren't afraid to get too personal." Tamara pauses and shakes her head. "I remember seeing one of her regulars hanging out for most of the night. He'd just sit there and talk with her, but he always seemed to nurse his drink instead of downing it like some of the other guys."

"Do you remember what he looked like?"

Tamara grimaces. "Like all the other guys? I don't know. There wasn't anything that stood out about him. He wasn't bad looking by any means… White guy, maybe in his 40's, but I've always been a bad judge of age. Hell, I thought Clara was in her 20's but she turned 34 a couple months ago, so take that for what it is."

Cruz looks up from his notepad, and I watch as his eyes scan the interior. I know what he's thinking. He wants another look at the surveillance cameras from that night. Maybe we can find the guy on video, this regular who came in often, seemingly just for Clara. He directs his gaze back at Tamara, ready to continue his meticulous note-taking. "Is there anyone in Clara's life who may have a grudge against her? A family member? Boyfriend? Ex-boyfriend?"

This time when Tamara shakes her head, she does it emphatically. "No. No way. Like I said, Clara is the sweet-est. She's the most genuine person I've ever met. She, uh, is estranged from her family. I don't even think they live in the area. Or the state. She never spoke about them except for once when she said they had a falling out about five years ago. Religious shit, you know? But she didn't have a boyfriend. That girl's a damn workaholic, which is why she never would've missed a shift on purpose. She never called out. I had to practically block her from scheduling extra shifts sometimes. All she wanted was to save money to open up her own coffee shop-slash-bar. She didn't make time for anything else. Except for me. She always made time for me. We always joked that she'd host yoga nights, and I'd run the classes."

The smile on Tamara's face is full of emotion as she reminisces, but the sadness in her eyes speaks volumes.

"I'm sorry," Tamara says as she glances down at her watch. "I have to get ready for my shift. Will you let me know if you find anything?"

"Of course. Would it be all right to contact you if we have any more questions?" Cruz closes his notepad and slips his pen in his pocket.

"You have my number. I'll be here if you need me."

We thank Tamara for her time before she slides out of the booth and disappears behind a door marked *Employees Only*.

Cruz and I are both silent as we process the conversation with Tamara. She didn't have much for us to go off of, but she did mention that regular. The one who nursed his drink while talking to Clara. I know Cruz has already thought about pulling the surveillance cameras around the bar to see if we can find him. I have no doubt that's where we'll be headed next.

Tamara made one thing all too clear: Clara's circle is practically non-existent.

No family.

No boyfriend.

Only her job, her dream, and Tamara.

CHAPTER 4

MAVERICK
DOWN SO LOW

BY THE TIME I make it to the FBI resident agency office the next day, my team has already commandeered a large conference room and set up our evidence board. One of them—Spencer, most likely—painstakingly recreated the board just as it was in Minneapolis.

No.

Not just as it was. This evidence board has more pins.

More locations.

More photos.

More failures.

Except for Clara's photo. It doesn't represent failure.

Yet.

Right now, it represents hope.

A lead.

We just have to find her.

I lean against the door frame and take in the activity.

Arlo and Spencer work side by side, sitting closest to

the evidence board, lost in their laptops. The headphones are a clear indication they're deep in a surveillance dive. When Arlo texted me back after Tamara's interview, he said he was still sifting through the footage. He didn't have anything then, but maybe he does now.

Evie and Jesse are standing at the edge of the table, poring over the photos of the crime scene. Jesse's laying out photos of evidence—they're marked and out of evidence bags. The real evidence is stored safely in the lab, but it's always been helpful to pair evidence photos with crime scene photos.

"I just got off the phone with the ME a few minutes ago." Riley looks up from a photo of the holes left by the portable table near the grave. She's comparing it to the ones left at previous crime scenes. They're not damn near identical; they *are* identical. She rolls her shoulders as though she's been leaning over for a while before continuing. "That woman moves fast; she's already completed the autopsy. The RPD must want to get ahead of the press on this one, considering this is victim number seven. The victim died of asphyxiation approximately three weeks ago, based on the body's stage of decomposition, which lines up with Sammie's preliminary observations."

Riley's eyes catch mine, and immediately I know I'm not going to like what she says next. Her pause has me on edge, and I raise my eyebrow to get her talking.

She sighs and glances at Evie before looking at me once again. "There were signs of sexual assault: pelvic bruising and lacerations. Internal and external."

I close my eyes and breathe through my nose, attempting to center myself and push down the rage threatening to escape.

This sick motherfucker.

Clara's face takes over my vision—dark hair framing delicate features and deep, penetrating brown eyes. Suddenly, she's all I can think about. Is that what he's doing to her right now? The thought is enough to make my knees buckle, and I move from the door frame to take a seat across from Riley.

"What else?" My voice is rough; it sounds as if sandpaper has been rubbed against my throat.

"The victim is estimated to be between 29 and 33 years old. She appears to have been healthy, if not a little malnourished. Sammie was able to take a dental impression and send it off for ID. Jesse collected her DNA last night, and we should have it processed within forty-eight hours."

"Thanks, Riley." She nods and goes back to her photo comparisons as I shift in my seat, turning toward Arlo and Spencer. "Where are we at with the surveillance cams?"

Arlo removes his headphones and places them in their case. "We haven't pulled any definitive information from the cameras. Not from inside The Pour House or outside along the strip."

He pushes away from the table and stands, walking to where I'm seated. After setting his laptop down in front of me, he presses play and points at the screen. "This is the ATM feed from that night. See here?" He points to the timestamp in the upper right corner. "It's 2:08 a.m. when

Clara exits the building and crosses the street to the parking garage. She has everything with her, but she's alone. And then here." He waits a few seconds before pausing the video. "She's waving at someone in the garage. I wasn't able to get a good view inside the parking garage from The Pour House's exterior cams, and they're the only ones with a direct view of the ground floor. There's only a running vehicle and a shadow behind the wheel. I can tell it's a man, but I can't make out anything else."

Dejection fills Arlo's voice as he speaks. There isn't much he can't do, so I know it grates him when he can't get the evidence clean enough for an ID.

"Here." Arlo leans over me once again and restarts the video. "1:30 a.m. Two groups of men walk out of the pub and disappear into the garage. It's possible our unsub was one of them, but we can't be sure. Cruz sent over the surveillance feed from inside the bar, so Spencer is cross-referencing the patrons with these men. He's looking for the regular Tamara mentioned."

At that, Spencer turns his laptop toward us and hits a button on the keyboard. "I think this is him. If I'm right, he's one smart son of a bitch. This guy was in the same seat for hours. You can clearly see Clara filling orders, then going back to talk with him. He chose a blind spot—right on the other side of the beer taps. His face is hidden."

"Jesus Christ. How far back does that feed go? Are you able to see how many times that regular showed up during Clara's shifts?"

"That's what I'm doing right now."

"Good." I knock my knuckles three times against the

table before standing and heading toward the door. "Good work. I'm going to let Juno out before he destroys the rental, then I'll check in with Cruz."

Another day without answers, without leads. We're chasing shadows, and the endless frustration is damn near suffocating.

My feet pound the pavement as Juno leads me down the running trail. This is our third run since yesterday's meeting, but I needed to expel the fury taking residence in my veins, and physical exertion is all I have. Cruz didn't have any updates, the ME said the toxicology report could take weeks, and any solid lead I thought we had is starting to feel like a dead end. A run sounded like the perfect outlet to clear my mind and calm my nerves. The burn in my lungs and calves is a pain I embrace; it brings me clarity, pushing me harder.

In Minneapolis, Juno and I often take long runs down the city streets. The current view of Silver Lake Park is a welcome change from the concrete and tall buildings that I'm used to. Its serenity lies in the calm waters to the left of the running trail and the woods to the right. It's quiet. Peaceful. Just what I need. I breathe deeply, inhaling the overpowering scent of the lake and trees.

There's a wooden bridge up ahead with a small creek running beneath it. I head straight for it, deciding we can slow down once we get to the other side. I loosen the slack on Juno's leash and pick up my pace. He takes the cue to push as far as I'll let him, his tongue hanging out of his mouth as he pants heavily.

Almost as soon as we step off the bridge and back onto the trail, Juno lets out a series of loud barks and veers off the path. He's running so fast that I have no choice but to follow or drop the leash.

"Juno! Juno! Slow down!"

What the fuck has gotten into him?

"Goddamn it, Juno! Stop!" I try to rein him in, but he's not having any of it.

Something's off—he's never done this before. But I trust his instincts just as much as I trust mine.

I take in the area as I fight to keep his pace. The sun has set; the only light comes from strategically placed lamp posts and the full moon's reflection on the lake. Juno and I are the only ones on this side of the water, but I spot the silhouettes of runners further ahead beyond a second bridge. Dense trees span the length of the trail to my right, only a few yards from the pavement. Juno heads in that direction.

I no longer make an effort to reel in Juno's leash. There's no stopping him. When he does stop abruptly, approximately 100 yards off the trail, I nearly topple over him.

"What the fuck, Juno?" I breathe heavily and lean forward, my hands grasping my knees as I try to catch my breath. A stitch in my side makes me grimace. Fucking dog.

Juno whines in response and begins pawing the dirt. He

presses his nose to the soil then continues digging. What's he found?

It takes a minute before I can hear anything besides Juno's whining and my panting. When I hear it, my body goes rigid. I straighten and turn my head to look around. We're a few feet into the woods. I can see the path from where we're at, but I see nothing else; no one else.

But I heard it.

It was faint and muffled.

A scream.

"Hello?" I call out. I expect the screams to get louder—closer—but they're still muffled, and I can't seem to pinpoint the origin.

"Can you hear me?" I call out again, louder this time. The responding screams sound more frantic, and I notice Juno nudging the dirt with his nose. He places his head down, ear on the ground, and lets out a high pitched whine.

No fucking way.

There's just no fucking way.

I drop to my knees next to Juno and follow suit, placing my ear against the earth. "Can you hear me?" I repeat.

Help me! That's what it sounds like, but it's almost indiscernible.

Jesus fucking Christ.

My eyes widen, and I reach for my phone in the pocket of my arm sleeve. It's only years of training that keep the panic at bay long enough to dial 911. I'm practically yelling at the operator, identifying myself and telling them to contact Detective Jonathan Cruz and my team. "Tell them to bring fucking shovels!"

I toss my phone down unceremoniously, keeping the call connected for the trace, and begin digging with my hands. I don't have anything else, and I know I'm running out of time.

She's running out of time.

CHAPTER 5
MAVERICK

CANNONBALL

BLOOD COVERS MY HANDS, making the dirt clump wherever I touch it. The constant friction and pressure tear up my skin and fingernails, but I can't stop.

I won't.

I don't even know how long it's been since I requested backup nor how long it's been since I started digging.

It's Clara.

I can feel it in my bones. There's nothing but desperation driving me—a deep-seated need to get to her before it's too late.

I look up to scan my surroundings one more time. I need something I can use as a shovel because my hands just aren't cutting it. I nearly give up and resign myself to using my hands when I see it: a broken branch. The widest point might just be enough to shovel the dirt faster than I can do it manually.

I hesitate to leave, even though I know it'll only take me thirty seconds to grab the branch and come back.

Fuck.

I need to do this.

"Keep digging, Juno. I'll be right back." Poor boy is out of breath, but he's just as determined as I am.

I make a mad dash to the tree a few yards away and snatch the branch from the ground. It sticks uncomfortably to my bloody hands, but I push back the pain and discomfort. None of that matters.

I resume digging, this time with the makeshift shovel that does a hell of a lot better than I could on my own.

I'm not a religious man. I've never been to church. I've never prayed, but I find myself praying that I make it in time. *If there is a God, please let her be alive.*

Hold on, Clara.

Please hold on.

I'm coming.

10 minutes later

Red and blue flashing lights cast ominous shadows against the trees.

An ambulance is parked directly on the running trail. The paramedics stand outside of the truck with the back doors fully open. Pacing. Waiting. They're frustrated, and I can feel their eyes on me. I denied their many requests to treat my hands. I'm pretty sure I told them to fuck off at one point, which definitely goes against my character. I've always been the one that pushes people to be seen if they need treatment. But tonight? Nothing can make me stop.

Dirt flies up haphazardly from the hole the six of us are

standing in. There's nothing graceful about the way the RPD officers and I are shoveling.

It's a race against time. All else be damned. Evie and Jesse will curse my name with all the evidence I'm likely ruining.

But in this moment, all I can say is *fuck the evidence*.

I need to reach Clara.

I need to see her breathing.

The longer it takes us to reach her, the less of a chance she has.

I can't let her down.

I can't fail her.

Her screams have lessened and become more sporadic. The fact that they're fewer and far between has me moving with more urgency despite the burning and tingling sensation in my arms.

"I hit something!" An officer shouts.

It's just what we need to scramble and pick up our pace.

Almost there.

As soon as I'm able, I toss the shovel aside and reach down to lift the lid. "Help me get this off!"

Two RPD officers rush to help me, then heave the lid onto the ground beside us.

Juno crowds me, wanting to take a look inside, but I lightly push him away. "Go rest, boy. You earned it."

I shift my attention back to Clara, but the sight that greets me brings me to my knees.

My tenure as a Special Agent, and as a detective in Minneapolis before that, has brought me face to face with unimaginable things. The darkness I've seen is a constant presence at night, but I'm not prepared for this.

It's her. It's Clara.

Her face is streaked with dirt, though I can still make out her pale, golden skin underneath. The tear tracks cutting through the grime on her cheeks. The blood on her hands.

But she isn't screaming anymore.

Her chest isn't rising.

She isn't moving.

No.

I won't accept that I was too late. That I failed her.

"Clara! Clara! We're here!"

The paramedics reach me and gently shove me out of the way. I watch helplessly as they attempt to resuscitate her.

I haven't allowed myself to truly panic yet. I've done my best to keep my composure, though there were intense moments where it slipped. Knowing that I failed *again* is a punch to the gut.

I can't bear this weight anymore.

"Maverick!"

Just as I'm about to lose myself to the spiral, I hear my name. I look toward the sound and see Cruz and my team rushing onto the scene.

Evie's eyes are huge as she takes me in, lingering on the bloody mess I made of my hands. "Maverick! Oh my god, Maverick! You need to get those taken care of!"

I hold my hands out, flipping my palms up and down,

then shrug. I'll get them treated eventually. "Clara's more important."

"What the fuck happened, Maverick?" Cruz barks.

I recount the events after Juno ran off the trail, but my eyes never stray from the paramedics who are still working on Clara.

Come on, Clara, come on.

"Jesus Christ, Mav." He wants to tell me I should have waited—I know he does—but he knows better. He would have done the same thing if he were in my position. They all would have.

My eyes narrow at the look the male paramedic shoots his colleague. He's going to call it. I just know it.

He looks at his watch. With a heavy sigh, he says the three most damning words I've ever heard: "Time of dea—"

A large, chest-deep inhale and series of sputtering coughs comes from inside the box and interrupts his announcement.

Alive.

She's alive.

CHAPTER 6
CLARA

HEAL ME

THE SOUND that wakes me is incessant. It's a steady *beep, beep, beep* that makes me scrunch my eyebrows in confusion. Why is there an alarm clock going off? And whose alarm is that? It can't be mine—my alarm isn't nearly that obnoxious—and I definitely don't want to wake up right now. My body feels so heavy, like I could sleep for thirty more hours, which is precisely what I plan to do.

But the beeping doesn't stop. It's almost as if it's taunting me, telling me to *get the hell up or you're going to be late*. Though I don't know what I'd be late for. Isn't it Saturday? I don't work today.

Slowly, so slowly, I peel my eyes open—holy shit, that takes some effort—only to immediately close them again.

Ugh, it's bright. The burn-your-retinas-blinding-white kind of bright.

It's never this bright in my room. Not even when I leave the curtains open and the sun shines through the bay windows, which is never because I don't like bright lights.

Tamara always jokes that I'm like a vampire, preferring to hide away in the dark, but she's not wrong. Give me a dark room any day.

I attempt to grab my phone from the nightstand but come to a full stop when my arm gets stuck halfway across my body. There's a sharp pain radiating from my elbow and a dull ache from my wrists to my fingers.

What the hell?

I'm forced to brave the light and open my eyes to find out why my arm won't move any further. I blink through the bleariness and squint through the sunshine.

Wait a minute. It's not sunshine. And this isn't my bedroom.

I feel my eyes bulge as I frantically glance around a room that isn't mine. Three walls are a crisp, boring white and a large window spans the entire length of the last wall, the one to the right of the bed. The curtains are drawn wide, and I can see the busy streets of downtown Rochester easily.

It occurs to me that it's still dark outside, and I have no idea what time it is.

The air smells sterile, like antiseptic.

I glance down at my arm, following the wires to the IV inserted in my elbow. Huh. No wonder it hurts. I continue following the wires because they don't stop at the IV. There's more. Four cords are attached to my chest beneath a starchy hospital gown, running all the way to a machine illuminated with steady beats. A pulse oximeter is wrapped around my finger, seemingly connected to the same machine as the others.

A hospital gown.

I'm in a hospital.

The thought is so jarring, I let out a loud gasp. I move to sit upright and instantly regret the decision. The pressure I apply to my hands in a poor attempt to sit up is excruciating. I look down and find my wrists and fingers bandaged in white gauze.

My heart beats rapidly, matching the pounding in my head. I try to make sense of how I got here and what happened, but all I get is a sharp, shooting pain behind my eyes. I squeeze them shut, then take a deep breath.

I'm lying in a hospital bed.

Despite the pain in my head, I somehow manage to find my bearings. Reopening my eyes, I scan the room nervously. There's a TV above a board that welcomes me to Clinic Hospital and tells me which nurse is happy to care for me today.

The loveseat in front of the window is empty. So is the chair in the corner across from it. For the first time, I notice that I'm alone.

There's no one here.

I don't remem—oh, god.

Tears fill my eyes and fall rapidly down my cheeks. It's as if a dam has broken and there's no stopping the flow. The once rhythmic beating of the heart rate monitor increases two fold, a warning that my heart is beating much too fast. It only causes a sob to lodge itself in my throat.

The wires.

This small bed.

I feel trapped.

Not again.

The beeping is getting louder; the cadence of my heart impossibly fast. There's no lack of air in this space, yet I'm finding it hard to breathe.

The feeling is familiar. Too familiar.

A door swings open. The handle crashes against the wall so loud, I nearly fall off the bed.

That sound. That bang.

It's all too familiar.

I turn my head to look toward the door, but my vision is cloudy, speckled with black spots. All I can see is the silhouette of a person walking towards me; he's framed by the fluorescent light in the hallway.

The thought of *him* takes my panic to another level. I choke on a scream and shake my head profusely, begging him with each turn of my head to not come any closer.

He stops halfway between the door and the hospital bed. I think he's talking to me. I can't hear him; I feel as though I'm under water.

His face isn't clear, but his warm brown eyes meet mine from where he stands.

Just for a second.

And then there's nothing at all.

Two days ago

I hear a loud crack. It's bone-rattling and causes me to flinch. It takes a few seconds to register that the noise preceded the stabbing pain in my temple, throwing my world into complete darkness.

———————

My head throbs.

It feels like a heroic feat just to open my eyes. I can't see. There's no light; no sliver of brightness to penetrate the black depths of my surroundings.

My chest feels heavy. There doesn't seem to be enough air, and I can feel the burn in my lungs with every inhale. Why is it so hard to breathe?

Where am I? Why can't I remember anything before right now?

Darkness overloads my senses; the taste and smell of loam envelop me. It's so strong, I have to fight back a gag. I can feel my heart racing against an invisible force, beating what feels to be hundreds of miles per minute. I need to fight the panic long enough to think straight, but it's nearly impossible.

I take a small breath to steady myself and make a concerted effort to take stock of my body. Maybe I can figure out where I am.

Restraints.

Coarse, thick rope cut into my wrists. The skin beneath the rough fibers feels raw. I attempt to break free from the bindings, pulling my wrists apart, but it only hurts more. Nothing I do loosens the rope—no matter how I maneuver my fingers and hands, it won't budge.

Abandoning thoughts of breaking free, I wiggle my

legs. They're untied. I kick out, my feet colliding with something hard above me. Next to me. Beneath me.

Wood. The sound of my bare feet hitting the planks is unmistakable.

It's everywhere.

I'm trapped.

Heart quickening, I close my hands into a fist and pound what solid surface I can reach. The sound ricochets in the small space, causing me to wince. Dirt drifts down, settling on my face and making me cough, forcibly expelling what little breath I have left.

I still.

No, no, no.

This can't be happening.

How long have I been down here? How much time do I have left?

Memories flash. A cloth on my face. The distinct sweet smell of chloroform. Rough hands bruising my arms. A sharp pinprick in my neck. Then, nothingness.

Oh, god. I can't breathe.

I know I should save my breaths, but the panic doesn't abate; it only heightens to a fever pitch until I swear my heart will give out.

I just need someone to hear me.

So I scream.

Someone help me.

Please.

I startle awake.

My face feels sticky and wet, so I swipe my bandaged fingers beneath my eyes. The movement hurts, but the pain brings me back to reality.

A sob wracks my chest. I fist the thin blanket and cover my mouth in a futile attempt to silence the cries.

Oh, god.

It wasn't a dream.

It really happened.

I wanted it to be a nightmare.

I *needed* it to be a nightmare.

The coffin. The warehouse. All of it.

"Hey, hey, hey." A soft, smooth voice shocks me out of my stupor. "Clara. You're okay. You're safe now." His voice is deep and calming. It makes me want to believe what he's telling me. That I'm safe. It makes me look up, where I find warm brown eyes staring back at me.

They belong to a man sitting in a chair next to my bed. I glance at the corner where the chair used to be and find that it's no longer there. Its new home is right here, right next to me.

He's close. His hands rest on top of the blanket just outside of my knees. They're wrapped in gauze. His fingers would be centimeters from mine if I dropped my hands. But I don't. I squeeze the blanket tighter and ignore the ensuing pain.

I don't speak. Instead, I resume my silent perusal of the stranger sitting at my bedside. He's older than me by a few years. By all accounts, I should be afraid of him. The last man I saw betrayed me in unspeakable ways, but there's something about this stranger that calms me.

Maybe it's his eyes. They're warm and brown; the color of espresso. The intensity I see there only reinforces the sensation of safety I'm feeling.

His hair matches his eyes perfectly: dark brown with streaks of gray along the sides and in his trimmed beard. It's longer on top and slightly wavy. Messy. Like he's been running his hands through it.

He's wearing a deep blue sweatshirt and matching sweatpants, showcasing 'FBI' in yellow letters at the center of his chest. This man is strong; it's easy to tell, even through the bulkiness of his clothes.

After a few beats of silence, the stranger takes his cue to speak, his voice soothing. "My name is Maverick. I've been here since you woke up the first time. I hope you don't mind." A small smile graces his lips before a serious expression overtakes it. "You, uh, had a panic attack. They had to sedate you to bring your heart rate down. How are you feeling? Are you in any pain?"

I consider his questions then shake my head. I mean, yes, I'm in pain. My entire body hurts, but the throbbing and aching of my hands, wrists, and fingers take center stage. I concentrate on that pain so I don't have to think about the other pain—the one *he* caused when he forced himself on me. Every time I shift my legs, I feel it.

I still don't speak.

"Okay. That's good. I bet you want to know what happened. How you got to the hospital. Would you like me to explain or—"

I'm already nodding before he even finishes the question. I don't want to wait. I want to know what the hell happened, and I want to know it now.

"A little over two weeks ago, you were taken," Maverick starts. His voice is soft and his eyes are locked on mine. I give him a slow nod to continue, choosing to disregard the way my lip trembles and my eyes swell with tears. "Your friend Tamara reported you missing when you didn't show up for work. They, uh, they couldn't find you." He ends on a tortured whisper.

The tears flow freely now. I do nothing to clear them.

They don't know. They don't know what *he* did. What I've been through. I know it isn't their fault that they couldn't find me. I didn't even know where I was, but I can still feel the anger sweep through me.

Maverick pauses, watching me intently with glistening eyes. He sighs and tilts his head down, clearing his throat before he begins anew. "I was out for a run with Juno, my dog. We were running the trails at Silver Lake Park when Juno started for the woods. I didn't know what he was doing, but he heard you." Maverick shakes his head and repeats himself, as if in disbelief, "He heard you. We started digging until backup arrived. We barely made it in time, Clara."

The crack in his voice coupled with his words elicits a whole body sob. I hide my face in my hands, soaking the bandages with tears.

"I can stop. We don't have to go over this right now."

"No!" My protest is a whisper, but Maverick appears shocked at my voiced response and dips his chin.

"Okay." He takes a deep breath, as if he's preparing himself. "The paramedics were on site. As soon as we got you out of there, they tried to resuscitate you. One of the paramedics almost called it, but you finally came to. That was two days ago. You were in a coma. The doctors weren't sure when you'd wake, but here you are."

My head is spinning with everything he's said, but I focus my gaze on one thing: his hands. They're bandaged. Because of me.

"You dug me out? With… with your hands?"

Maverick looks down at his hands, still on the bed, and turns them palm up. "I found a branch to help. Until RPD came with shovels."

"Are you okay?"

I'm surprised when Maverick lets loose a laugh. I simply stare at him. What the hell is so funny?

"Oh, man," he says with a chuckle and wipes his eyes. "After everything you've been through, you're asking me if I'm okay? I'm okay, sunshine. Don't worry about me."

A knock on the door saves me from thinking about what he called me. *Sunshine*.

The door opens just enough for a woman to slip through, dressed in scrubs and a wide, genuine smile on her face. She's older, in her sixties at least, with gray hair thrown in a bun on top of her head. She has a youthful appearance and easy persona about her. I like her already. "You're awake! I'm Rosie. How you feeling, darling? The doctor will be in to see you in a little bit, but I'm going to take your vitals. And I just want to check on you."

Rosie stops beside my bed to check the monitors and IV

line. When she's satisfied less than a minute later, she places a hand on the guardrail and turns to face me. "How about we get you sitting upright?" She waits for my nod before she presses a button on my side of the rail, only letting up when I'm fully seated.

Oh, bless her heart. I didn't realize how much I needed to sit until this very moment.

"I bet you wanna get up and walk around, but I should probably get that catheter out of you first, darling."

I cringe at the idea. Couldn't they have done that when I passed out earlier? I don't want to be awake for this.

I swallow thickly and clear my throat. "Oh. Uhm. Yes, okay." I glance at Maverick and wish I hadn't. He's watching me, but there's a lift to his lips as if he's amused.

"Now, you, mister, need to leave," Rosie says to Maverick. "I'll let you know when you can come back in." She points to the door and waits for him to acknowledge her demand before collecting what she needs from cabinets along the wall.

Maverick pats the mattress three times before he stands and walks toward the door. "See you soon, sunshine."

There it is again.

Sunshine.

CHAPTER 7
CLARA
WICKED

AS SOON AS Maverick closes the door, Rosie pushes a cart with the collected items to the foot of the bed, then gives me a long look reminiscent of my mother. "Okay, darling. We're gonna get this catheter out." The smile she had on her face just a second ago disappears. "Before I do that, I need to ask you a question."

My brows furrow, and I tilt my head, attempting to process what she just said and what question she needs to ask me. She went from jovial to serious in half a heartbeat. "What is it?" I can't seem to raise my voice beyond a whisper, and I'm reluctant to speak.

I'm overwhelmed.

"The handsome gentleman tell you what brought you here?" Rosie nods in response to mine. She mindlessly rearranges the cart items for a moment before she continues. "The doctors did a physical exam when you came in, just to assess your injuries and make sure everything was as it should be."

Rosie pauses, causing my anxiety to increase. At the rate my heart's been beating tonight, I worry it'll give out soon.

"Your physical exam... suggested signs of sexual assault, my darling. Dr. Callahan would like to do a forensic exam for DNA. We can usually get viable evidence within 72 hours, and she wanted to wait as long as she could. She was hoping you'd wake up and consent. We're nearing the end of the 72-hour window now... What do you think?"

"What would've happened if I didn't wake up?" I answer her question with a question because I need to know.

Rosie sighs. "If you didn't wake up, Dr. Callahan would've asked the ethics committee and medical team for consent."

My eyes look in her direction but stare at nothing as I process the implications of that. They want to do a forensic exam to see if I'd been raped. To see if he left any evidence inside me.

I was.

And he did.

I'm scared, and I wish Tamara were here to hold my hand through all of this. I don't even know if they called her to tell her they found me. I want to ask Maverick when he comes back.

The silence is heavy for a few minutes, but I break it with an almost inaudible "Okay."

Rosie looks relieved. She dons a pair of gloves and starts removing medical items from their sterile pouches. "I'll make this quick, darling. I'm gonna remove the catheter. It shouldn't hurt, but you might feel some discomfort."

I nod and squeeze my eyes shut. I just want to get this over with.

"I'm gonna lay your bed back, then I'll sit you up again after the exam." She presses the button that lays me flat and moves the blanket from my legs.

I wince when Rosie removes the catheter, but she makes quick work of the procedure.

"Alright, my darling, we're done! I'm gonna call Shelly. She's our trained Sexual Assault Nurse Examiner, so she'll come in and do the exam. She'll take care of you."

The idea of someone new in the room is too much. I start to shake my head, keeping my eyes closed, when I feel a warm touch on my hand. "Would you like me to stay with you while she's here?"

"Yes, please." I feel like a child. I haven't spoken to my mom in a little over five years, but in this moment? I really, really fucking want my mom. I can't tell if the tears are from loneliness, fear of the exam, or both.

Both.

Rosie gives my hand a gentle squeeze and tells me she'll be right back.

And she is. Within moments, the door opens again, but this time another woman follows Rosie into the room. She's younger—possibly the same age as me—and tall with blonde hair cropped close to her head. As she moves closer, I notice her hospital badge has her name and picture with "SANE" in bold, white letters beneath them.

"Hi, Clara. My name is Shelly. I'm a Sexual Assault

Nurse Examiner. Rosie told me you consented to the forensic exam?" Shelly poses the statement as a question.

"Yes," is all I manage to say.

"You'll be in control of this entire exam, Clara." Shelly speaks softly and cautiously, the way someone would to a wounded animal. I'm not sure how I feel about that, despite knowing she's just trying to keep me calm. "You can refuse any part of it. If you'd like to collect the evidence yourself, I can walk you through that."

Wait, what? Collect the evidence myself? No. I don't want to do that.

The look on my face must broadcast what I'm thinking because Shelly quickly adds, "You don't have to do it; it's just an option available to you if at any point you're uncomfortable. Remember, you have full control over the exam. I'll ask permission before we start and before I collect any evidence. I'll tell you exactly what I'm doing and explain every step. If any part of the exam is uncomfortable, tell me, and I'll stop."

Maybe I do like Shelly.

"You also have the option of getting an STD test. I can do that for you while I'm here, if that's something you'd like. We can also talk about birth control if you aren't on it."

My head is reeling. I hadn't even thought about any of those things. I have a birth control implant, and I've never been more thankful for it. But an STD? That bastard could've given me something.

"I'm on birth control. I have an implant." My voice cracks as I speak. "And I'd like an STD test, please."

"Okay, Clara. We can do that. Are you ready? Remember, you have full control."

No.

No, I'm not ready, but I nod reluctantly anyway.

I've read books where the female main character disconnects from her body during traumatizing events. She would somehow dissociate and find solace in her mind. It's a survival strategy. A coping mechanism. I tried to do it when Shelly was collecting evidence from me, but I suppose there's a reason it's called fiction.

It didn't work.

Or maybe I just couldn't *not* focus on what she was doing. It was hard to disconnect when she was constantly asking for permission to touch me. I appreciated it, but I also just wanted to pretend it wasn't happening.

I felt raw.

Exposed.

Once the exam was over, Rosie helped me shower. She brushed my hair, then gave me a hug and told me she'd be back to check on me soon. She said she'd ask Dr. Callahan about food. I nodded, but I'm not hungry. I don't even think I can eat. I hope she doesn't come back with a food tray.

I asked her to turn off the lights before she left, but as soon as the room went dark, my heart rate skyrocketed, and my breathing turned shallow. She had to turn them back on.

The lights illuminate every inch of this hospital room, and the bathroom door is wide open. That light is on, too. None of it brings me comfort.

My body is exhausted. Hell, *I'm* exhausted. I'm terrified of sleeping. What if I wake up and find that this is all a dream? That I never left that godforsaken wooden box? Or maybe *that* was a nightmare, and I'm really still in that warehouse. I don't want to chance it. So, instead, I lay the bed back and pull the sheets over my head, curling into a ball with my back against the guard rail.

Beneath the blanket, tucked in my cocoon, I crumble. The pillow is soaked with tears, and I shake uncontrollably.

I hate what he's done to me.

I hate that I don't feel like myself.

I'm deathly afraid he's taken pieces of me I'll never get back.

CHAPTER 8
MAVERICK
MIND OVER MATTER

THE LAST TWO days have felt like the longest days of my life.

Forty-eight hours.

That's how long Clara was in a coma.

I drove the nurses and doctors crazy each time I asked them for an update. *When will she wake up? How long will she be like this? Isn't there* something *you can do?* I couldn't be satisfied with their answer—that this is normal after the trauma she's been through, that her body needs time to heal. Not when every time I walked into that hospital room, she was lying so still in that bed.

Practically lifeless.

It was only the constant beeping from the monitors that reassured me. As long as the beats were steady, she was alive.

I was on my way back from checking on Juno when I saw hospital staff rush toward her room. I started running before my brain had a chance to catch up. I made my way through the throng of doctors and nurses, utterly desperate and forgoing all niceties.

That's when I saw her.

The monitor alarms were going haywire, but it was the look on her face that stopped me dead in my tracks. She had tears running down her cheeks, and she was shaking her head *no* so forcefully, I felt a pang in my chest.

The moment her brown eyes locked with mine, I knew I wouldn't leave her side again. I stood sentry in the corner of her room as the doctor assessed her and the nurses administered a sedative. To calm her and bring her heart rate down, they told me.

Seeing Clara in that coffin looking like I was too late to save her... Knowing that she would've been lying in the morgue instead of a hospital bed if Juno and I hadn't gone for a run. If we hadn't gone to that running trail. If Juno hadn't heard her. Just the thought of any other outcome where Clara isn't here is enough to wreck me.

A deep sigh escapes, unbidden. I lean my head back against the wall and close my eyes. These stiff plastic chairs are torture on my body; there's no comfort to be had. I'm getting old.

The waiting room is only two doors down from Clara, but I feel antsy being even this far away. What if she has another panic attack and no one is there for her? I don't like the thought of that.

A buzzing against my leg brings me back to the present. I shift and reach into the pocket of my sweatpants for my phone.

Spencer.

My team has kept me in the loop over the last few days. I've pretty much taken residence in Clara's room, working on my laptop from the corner and only leaving to eat and spend some time with Juno. He's been staying at Arlo's house in Rochester, but he's been a little high strung since the other night. Evie and Jesse cursed my name, like I knew they would, when they went back to collect evidence from the crime scene. Cruz cordoned off the entire section of the park, and those two worked double time.

"Spencer, talk to me."

"We got the surveillance videos from Clara's apartment. A black Toyota Camry pulls into the parking lot and stops right in front of her building at 2:28 a.m. It's difficult to see inside the car with the camera's angle, but we can see through the back windshield. It looks like a possible scuffle. The passenger moves to exit the vehicle as the driver leans toward them. The car drives off at 2:31 a.m. No one got in or out."

"Those timestamps are in line with what Cruz said about the last location of Clara's phone. That's gotta be her in the car. Were you able to get plates?"

"A partial. Cruz is running it through the database. Is Clara awake yet?"

"She woke a few hours ago, but she had a panic attack and they had to sedate her. I was there when she woke up again. Been about an hour."

"Did she say anything?"

"No. I didn't ask. I asked her if she wanted me to explain how she got to the hospital."

"You told her?"

I nod, even though he can't see it. "She asked me if I was okay after I told her about Juno. She saw my bandages. A nurse came in and kicked me out, so I'm waiting until I get the all clear to head back in. I texted Cruz to let him know, and he'll be here within the next few hours."

"Hopefully she's able to identify the fucker. Speaking of identification, the DNA results came back on our Jane Doe."

"That was fast."

"Yeah, seems they move pretty fucking quick when a serial killer is involved. Jane Doe came back as Catherine Bennett. 31, single, worked as a cashier at Walmart in Chatsworth, Iowa. As far as we know, she has no family or next of kin."

"Fuck. She matches every single criteria."

"Yup. It's him. No doubt it's our unsub."

"We need to find this son of a bitch," I growl. I will do everything in my power to make sure this bastard goes down. And I'll never admit it out loud, but I wouldn't be opposed to finding him a permanent place six feet underground. It'd be more than he deserves.

"It'll be easier when we know who we're looking for."

"I'll call you after Cruz and I talk to Clara. Keep me updated with anything else."

Spencer makes a sound of acknowledgment then hangs up the phone.

How the hell did one man dig a six foot hole *by himself* in a public park without being seen? And then to bury a body and cover the grave on his own? I'm struggling to understand it. It's like this guy is a chameleon, blending seamlessly into his surroundings and going completely unnoticed.

I take a deep breath. The hatred I feel for this guy grows by the second. Every time I learn something else, every time we have new evidence, the hatred just festers.

Now that Clara's been found? The manhunt is on.

And I intend to hunt.

It's been about two hours since I got off the phone with Spencer, and I'm still in this damn waiting room. The nurses gave me an exasperated look when I approached to see if Rosie was still with Clara. Apparently, the fact that I'm an FBI agent does nothing for these women. No blurred lines. No special treatment. I suppose that's a good thing. Except for right now.

Just as I consider checking in with the nurse's station *again*, Rosie pops her head in. "Maverick?" We're on a first name basis now, considering I refuse to leave. "You can go in now. She might be asleep, though."

"Thank you, Rosie." I flash her a smile as I make my way out of the waiting area and down the hall.

By the time I make it to Clara's room, she's curled in bed, completely covered with the blanket and positioned right up against the guard rail. I move to turn the lights off but notice the human-sized ball is moving.

No, not moving. Shaking.

I abandon the light switch and reach Clara in three strides. She's still shaking, and I can hear sniffling.

Fuck. She's crying.

"Clara?" I keep my voice low, almost a whisper. My hand automatically goes to pull the blanket back so I can see her face, but I stop myself before I make contact. She might not want me to touch her. "Clara, sunshine, it's Maverick."

"Maverick," she whimpers as she lowers the white fabric down to her chin.

The sight of her breaks my heart. She looks fragile. Her face is tear-streaked, her eyes puffy and bloodshot. How long has she been crying?

"I'm here, sunshine."

"Will you stay?" Her question trembles with emotion, and I immediately make my way to the chair beside her bed.

"Of course I will. Are you okay?" It's probably a dumb question, but I've never been very good with women in tears.

She shakes her head, then surprises me by flipping onto her other side—the side facing me—and reaching for my hand. I thread my fingers through hers and rest them on top of the mattress.

"I don't know how to describe how I'm feeling. A nurse came in with Rosie. She did an exam... to, uh, collect evidence." Clara wriggles her other hand free from beneath the blanket and wipes the tears from her eyes.

I have to make an effort to keep my hands relaxed. The fact that she had to undergo a forensic exam makes my blood boil. This woman has been through so much. Despite her fragility in this moment, Clara is strong.

"You don't have to describe how you're feeling, Clara. You just need to let yourself feel it. I don't know everything you've been through yet, but I know you're strong. You're a fighter."

"I don't feel strong." She keeps her eyes locked on mine as she speaks, letting me see her vulnerability. "I hate bright lights, but I can't stand the dark anymore. I almost had another panic attack when Rosie turned them off. I feel… violated. Like a different person. And I'm really fucking tired."

"I'm not really good at this, and I don't want to say the wrong thing…" After all the death and violence I've seen, talking to this woman at her most vulnerable is harder than I thought. "You've been through hell. No one walks away from that feeling the same. But you're still you."

"You don't know me," she whispers, but there's a small smile on her face that tells me I might've said something right.

"I know enough. Why don't you get some sleep?"

"I can't." I have to strain to hear her, as if she said it more to herself.

"Why can't you?"

"I'm scared that I'll wake up and this will all be a dream."

"It's not a dream, sunshine. You're safe. I've got you." I tighten my fingers around hers, hoping she finds comfort. "Sleep, Clara. I'm not going anywhere."

She closes her eyes and keeps her hand in mine. Within minutes, the steady cadence of her pulse tells me she's asleep. Good. She needs it. There's this innate sense of protection I feel for her. More than that, I feel responsible for her. For her well-being. For her happiness.

Carefully, I use my free hand to pull out my phone and send a text to Cruz.

Maverick
Don't come tonight. She's asleep.

Cruz
I'll be there tomorrow morning.

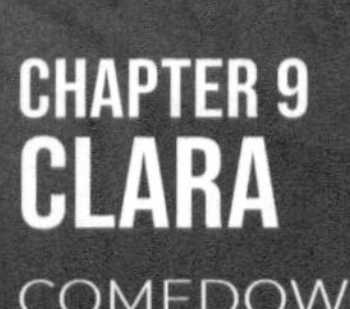

CHAPTER 9
CLARA

COMEDOWN

IT'S STILL EARLY when I wake. Through the half-drawn curtains, I can see the sun beginning to crest over the horizon. The city below starts to stir with activity. And here I am, lying in a hospital bed. When was the last time I breathed in fresh air? God, what I wouldn't give to sit outside right now.

A heavy weight across my legs brings my attention from the window to the man slumped over me. Maverick is snoring lightly, his head resting on his arm. He's facing me, and my eyes linger on his soft, unguarded expression. His hand is still in mine, and the warmth from his skin is grounding. Miraculously, I don't feel trapped.

I feel safe.

But I really need to use the bathroom.

"Maverick," I whisper while attempting to stealthily pull my hand from his.

Apparently, I'm not very stealthy because Maverick

jerks awake as soon as he feels my fingers slide against his palm. "Clara? What's wrong?"

"Nothing. Nothing's wrong. I just have to use the bathroom."

"Oh. Right." He sits up and leans back in his chair to give me space. As I gingerly climb off the mattress, he raises his arms above his head and stretches with a groan. A series of small pops and cracks has my eyes widening, and I pause to look at him. "I'm getting old and rusty," he tells me with a sheepish smile.

I shake my head and roll my eyes, heading toward the bathroom. Old and rusty. Sure, there's some salt in his pepper, but Maverick can't be older than 42. Hardly old and rusty.

I quickly use the bathroom and wash my hands. I'm careful to keep my wrists out of the water; Rosie removed the bandages on my fingers, but she re-wrapped my wrists after the shower. They still ache, and I can feel the tender skin beneath the gauze.

A couple of fresh toothbrushes were left on the counter yesterday, and I take the time to brush my teeth. I ignore my reflection in the mirror, fixating my gaze on the running water instead.

I don't feel like myself, and I know I don't look like myself either. I don't particularly want to see what a mess I am right now.

A knock startles me. "Clara? You okay in there?"

Maverick.

"I'm fine," I call out, rinsing my toothbrush and wiping my hands on the towel. I must've zoned out.

Two nurses—Rosie and a woman who looks like a younger version of her—are standing next to my bed when I step out of the bathroom. I glance around, searching for Maverick. When I see him sitting on the loveseat, phone in hand, my shoulders drop, releasing tension I didn't know I was holding. He gives me a reassuring nod.

Rosie is the first of the nurses to spot me. "Clara, darling. This is Sarah. She's gonna be your nurse today."

I try to hide my frown, but I'm pretty sure I fail. I didn't consider the fact that Rosie would be going home today and I'd have a new nurse.

"Don't you worry. I'll be back this evening, if you're still here, and Sarah will take good care of you. Now come over here and let me take your vitals." She pats the bed, signaling where she wants me.

I do as she says and maneuver my way back into bed, simultaneously pulling up the covers. While Rosie takes my blood pressure, checks the bandages, and gives Sarah her report, I notice a tray of food on the table. My stomach takes that as a cue to let out a loud rumble.

"We're almost done, then you can eat. And eat it all, darling. You need the energy," Rosie tells me, amusement lacing her tone.

"Your wrists are looking good," Sarah observes. "How's your pain? Do you need any pain meds?"

"No, I think I'm okay. It's manageable." There's a throbbing in my head that hasn't quite gone away since I woke up yesterday, but I don't need anything for it.

"Okay, well. If you need anything, press the call button, and I'll be right here."

"Thank you. And thank you, Rosie." I'm going to miss her today. Her kindness last night brought me back from the edge.

She made me feel human again.

"Of course, my darling." Rosie gives my arm a light squeeze, then fixes her face into a stern expression. Like a mother scolding her daughter. "Now eat up. You haven't eaten."

I nod and smile in her direction, watching as both nurses leave my room.

The moment the door shuts behind them, Maverick is there, pushing the table over my legs and sitting my bed up. "You heard the lady."

"I could've done that myself, you know." I reach for the lid and set it to the side. I can't help the involuntary jig of excitement when I take in the food. Eggs. A yogurt parfait with granola. Toast. Orange juice. And coffee. It's hospital coffee, which likely equates to watery black bean juice, but it's still coffee. I dive in.

"You absolutely could've."

I'm stuffing my face, ready to bring the next bite of eggs to my mouth when I pause. Shoot. He doesn't have breakfast. Here I am eating in front of him, and he doesn't even have breakfast. "Uhm... Do you want some? Are you hungry?"

"I'm not eating your food, sunshine." There's mirth in his eyes when he looks at me, and he reaches out to lightly tap my bent elbow. A silent command to take the bite. He doesn't have to tell me twice. "Detective Cruz is going to stop by, if that's all right. He's a friend of mine, but he's also working on your case. And he's bringing me breakfast, so don't worry about me."

"I'm glad because I would've shared, but I didn't really want to." I pause and consider the fact that his friend is a detective, working my case, and he's coming here. There's no way it's just to drop off something for Maverick to eat. "He's going to want to question me, isn't he?"

Maverick nods. "Yes. If you don't think you're up for it, we can wait a little longer. But your statement might give us a break in the case."

"Okay. I'll try. But first, do you know if Tamara knows I'm here?"

"We can ask Cruz. He's kept in contact with her."

Thirty minutes later, there's a tap on the door. Maverick must know it's Cruz because he stands up to let him in.

"Clara, this is Detective Jonathan Cruz." Maverick introduces the detective who trails behind him, a white bag in one hand and a tray of coffee in the other. He's as tall as Maverick, who looks to be nearly a foot taller than me. Hispanic, with dark hair and kind, light brown eyes. He looks like a detective with his trimmed beard and gray suit.

I spy three cups and immediately decide I like him. It's probably a consolation coffee because he's going to make me relive the nightmare I've been through, but it's from one of my favorite coffee shops so I'll take it. That is, if the third cup really is for me. If not, he'll get the silent treatment.

"Hi Clara. I'm Detective Cruz. You can call me Jonathan or Cruz, like this guy does." He sets the coffee tray on the side table next to the loveseat, then shoves the bag at Maverick's chest. "Here. I don't want any complaints. You get what you get."

I roll my lips between my teeth to stifle a grin. Cruz notices and winks, then lifts one of the coffee cups and raises it in my direction. A wordless question. Do I want it? I'm already nodding. Yes, please.

Maverick takes the coffee from Cruz and sets it in front of me, then takes a seat and pulls out whatever Cruz brought him. A breakfast sandwich.

"I know it's still early, but I need to ask you a few questions," Cruz starts.

"And you brought me coffee in hopes I'd answer them all." I level him with a look, but there's no heat behind it.

"Guilty." He waits until I gesture for him to get on with it, then digs a hand in his suit jacket and removes a small notepad and pen. "What can you tell us about the night you disappeared?"

The night I disappeared.

The night *he* drove me home after work only to drug me and hold me captive.

The night I learned that I'm not as great a judge of character as I thought.

Two weeks ago

I've been on my feet all night, unable to take a break since I clocked in.

Fridays are typically busy for us at The Pour House. So many customers come in to drown out their sorrows and shitty work weeks. I don't judge them; I'd do the same thing if I weren't slinging drinks behind the bar. But tonight? Tonight is unusually busy, and I'm ready for a little respite.

I spy Tamara flitting between her tables, hustling to pick up food from the kitchen and drinks from the end of the bar. Any other night, we'd have time to gossip and give each other shit, just because we can. The long hours pass by much faster when we can spend them laughing.

From the corner of my eye, I spot a familiar head of dirty blonde hair and smile in anticipation.

Samson has been coming to The Pour House for a couple of weeks now, always during my late shifts. He's claimed the spot to the left of the beer taps tucked between the dispenser and wall post, giving us the illusion of privacy. No one typically sits there because it's relatively closed off. They want to socialize with their friends and other patrons. So when Samson comes, it's always available.

Excitement courses through me at the sight of him taking his usual seat. If I can't spend the night talking with Tamara, my new regular is the next best thing. He's charming and handsome with his man bun and brown eyes. I've found myself wondering what he looks like in glasses. I can see the outline of his contacts, and I think Samson in glasses would be a dangerous combination.

I finish drying a glass and set the rag down, making my

way to his spot and stopping directly in front of him. "Hey, you. Want your usual?"

"Yes, ma'am." Samson has a bad habit of calling me ma'am, no matter how many times I tell him not to. I think he does it just to get a rise out of me; the banter comes easy with him. Sometimes he calls me Clar, and I find I miss the amused tone he uses when he calls me ma'am. Like I'm some well-to-do woman.

"I'm not an old lady, Samson. In fact, I'm pretty sure I'm younger than you. Stop calling me ma'am." I roll my eyes, swiftly moving to prepare his usual order: A whiskey neat. Blanton's. Three fingers. He spends most of the night sipping it while we talk in between serving other patrons, and he never orders more than two.

His chocolate brown eyes watch every move I make. It was unnerving when he first showed up, but now I enjoy the way he watches me. Almost as if it's all he wants to do. I slide his drink toward him and signal that I'll be right back.

With practiced ease, I fill a number of orders and place them down along the bar. I can still feel his eyes on me while I work. By the time I make my way back to him, it's been ten minutes of nonstop movement, and I eagerly rest against the counter.

"Busy night?" he asks. His voice is deep and husky. I like it.

"God, like you wouldn't believe. I think this is the first time I've been able to stand still since I got here, and I'm not even sure how long this will last."

"You need a night off, Clar."

"I know, but I can't. My car is in the shop. It needs a new battery, and lord knows what else they'll find while it's there." I've had my car for ten years now, a little Mazda CX-3. I'm thankful it's lasted me this long, but buying a new car—or spending a shit ton on repairs—is not on my list of things to do.

Samson straightens when I tell him about my transportation predicament, and I pretend not to notice the look of disapproval on his face. "How are you getting to work and back if your car is in the shop?"

"Oh, I hitch a ride with Tamara. She's like my own personal chauffeur," I say as I search for her in the crowd. She's flirting with a table full of frat boys, earning her tips like the bad ass she is. "Sometimes I take an Uber when I have to close and she gets off earlier, like tonight." I bring my attention back to Samson and shrug. "It's not a big deal."

"How about I give you a ride home tonight?" At the look on my face, Samson lets out a chuckle and quickly adds, "Just a ride home. It'll save you money, and you won't have to wait for an Uber."

I hesitate. I like Samson, and he's been nothing but kind to me since the very first drink I served him. He's shown an interest in my life and knows my dream of owning a coffee shop. He's easy to talk to. Comfortable.

"I don't want you to go out of your way for me. I'm here until two. That's a couple more hours."

"I wouldn't have offered if I didn't want to do it, Clara." When I simply look at him, he adds, "I insist, ma'am."

Taking an Uber and trusting a stranger to bring me

home safely has always made me anxious. At least Samson isn't a stranger. What could it hurt? And hell, maybe this could be the push he needs to see me outside of work. I think I might like that.

"Okay. Sure, you can give me a ride home."

Two hours later, I say goodnight to my shift manager and head out. I'm not sure why I'm nervous, but I am. I try to shake the feeling as I walk across the street to the parking garage where Samson said he'd be waiting.

Halfway there, a man steps out of a dark Toyota Camry and waves me down. It's Samson. I smile and wave back, hustling over to him. He opens the passenger side door, letting me slide inside before he closes it and walks around the car.

The ride to my apartment isn't uncomfortable. Samson continues to be his charming self and engages me in conversation, asking me how the rest of my night went and if I work tomorrow. The nervous feeling from earlier is gone, and I'm content sharing stories and sitting in occasional silence.

When Samson pulls up in front of my apartment building, he parks and turns toward me. "Would you like me to walk you inside?"

"I think I can make it." I offer him a smile and reach over to squeeze his hand resting on the gear shift. Any other night, I'd entertain the idea of inviting him inside. Not tonight, though; I'm too exhausted. My bed is calling me. "But thank you so much, Samson. You have no idea how much I appreciate you."

An emotion I can't name flickers over his face before he

hides it with a smile. "You're welcome, ma'am. Any time you need a ride, you let me know. I'd be happy to do it."

I shake my head at his antics, then, before I can talk myself out of it, I lean forward and press a kiss to his cheek.

"Thank you again, Samson." As soon as the words leave my lips, I collect my purse and move to get out. The passenger door isn't even halfway open before I'm jerked back. A cloth is pressed tightly against my face, covering my nose and mouth. I fight to free myself, attempting to remove the hand holding the cloth in place. Just as I think I might succeed, I feel a sharp twinge in my neck and my vision starts to blur.

"You should've let me come inside, Clara."

His voice is the last thing I hear before the world goes dark.

CHAPTER 10
CLARA

TITANIUM

A LONG SILENCE stretches between us. Maverick's hands are clenched so tightly, his knuckles are turning white. I can't bring myself to look at him right now, so I fixate on Cruz's notepad.

It's full of notes.

Full of the night I trusted the wrong person.

"Did he ever say where he worked or where he lived?" Cruz's voice is gentle, a balm to the heavy silence.

"No. Now that I think about it, he never really talked about himself. He always asked me questions and wanted to know more about me. I don't remember him sharing anything personal about himself at all, only that he's an only child. Like me."

"Do you remember what happened when you woke up? Where you woke up?"

This is the part I dread the most.

This is the part where I have to relive both the devil and the hell he kept me in.

One week ago

This small room has become my prison.

I feel as if the gray cinder block walls are closing in on me. There's a pedestal sink, toilet, and dirty shower stall in the corner of the room, surrounded by unfinished walls. The stall is completely visible, lacking a rod or shower curtain. There's nothing but a single bar of Irish Spring soap and a bottle of shampoo sitting next to the drain. A twin bed is set up directly across from it, covered with a threadbare blanket and a single, thin pillow.

I'm not sure how long I've been here. A week? If it weren't for the tiny window, the one just barely within reach of the chain around my ankle, I wouldn't be able to tell if it's day or night.

After I woke up the first time, I found Samson hovering over me. I was lying on the mattress, bound to a chain connecting the metal bed post to my foot. The frame is soldered to the concrete floor, making escape virtually impossible. "Welcome home," was all he said. It's the only thing he's said to me in days. When he visits, he ignores my questions. My screams. My sobs.

After a few days of being ignored, I stopped begging to be set free.

I stopped asking what he wants from me.

He never answers.

He only brings food and water. A towel and washcloth every other day.

He's always watching. It's hard to imagine that I used to

enjoy the feeling of his eyes on me. Now, it makes me sick to my stomach.

I dread the days when he has a towel and washcloth in hand. I can only shower with him present. He never leaves me alone; never turns his back to give me a semblance of privacy. I've never moved so fast to wash and get dressed in my life. What was once a luxury is now strictly a necessity. He doesn't like it when I'm unclean. And he always hands me a large t-shirt and boxers. No underwear. No bra. Always a large t-shirt and boxers. They might be his, and the thought makes my skin crawl, but I'd rather wear his clothes than be trapped here naked. The used towel and washcloth always leave when he does.

The chain stretches as far as it'll go as I peer through the rectangular opening, studying the empty space beyond. It's vast and industrial-looking with concrete floors, pillars, and half-constructed walls. I think I might be in an interior office of a warehouse or unfinished building, but I can't be certain.

I watch for him now. I feel as though that's all I do—stand at this window and keep watch. It isn't as though I have anywhere to hide in this room, but I suppose it helps me prepare myself.

The door outside opens and closes with a bang. I see him cross the threshold and scamper back toward the bed.

It's shower day.

He doesn't knock; he just opens the door to my prison and enters.

Like the devil entering his kingdom.

He glances at me, curled in the corner of the bed, but

says nothing as he walks toward the shower stall. I watch him turn on the water and check the temperature with his hand. I wonder if he thinks he's being gentlemanly by testing the water for me so I don't scald my skin.

I know what comes next, though. If I don't hurry to undress and get in, he'll force me. It wasn't a pleasant experience the first time, and I don't intend to give him that power again.

Standing quickly, I remove the two articles of clothing I'm wearing and leave them where they fall. He takes them with him anyway.

My legs shake with every step I take, but I make it into the shower without falling. I wash my body and hair with hurried determination. The sooner I get clean, the sooner I get dressed.

He stands at the edge of the shower stall, leaning against the pedestal sink. As silent as ever.

Something feels off.

Different.

Wrong.

The way his gaze devours me fills me with equal amounts of unease and terror.

I rinse the suds from my hair, then turn off the water. I wait for him to hand me the towel, but instead of giving it to me like he usually does, he walks closer. He holds the towel in both hands, raising it for me to step into.

I don't move.

"Come here, Clara." His voice is stern. Still husky and deep.

I fucking hate it.

My feet move before I realize what I'm doing, but maybe that's my body trying to keep me alive. If I do what he says, maybe he'll let me go.

Maybe that's wishful thinking, but wishful thinking is all I have right now.

Once I'm within reach, he dries me off. Tears escape as he takes his time and runs the rough towel over every inch of my skin, paying attention to my chest and legs. He drops the towel when I'm completely dry and grasps my arm tightly, pulling me toward the bed.

No.

No, no, no.

No.

"I can't wait anymore, Clara," he whispers gruffly in my ear. "You've had time."

I panic and attempt to pull my arm from his bruising grip, but he presses me forward, effectively trapping me between his broad body and the bed. "Please don't do this, Samson. Please don't do this to me. I'm begging you."

Samson. I never want to hear or speak his name again.

He's the devil.

I'm back to begging and pleading. I ratchet my attempts to break free when I hear the sound of his belt unbuckling. Of his pants hitting the floor.

"Stop moving," he yells, yanking me back against him so hard I fear my shoulder might dislocate. His hand shifts from my arm to my wrists, awkwardly pulling both of my arms behind my back. "Keep still and I won't have to make you. You don't want that, do you, Clara?"

I shake my head, my entire body quakes with the force of my sobs.

Though dying would release me from this hell, there's a part of me that still holds out hope. A flicker inside me that thinks I might survive—might find a way to escape.

So I stop fighting and take refuge in the one place he can't breach: my mind.

I can't see Cruz or Maverick through the tears, but I hear the sharp scrape of Maverick's chair as he pushes himself away from the hospital bed. His heavy footsteps move back and forth, the telltale sign of pacing.

"That's enough. No more, Cruz," he all but barks at the detective. Cruz looks at me, his light brown eyes full of sympathy, and moves to close his notepad.

"No!" I rub my eyes with the palm of my hands, clearing my vision and focusing on Maverick's face. He's angry. It should scare me, but it doesn't. "I need to do this. I need to finish this, Mav." My voice is shaky but firm.

Maverick stops beside my bed but doesn't look at me. He looks like a sentinel with his legs in a wide stance and his arms crossed over his chest.

"Please sit down, Maverick," I whisper, and the sound of my voice draws his espresso eyes to mine. "You're making me nervous… just standing there like that."

Reluctantly, he folds his body into the chair. As soon as he does, I reach out and grasp his hand. The strength of his hold anchors me to the present.

. . .

Three days ago

I watch, motionless, as he buckles his belt and leaves the room.

My hope that he won't return today is slashed when he walks back in a few minutes later holding a plate of food and a bottle of water.

He shoves the ham and cheese sandwich at me before I even have the chance to sit up. "Eat."

I stare blankly at the layers atop the styrofoam plate. White bread. Ham. Cheese. Mayo. Another slice of white bread.

I hate mayonnaise. And I'll forever hate ham and cheese sandwiches. In this moment, I swear to myself that I'll never eat another one.

If I live long enough to see that through.

Any flicker of hope that I could survive this, that I could escape, is long gone. He killed that flicker within days of the shower that went wrong.

"Eat, Clar. Or do you want me to feed you?" He leans toward me, reaching for the plate, but I bring it closer to my chest.

"I can do it. Thank you," I keep my tone even. Soft. I learned that he doesn't like it when I'm firm with him. He doesn't like it when I don't thank him for feeding me or letting me shower. Dressing me. *Touching me.* The healing bruise on my cheekbone is proof of that.

I eat but taste nothing. When he uncaps the water bottle and shoves it into my hand, I drink.

Minutes later, he takes the plate and water from my lap then leaves me alone in the room. In my prison.

It isn't until the door shuts completely and I hear the lock snap into place that my world starts to spin.

I lean back against the cold metal bed frame and close my eyes, trying to soothe the dizziness.

Maybe if I take a little nap I'll feel better.

A rhythmic rocking lulls me. I'm floating in that space between waking and dreaming, momentarily forgetting the hell that has become my life. It's only when the rocking stops and the trunk lifts up that I regain consciousness.

Trunk?

Before I can process what's happening or what it means that I'm inside a trunk, his face hovers above mine. I move to sit up—to possibly make a run for it—but he's lightning fast. There's a pinch in my neck, and then I'm being lifted out of the vehicle.

He has my arms pinned to my sides in an ironclad hold, manhandling my body so that I'm pressed against him and suspended just above the ground.

"You've been so good to me, Clara."

I can't move, I can't pull away, but I feel him trace his nose along my neck and jaw.

He brushes his lips against mine before trailing them toward my ear. "I'm going to miss you."

I stare into the face of a monster before darkness consumes me.

The devil in disguise.

"And then I woke up in the hospital." The rawness of my throat mirrors the rawness in my soul.

I stare out the window, though my sight is unseeing. I'm lost in my head. Set adrift in places I don't want to be. The coffin. The warehouse. The moments where pieces of me were pilfered and stolen.

"Hey. Look at me, Clara." I turn my head toward Maverick's voice on command, but I don't see him. "Look at me, sunshine."

I refocus on his face. What is it about this man that calms me instead of scares me?

"You're safe now. Do you hear me? You're safe."

I nod absently and notice Cruz watching us curiously.

"He's right, Clara. You're safe now. You'll be protected until we find him. Did you ever catch his full name?"

"Smith. Samson Smith." It takes everything in me to say his name, but I remember it from his driver's license. "I looked at it when I carded him."

"You're a brave woman, Clara Santos. I'm going to leave you alone now, but is it okay to reach out if I have any more questions?"

"Uhm, sure. I don't know what else I can tell you." Cruz has been patient and understanding, but I really don't want to talk about this anymore. Ever.

The detective is just about to open the door when he turns toward us again. "Maverick, can I talk with you outside? It won't take long." He aims the last comment at me.

"I'll be right out," Maverick grumbles. "I'm going to be just outside, Clara. Yell if you need me."

"Okay." I won't. Because as much as Maverick's presence calms me, I need some space. Recounting the horror of my captivity has left me empty.

They're about to walk out the door when a beautiful face surrounded by curls pops into my head. "Wait! Detective… er, Cruz, did you let Tamara know where I am? Could you tell her if you haven't? I don't have a phone or I'd do it myself."

"I'll call her. Get some rest."

Suddenly, a rest sounds like the best idea I've ever heard.

CHAPTER 11
MAVERICK

SOMETHING TO BELIEVE IN

I FOLLOW Cruz down the hall to the waiting room, but I don't sit. I lean against the door jamb, keeping the door to Clara's room in my line of sight.

I'm unsteady—untethered—after hearing Clara describe the details of her captivity.

That sick son of a bitch.

"What the fuck was that, Rhodes?"

"I don't even fucking know. I don't know what I was expecting, but it wasn't that."

"That's not what I meant. I meant what the fuck was with you calling her *sunshine*? You're getting attached."

"Fuck off, Cruz." I have no answer for him. Hell, I don't even know what possessed me to call her sunshine in the first place. The endearment just slipped out of my mouth, but it's here to stay. It fits her. I see glimpses of the light she exudes before she falls into dark memories. She may be caught in the shadow of an eclipse, but there's no doubt in my mind that she'll come out stronger.

"I hope you know what you're doing, Rhodes." His stare is sharp enough to cut, but he simply shakes his head. "I'm going to run this fucker's name through the database. I can send it off to my contact at the Minneapolis PD, see if he can get a hit on the N-DEx. Unless you want Arlo to run it."

I already have my phone out and the text app open before Cruz finishes speaking. "I'll have Arlo run his name through our databases." Rochester isn't exactly a small city, but its PD doesn't have access to the National Data Exchange the way Minneapolis does.

Maverick
Got a name. Samson Smith. Let me know if you get a hit ASAP.

Arlo
On it.

"Ask Clara if she'd be okay talking to a sketch artist tomorrow? No one's been able to get a clear picture of this guy except her." Cruz shifts gears seamlessly, knowing Arlo will find any and everything he can on this piece of shit.

"Yeah, I'll ask her." As much as I hate to put this on her —to ask her to describe him again—we need this. "The make and model of the car she described matches what Spencer found on the surveillance video from outside her apartment. Toyota Camry. He has a partial plate. Should be getting a text sometime soon with a report. I'll forward that on to you."

"Good. We'll need to look into any warehouses or unfinished construction buildings. Fucking needle in a haystack, man. The entire warehouse district is under construction. That's a lot of fucking ground to sweep."

"Let's send some teams out. We're looking for a building that has an interior room with a small window. Didn't sound like she was able to see outside, just into the main space."

"I'll get some guys out there. One more thing, Rhodes." He scrubs a hand down his face and pinches the bridge of his nose. "She's going to need protective detail. We don't know what this guy will do when he finds out she's alive. Think she'll go into WITSEC?"

Fucking hell. Between the FBI and local PDs, we've succeeded in keeping the media at bay. But now, with a body and live victim found in the same city, it's only a matter of time—a real short fucking time—before the news broadcasts coverage of a serial killer and the victim who survived. It'll be a fucking media frenzy.

"I'll ask her. Something tells me she won't go for it. And hey, you tell Tamara that Clara is here?"

"No, I wanted to talk to her first. I'll call Tamara when I get back to the station."

"Do that. She needs someone."

"Oh my god! I feel like a new person. Will you thank Riley and Evie for me?" Clara walks out of the hospital bathroom, freshly showered. She runs a hand down the front of her new charcoal gray lounge set before lifting a foot and wiggling it in my direction on the couch. "Look! They even got me fuzzy slippers! I freaking hate when my feet are cold."

I can't deny that she looks like a different woman. With her dark brown—almost black—hair swept into a bun at the back of her head, her natural beauty is exposed, drawing me in. Her full cheeks are flushed from the hot water, mirroring the soft pink of her lips. She looks happy and at ease. I like seeing her like this. There's a playful side to her that comes out every now and again, and I'm thankful she hasn't lost that despite the trauma she's endured.

"I will." I shake my head and laugh under my breath. "I'll text them right now."

I retrieve my phone from the side table and send a text to Riley and Evie. After they respond, I wave my phone at Clara. "Here. They said you're welcome. See."

Maverick
Clara says thank you for the clothes.
Especially the fuzzy slippers.

Riley
She's so welcome! I wish I could have
met her.

Evie
Me too! Next time! When I'm not
drowning in all this evidence.

I asked Riley and Evie to pick up a couple of items for Clara, including something to wear besides the hospital gown. They dropped the bags off on their way to the FBI office, but she was still in the shower. Evie said she's knee deep in forensic analysis or else she would've stayed for a meet and greet.

Evie and Riley have been comparing evidence from the most recent crime scenes to the six others. Jesse's been in the lab, processing DNA and trace evidence. He confirmed receipt of the samples from Clara's forensic exam and is currently running it against the DNA collected from Catherine Bennett's body.

"You said we could talk after your shower, sunshine. It's after your shower, and I have some things I need to go over with you." I track her as she moves across the room, toward her bed, so I don't miss the eye roll she gives me.

"Fine, fine," she huffs. Situating herself against the pillows, she sits criss-cross and uses the blanket to cover her legs. "Talk."

"When I stepped out with Cruz earlier, he asked about a forensic sketch artist… and if you'd be willing to work with one tomorrow. We didn't have a description of Samson until now."

Clara flinches the moment I say his name. She's a well of emotion, and I watch as the light swirling in her rich, dark chocolate eyes—the one she had moments ago—extinguishes.

"Please don't say his name." Her whisper is barely audible and full of anguish. "If I never hear that name again, it'd be too soon."

"I'm so sorry, Clara." Guilt for being the reason she's shut down again weighs heavy on me.

"It's okay." Her breaths are measured, as though she's actively staving off panic.

It's definitely not okay.

"No, it's not," I urge. I'm on the verge of standing up so I can sit next to her—hold her hand, comfort her.

"I promise, Mav. You didn't know," she says, her voice stronger than before. "Now you do."

"It won't happen again," I promise. And I'll make sure no one says that fucker's name in front of her.

"Thank you. Truly." She offers me a smile, then sits up straighter. "I'll do it. I'll meet with the sketch artist. I just… I just want to move past this."

"I know you do, sunshine. And you will." I clear my throat, knowing she won't be as amenable to what I say next. "When you're discharged, Cruz is going to have a protective detail on you. At home, at work. It's for your safety until we find him." Clara's eyes widen, the color of her golden skin paling slightly, but I continue. "The safest place for you would be in witness protection."

"No, absolutely not, Maverick. You aren't listening to me. I need to *move past this*. I need to get back to my life— back to normal. My apartment. My job. I can't do that in witness protection, pretending to live a life that isn't mine." She shakes her head vehemently. "No."

"Okay, okay." My hands immediately lift in surrender. "I told Cruz you wouldn't go for it. But the protective detail won't be an option, do you hear? We need you safe."

"Fine." She relents, though I know she doesn't want to. But at this point, I'll take any win I can get.

Arlo

Samson Smith doesn't exist. No bank
accounts, no credit cards, nothing.
He's a ghost.

Spencer

Toyota Camry checked out to be a
rental. Paid for with cash and
registered to S. Smith. Rented for two
days.

Maverick

Send a team to pick it up. Need
forensics to comb through it.

Spencer

Already done. Rental company had it
cleaned weeks ago, though.

Maverick

Shit. Let's hope their guys were feeling
lazy that day.

Fuck. Samson Smith has got to be an alias. We're back to square one when it comes to finding this asshole.

I'm reviewing the surveillance videos of The Pour House, zooming in on the man sitting between a wall post and beer dispenser. It's him. I just can't see his fucking face. I pause the video on his hands—on any visible skin— searching for noticeable marks: a scar, tattoo, anything.

Nothing.

It's only 6 p.m., but it feels like it should be a whole lot later than it is. I close my laptop and stand to check on Clara. The interview this morning took a toll on her, and she's been napping fitfully for the last hour. Hearing her whimpers and not being able to do anything about it has been nothing short of grueling.

Just as I reach her side, I hear a sharp rap on the door. My guard is up instantly. I'm not expecting anyone; the nurse and doctor have already made their rounds, and Cruz or my team would have messaged first.

"Who is it?" Clara whispers from beneath the blankets. I look down at her, sleep-laden eyes now wide and alert.

"I'm not sure." The rapping comes again, more impatiently this time. I unholster my weapon, keeping it low as I move to open the door.

I barely have it open when I recognize the person's coily hair and wide, misty eyes. Tamara. She looks right past me and through the small opening, her voice faltering with disbelief. "Is she here?"

Securing my gun in its holster, I respond by opening the door wide and moving aside to let her through. She takes the invitation and steps inside the room.

The moment Tamara's eyes land on Clara, who is now sitting up in bed, she lets out a loud sob and runs forward.

Clara's gaze lands on mine, and I give her a nod before closing the door gently behind me.

They need time.

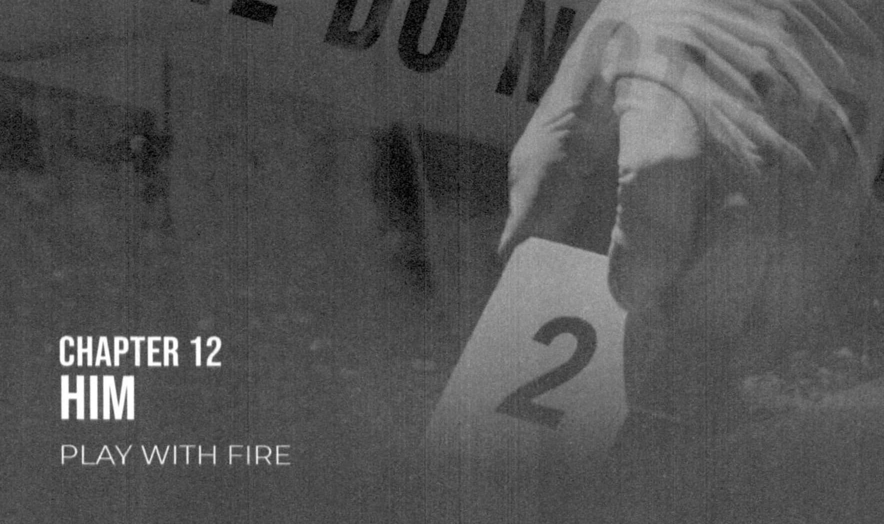

CHAPTER 12
HIM

PLAY WITH FIRE

GOD, she's perfect.

The others were, too.

She weaves gracefully between the tables, holding the serving tray steadily above her shoulder. Glasses full of beer clink together, but she spills nary a drop. It's beautiful to watch.

She's beautiful to watch.

I claimed the furthest booth from the front door, tucked away in shadows and just out of the restaurant camera's line of sight.

Her full lips stretch with a smile as she carefully adjusts the tray, wrapping those dainty fingers around my glass. "Here you are. Your usual, the house lager." When she sets my beer on the table, directly in front of me, her smile seems to widen, and those perfect brown eyes sparkle.

At me.

"Thank you, ma'am." Smiling in return, I lift the glass and take a sip, making sure to swipe the foam from my upper lip with my tongue. She's watching every move I make.

A blush creeps up her neck, settling in her cheeks. "Well, let me know if you need anything else." She glances at me one more time before she turns on a heel, leaving to deliver drinks to other tables.

I do need something from her.

But I'm a patient man.

CLARA

FEAR ON FIRE

"YOU HEIFER! I can't believe you've been here for two whole fucking days, and I'm just now seeing your face." Tamara's puffy eyes are narrowed into slits, but I know she isn't really mad at me.

I broke down when Tamara walked through the door, and I'm so thankful that Maverick slipped out before he saw the absolute ugliest cry ever.

Tamara immediately crawled into the cramped hospital bed, wrapping her arms around me and soaking my shoulder with her tears. She broke down harder than I did when I told her everything—the ride home, the warehouse, the coffin, the forensic exam…

"I don't even have my phone! I wish Cruz called you sooner…" Our hands are intertwined between us as we lay on our sides, but I dip my head closer to hers because I just need her. "I wish you were here when I woke up."

Tamara is all I have. She's been my champion, my person, ever since our first shift at The Pour House years ago. She's the sister I've never had, and it was her voice in my head that kept me sane. Talking to me. Telling me to fight. Cursing me anytime I wanted to give in to the suffering.

"I'm here, best friend, and there's no way in hell I'ma let a man get rid of me. That detective is gonna get a piece of my mind for not calling me right away. I told his ass to call me if he heard anything."

I can't help but laugh because she's dead serious.

"And that… that fucker better not ever show his face. He better fucking hope I never see him on the street because I'll fucking kill him. I'll cut off his dick and feed it to him." She stares me right in the eyes, telling me she'd do it, consequences be damned.

"Whoa, whoa, whoa. Calm down, tiger. Isn't that what Mav and Cruz are for? Maybe he'll do something stupid, and they will be forced to shoot him. I'd like to see that."

"Girl, they won't cut off his dick. It's probably against the law and shit. And you know that fucker should have it sliced right off. With a dull fucking knife, too. Or scissors. Kid scissors." God, she reads too many horror stories. She's freaking scary, but I love her. "So. Mav, huh?" She wiggles her eyebrows at me teasingly.

I awkwardly shoulder check her. "Shut up. But, honestly, Tam, I don't know what I would've done without him here. Whenever I spiral, he's there. You'd think I would've been afraid of him, but he makes me feel safe."

"Hell, girl, he'd make me feel safe, too." Tamara shimmies her shoulders, and I swat her before a yawn overtakes me. "Get some sleep, best friend. I'm not going anywhere."

"Promise?" My eyes are already closing, heavy with sleep.

"Promise," she whispers as she leans forward to kiss my forehead.

I believe her.

Tamara kept her promise. She stayed with me through the night, even though the bed was way too freaking small for both of us. I had to force her to go home before she missed her yoga classes. She's worked hard to build a clientele, and I'll be damned if she cancels because of me.

"You sure you're up for this?" Maverick hands me a cup of coffee, then pulls a breakfast sandwich from a white bag and places it on the side table, right next to my drink of life.

"The sooner I do this, the sooner I can freaking stop talking about him." I don't know if he will ever stop invading my mind or my sleep, but I can make the choice to never talk about him when this is all over. I feel like it's the only control I have, and I'm grasping onto it like a lifeline.

"Okay. Just remember we can stop if it becomes too much." Maverick opens the door and gestures for someone to come inside. He steps out of the way as a middle-aged woman crosses the threshold, offering Maverick a nod before he eases the door shut.

He follows her into the room and indicates for her to sit in the chair he positioned to face us. "Clara, this is Amy.

She's a forensic sketch artist who works with the Minneapolis FBI and police department. Amy, this is Clara."

"Hi, Clara. It's nice to meet you." Amy sits down and places her briefcase on her lap, quickly removing a sketchpad and pencil. "I'm going to ask you a few questions to help me visualize his face. Take your time—the more details, the better. Are you ready to get started?"

Short and straight to the point. I like her, even though the thought of picturing his face makes my heart race.

I nod and readjust my position on the loveseat, folding my legs beneath me and leaning against the armrest. Maverick sits down next to me, not too close yet not too far. His hand rests on his thigh, calloused palm facing up, letting me know his strength is there if I need it. "I'm ready."

"Alright." Amy's voice is calm and even. "Let's start with his face. Can you describe the shape of it?"

I exhale, tapping my fingers restlessly against the armrest. "Uhm… kind of angular. His jaw was defined, but I don't know how else to describe it."

Amy nodded and started sketching. "What about his hair? Color, length?"

"Dirty blonde. Whenever I saw him, his hair was up in a man bun, so I'm not exactly sure how long it was. And he was clean shaven." God, I really don't want to picture his face. I lean forward and pick up my coffee, needing to hold something. The warmth is comforting, so I bring it to my lips just to feel the steam.

"Got it. And his eyes?"

I swallow. "Chocolate brown." I have to close my eyes and breathe deeply through my nose, attempting to ward off the shiver threatening to run down my spine. I remember the feel of his eyes on me, the revulsion that coursed through my veins every time his gaze lingered. "He wore contacts. I used to wonder what he'd look like in glasses. And he, uh, had thick eyebrows."

The only sound in the room is the scratch of Amy's pencil on the sketchpad. She takes her time, but the pace is oddly calming. "Okay. How about his nose?"

"Uhm… normal? It was straight. It fit his face." I shrug because I don't know how to do this.

"His lips?"

I pause, involuntarily visualizing the way he pressed his lips against mine after he took me out of the trunk. Right before he buried me. Alive.

Maverick's warm hand slides against mine, pulling me from those terrible memories. "Uh," I clear my throat. "They were, uh, full. Even. Top and bottom. You know how the bottom lip is usually fuller than the top lip? His were even."

"Did he have any scars, tattoos, piercings, moles, freckles? Anything like that?"

I shake my head. "No, none that I saw."

"Okay." Amy is quiet as she continues her sketch. I watch her hands move while she works, taking care not to look at the sketch itself.

"Hey," Maverick whispers, his head leaning closer to mine. "You okay?"

Am I okay? I don't think I am. I suck in a breath then

shake my head. This feels worse than recounting what happened in that office with him. I'm going to have to see his face again. It doesn't matter that it's in the form of sketched charcoal, it's still his face. A face that fills me with terror and overruns my dreams.

I never want to see his face again.

Amy glances up and studies me for a moment, then turns her sketchpad around. The rough pencil strokes have taken shape—there he is, staring back at me. I feel my stomach twist. "Is this him?"

My breath hitches as I stare at the face of the devil.

"Yes," I whisper. "That's him."

———

"Knock, knock, darling." Rosie doesn't actually knock; she simply walks in with a smile on her face. There are times when she reminds me of my mom, and every time she does, it hurts just a little bit. But Rosie has a knack for making me smile when I don't want to. "Dr. Callahan says you can go home. How you feeling?"

"I'm okay. I'm ready." I look down at the bandages on my wrist and wrinkle my nose. "Do these come off now, too? Because I really want them off."

Rosie laughs at me before gently taking my hand and assessing the skin beneath the gauze. "They're healing nicely, darling. They can come off. I have your discharge paperwork. Do you have a ride home?"

"Yes," Maverick answers before I can. "I'll take her home."

"Of course you will." She winks at him, then turns her attention back to me. "Dr. Callahan doesn't have any prescriptions for you, but she said you can take ibuprofen or acetaminophen if you need to for any pain."

"Thank you, Rosie. For everything," I say. "You've been… amazing."

"Oh, darling." Her arms are soft and comforting when she wraps me in a hug and kisses my cheek. "You'll be okay." Patting my cheek before she steps back, Rosie shows me the discharge papers and points to a handwritten number. "That's me. I don't usually do that, but you seem like you need someone, darling. Call me if you need anything, you understand?"

I nod, blinking back tears at her kindness. "Yes, I understand." I kiss her cheek and watch her leave.

"I don't like that you'll be by yourself, Clara," Maverick says ruefully as soon as he hears the snick of the door.

"I won't be by myself. Remember, Cruz is putting a detail on me."

"You know what I mean. We're getting you a phone, and you're gonna call me if you need anything. Anything at all."

A loud ringing startles me, but Maverick fishes his phone from his pocket and brings it to his ear. "Rhodes."

I don't like the look he gives me. I like it even less when he starts pacing.

"She's just been discharged… Fuck." Maverick stops right in front of the window and pulls the curtain open just wide enough to peek through.

"How'd that happen, Cruz? … Fucking hell, this is

gonna be a disaster … Alright, alright. We're leaving in a few minutes." Maverick shakes his head and starts collecting his things and mine. "No, I'll take her through the employee garage. Thanks for the heads up … Do me a favor? Meet me at her house with a phone. She needs one … Thanks, man."

"What's wrong, Mav? What happened?"

"The press is outside. They know about him… and you."

CHAPTER 14
CLARA

LOVELY

MOST PEOPLE LOCK their doors at night and turn off all the lights before going to bed. And most people fall asleep in absolute darkness or with a guiding light plugged into an outlet.

That used to be me.

But I'm not *most people* anymore.

Shadows taunt me in the dark. It doesn't matter if the shadows are cast by moonlight, a nightlight, or the bath-room light—the dancing silhouettes twist and stretch across every surface. They taunt me, tease me, cause me to lose precious hours of sleep.

Sleep is hard to come by as it is. Every time I close my eyes, I'm back with him.

There's no reprieve.

No escape.

God, I'm so tired. All I wanted was to move past this. I wanted to move on with my life and dive back into normalcy. I didn't want his depravity to change everything —to change me.

Yet nothing is the same, and it's really messing with my psyche.

I check the locks no less than thirty times each day, and not just before I go to bed. I check them all the time; it's become an obsession. Whenever I pass a window, I stop to make sure it's locked and sealed tight. The curtains are always closed with the blinds pulled down and tilted inward. Every interior door remains open; I need to be able to see inside each room at any moment.

Once upon a time—like, three weeks ago—I used to revel in the dark. The only lights I'd have on in the house were single lamps. But now? Darkness is no longer a comfort. The entire apartment has to be lit up like the Vegas strip at midnight.

I haven't stepped outside. Hell, I don't think I've even opened the door—except to let Tamara in or to grab the groceries that were ordered online. The last time I breathed in fresh air was when I walked from Maverick's car to the apartment seven days ago.

By some miracle, I still have a job at The Pour House. Ronnie, the owner, has been surprisingly understanding and patient. She says I can return whenever I'm ready.

I'm not ready yet—I'm nowhere near ready. I can barely function.

A sudden chime from my phone makes my heart skip a beat. I've never been this jumpy, but every sound crashes against my nerves, making my pulse stutter.

> **Maverick**
> Hey sunshine. Just checking in.

Clara
I'm ok. Tamara's coming by in a bit to
keep me company.

> **Maverick**
> I'm here if you need anything.

Clara
I know, thank you.

Maverick checks in with me every day. I'm shocked that I miss him—his stalwart presence. I wish he'd come over, but I'm too afraid to ask. I don't want to appear needy, and he's already done so much for me. He practically lived in my hospital room until I was discharged. I'm sure he has mountains of work to catch up on.

It isn't his problem that I'm afraid of my own shadow.

A scream claws its way up my throat until it feels as though I'm going to suffocate.

I shoot straight up in bed, throwing the covers off my sweat-soaked body. My clothes are drenched with fear, clinging uncomfortably to my skin. I can't recall what woke me, but my breathing is ragged and my body is trembling as if I'm still caught in the nightmare.

How much longer can I do this? I collapse into quiet, shuddering sobs, wishing I had someone here with me. *Pull yourself together, Clara. You're stronger than this.* Taking a deep breath, I try to do what my head is telling me to do: get it together.

I glance at the clock on the nightstand, the neon glow revealing it's two in the morning.

Three hours of sleep. Well, that's an improvement.

Ugh, I need a shower.

Leaving the bed, I step over the blanket that was thrown onto the floor and make my way into the fully lit bathroom. As usual, I ignore the mirror and walk straight to the shower. One day, when I test the temperature with my hand, I won't think of him and the way he did this, too. Nausea swirls in my stomach, forcing me to swallow down the bile threatening to escape.

It's just a shower, Clara. And no one is here. No one is watching.

Without removing my clothes, I step inside and close the glass door. The steam envelops me completely as I slide down the tile wall, positioning myself directly beneath the shower spray. I pull my legs to my chest and lock my arms around them, then rest my chin on my knees and stare blankly at the swirling water running down the drain.

I just need to sit here for a moment and try to fit the broken pieces of me back together.

The water is cold by the time I step out of the shower, but I'm clean and feeling refreshed. I dry myself off and drape the soft, fluffy fabric around me, using another towel to twist my hair into place.

I'm still rubbing the lotion into my arms when I walk into my bedroom, aiming for the dresser next to the window. From my periphery, I notice how inviting the bed looks: the comforter is made, the pillow is fluffed. It looks so cozy; I can't wait to get in once I'm dressed.

I freeze, every muscle locking into place.

The comforter is made.

But that's impossible. It was on the floor. I distinctly remember stepping over it after throwing it off the bed.

I frantically look around the room, my eyes as wide as saucers.

Nothing else appears out of place.

I bolt to the dresser, throwing on the first shirt and leggings I can find. I nearly trip over my feet as I sprint to the nightstand to snatch my phone, then hightail it into the bathroom. The door slams shut with a deafening bang.

A barricade. I need a barricade.

Turning the lock into place, I pivot and push the vanity against the door. I struggle with its weight but adrenaline fuels me.

As soon as the door is barred, I run into the shower stall and attempt to call Maverick. My fingers are trembling uncontrollably, and it takes longer than it should to find his name and press call.

One ring.

Two rings.

Please pick up.

Three rings.

Please, Maverick. Pick up the fucking phone.

Four rin— "Clara?" His voice is gravelly with sleep, but I hear the blankets shift as he sits up. "What's going on?"

"Maverick." I keep my voice hushed, worried the person

who came into my apartment uninvited and made my bed might hear me. "Someone's been in my apartment."

CHAPTER 15

HIM

KING OF THE WORLD

HER HIPS SWAY as she walks up the stairs to her apartment building; the rhythm… hypnotizing. I can't look away. She's calling to me. The way her hand trails up the banister… Her palms, so soft.

Fuck me. I check my rearview mirror, then adjust myself through my slacks.

The itch inside… it's begging to be scratched; my skin feels too tight.

It's almost time.

If only I could find the perfect one who scratches the itch for longer than a few weeks at a time, I wouldn't have to keep doing this.

Driving.

Hunting.

Waiting.

Planning.

But the monster inside beats against my ribcage,

unhappy with no one to please him. I thought the last one was perfect. Just like this one. They all were.

Oh, but that last one…

She was fucking phenomenal. The way she smelled after her shower. How she trembled when she washed her body in front of me, knowing she would be devoured as soon as she stepped out of the water.

Goddamn, I feel myself throbbing just thinking about her. Mmm, the smell of her skin as I trailed my nose along her neck one last time. Her jaw. The decadent feel of her lips on mine.

When I laid her in that coffin, full of my essence, I felt powerful.

Invincible.

Still, I would have kept her.

But the monster wants someone new.

Always someone new.

I'm thrown from my reverie when a notification on my phone breaks the silence. I move my hand from my zipper —so close—and snatch the forsaken device from the cup holder. This better fucking be important.

The email app flashes with an alert from my assistant. I scan the subject line—Rochester PD Press Release—and frown, knitting my brows in confusion. Why the fuck does Rochester PD need to make a press release?

I read the email, my blood turning cold with each word.

FBI PRESS RELEASE

 MINNEAPOLIS FIELD OFFICE

 ROCHESTER RESIDENT AGENCY OFFICE

EMBARGOED UNTIL SEPTEMBER 16, 2024, 0830

ROCHESTER, MN — Federal and local law enforcement agencies in Rochester, MN have joined together to create a criminal task force to investigate the death of a woman found buried in Rollins Orchard and a second woman who was found buried alive in Silver Lake Park. The second victim is stable and remains in good condition.

The members of the FBI and Rochester PD Task Force will work the case jointly and share investigative, intelligence, technical, and forensic resources. An active search for the perpetrator is being conducted by both agencies.

Due to the ongoing nature of the investigation, no other information will be released at this time.

God fucking damn it!

She wasn't supposed to live.

None of them are supposed to live. Not once the monster is sated by their bodies.

But she *is* alive.

This is a fucking problem.

I can't have loose ends.

Everything needs to be done right. Everything needs to remain in order.

And her survival? It's chaos in my neatly organized plans.

It's unacceptable.

Though I can't deny… there's a part of me that's thrilled with this turn of events.

I can feel her again.

Fill her again.

Before I take care of her for good.

I slip my phone back into the cup holder, then glance out the windshield toward her apartment window.

She'll have to wait a little bit longer.

I'll have her soon.

After I take care of my little problem.

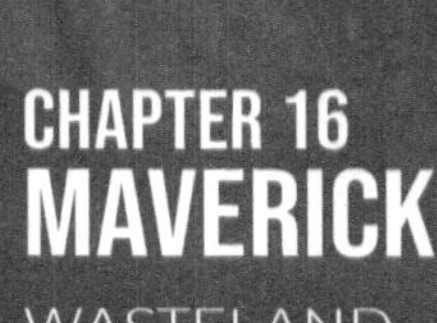

CHAPTER 16
MAVERICK

WASTELAND

"WHERE ARE we at with the DNA results from Clara's forensic exam and Catherine Bennett? Have they come back yet?"

"Came back this morning, boss," Jesse says hesitantly, likely remembering that my temper has been like a loose cannon since I came back from the hospital. "The DNA from Catherine's autopsy is the same DNA profile as the sample taken from Clara's exam. They also came back as a perfect match to the other victims when I ran them through CODIS."

God fucking damn it. I knew it. The one time I wish my gut instinct was off, it's not.

I dip my chin in a nod, attempting to control my expression even though I'm raging inside. I clear my throat and focus on the facts. "So our perp buried Catherine's body in Rollins Orchard roughly five weeks ago, then buried Clara three weeks later. That doesn't match his MO

—he's never buried two bodies in the same city. Not unless we missed a slew of vics where the others were found."

"I don't think we did." Spencer moves to stand in front of the array of victim photos, examining the newest additions before continuing. "Either he's closer to Rochester than we thought, and this is his home base, or something was different with Clara. Maybe he saw her when he scouted Rollins Orchard and couldn't help himself. This guy has raped and killed six women across four states; I think he got cocky."

I hum in consideration. Something is off with the timeline. This bastard has driven anywhere from one and a half to four hours to find his victims. He buried them in the same state—often the same city—from where he took them. Yet, Clara was taken while the soil over Catherine's grave was still settling. A heavy weight in my stomach forces me to face the realization that we might've been wrong.

We pinned the burial sites to the map and determined Minneapolis was the central point, linking each crime scene back to it. But what if the center radius isn't Minneapolis? What if it's Rochester? That changes things. I study the map on the evidence board, tracing each location and the connecting web of strings. "We have to recreate the map," I say, though mostly to myself. "He didn't drive from Minneapolis; he drove from Rochester. He's here."

There's a brief tap on the conference room's glass door before Cruz pokes his head in. "Chief wants a press con tomorrow morning."

My head snaps up. "Come again?"

"Press conference, man," Cruz repeats as he meanders to a chair and sits down. "The task force press release was sent out, but there's an embargo until 8:30 tomorrow morning. Chief said he wants to get ahead of it and do a conference."

Fuck me. I hate press conferences. Clara's face immediately fills my mind, and I'm not sure how she'll respond to it. She's the only survivor—the only one who managed to make it out alive before suffocating to death six feet below the earth. A press conference has the potential to reveal her identity and upend her life even more.

"And he wants us all there," Cruz adds. "The entire task force."

"Shit." I scrub a hand down my face and sigh wearily. "Okay. Let's go over the evidence from the Silver Lake crime scene." I shift my attention to Evie and Riley who are sitting across from me.

"We found four holes near the grave, identical to the other crime scenes," Evie says, picking up the conversation. "No footprints."

"The grave was in a semi-public area of the park. It was off the trail, just beyond the woods. Given the season, the trees weren't dense—he would've been seen by runners during the day," Riley chimes in. "Six feet is a lot for one man to dig by himself. We're guessing he started digging at night. It likely took him a couple of nights to dig deep enough. There were two mounds of shrubbery and branches that were out of place. I would bet he used one to cover the hole and the other to camouflage the dirt pile."

"He took a risk burying Clara without the cover of

midnight. How was he not seen filling the grave? She couldn't have been buried for long by the time Juno heard her, and there were runners off in the distance. They would've passed that area."

"You would think anyone on the trail would've noticed a man with a shovel, even out of the corner of their eye," Cruz remarks. "But, you have some people who aren't as aware of their surroundings as they should be when they're out running. They likely wouldn't have been paying attention to anything that wasn't directly on the trail and in their way."

"True."

It was pure happenstance that Silver Lake Park was the place I chose to release some tension. And blind fucking luck that Juno, with his keen hearing and training, heard Clara's screams from six feet underground and a hundred yards away. It was simply a matter of time and place that distinguished life or death.

The idea that she might not have been found if I hadn't been at the right place at the right time is enough to make my blood run cold. I retrieve my phone from the table and send her a quick text to check in.

I haven't seen Clara since I brought her home from the hospital. That was six days ago. There hasn't been a day I haven't wanted to stop by or call to hear her voice, but I wanted to give her space. So in lieu of unexpected visits and phone calls, I send texts. She always responds, but they're short and distant. I don't like it.

"The rental car came back clean." Spencer flips through a report prepared by the Evidence Response Team. "Either the rental company has some real good detailers or Samson wiped it before he returned it. It was pristine."

"Evie and I also ran through it with a fine tooth comb. Not a single speck of trace evidence," Jesse adds.

At this point, we might as well run a list of all the things we do have on this bastard. It'd be a hell of a lot shorter.

"Also," Arlo straightens before turning his laptop toward me. "We ran the forensic sketch through the database. No hit to any mugshots or photos. I'm ten thousand percent positive Samson Smith is an alias."

"Dude sounds like an alias," Jesse comments with a wiry grin.

"He's a fucking bastard." I think back to Clara's interview and an intense urge to cut off his hands for daring to touch her fills me. "Which reminds me. If you're ever in front of Clara, don't say his name. It's a trigger."

"Oh, I already heard—don't you worry." Cruz rolls his eyes and shoots me a look. "Tamara called and ripped me a new one for waiting so long to tell her about Clara. And she told me to never bring his name up if I wanted to keep my tongue. She's a violent one."

"Better stay on her good side, then."

Cruz laughs as his phone pings with a notification, drawing his attention. He scans the message quickly before looking at me. "Had a few officers do a sweep of the warehouse district. We haven't found anything yet, but they only canvassed maybe twenty-five percent of the place."

"We can help with the sweep. Start on the opposite end of the district."

"That'll get it done faster. When?"

"After the press conference tomorrow? Gives us time to prepare, and I can call in a couple of other teams."

My gut is telling me that fucking warehouse is somewhere in the district.

What a fucking day.

The press conference this morning turned into a media frenzy. It was a packed house; the floor completely full of reporters. Hell, even the mayor showed up and made a statement about the safety of Rochester's residents. Rochester isn't a sleepy town that hasn't seen violent crimes in decades, but the idea that someone is abducting women and burying them alive in their own city makes the fear spread like wildfire.

And to add onto an already chaotic morning, the warehouse sweep was a bust. The entire warehouse district is under construction—it's been a long standing project—but its overall real estate is vast. Between the Rochester PD and FBI, we were able to search fifteen more warehouses—only a dent in what's left.

I toss my keys onto the kitchen counter just as Juno rounds the corner and bumps his snout against my leg, demanding a head rub. I oblige. "Hey, boy. Have a good day? We'll go for a run tomorrow."

Juno huffs. Ever since we found Clara, I've hardly been home. Our daily runs have become practically nonexistent. "Bright and early," I promise, giving him one more scratch behind the ear before I make my way down the hall toward the bedroom.

Fatigue settles deep in my muscles after too little rest and nonstop movement. It's days like these where the ache in my shoulder is incessant and unyielding. What I need is a scorching hot shower and a good fifty hours of fucking shut-eye.

I follow the tactical unit into the abandoned barn, moving silently in formation and keeping my weapon poised at the ready. At night, the outskirts of rural Minnesota are pitch black, and the night vision optics are all that guide our way. We're here on a tip—one that suggests our primary suspect is using the barn as a hideout. Victor Townsend, a prolific serial killer, has been on the run for months. The FBI has spent years tracking the son of a bitch who has a history of murdering forty-nine women across the upper Midwest.

The air inside the barn is thick with the stench of manure and hay bales, and the barren interior is cast in eerie shades of green. Something isn't right. The quiet is disconcerting.

Out of the corner of my eye, I spy slight movement above us. With only a split second to react, I shout, turning and lunging in front of Spencer right as a single gunshot shatters the silence. A sharp, burning pain explodes in my left shoulder, knocking me backward. My vision blurs as I hit the concrete floor with a groan, the gun falling from my hand and clattering out of reach.

"Rhodes!" Spencer shouts at the same time the unit leader orders, "Contact front! Take cover!"

The agents respond instantly, spreading out and returning

fire toward the unseen shooter in the rafters. Spencer ignores the order and pulls me behind a stack of hay bales. "Stay with me, Rhodes!"

A grunt of pain escapes me when he presses down on the wound. I clench my teeth and manage to ask, "You good?"

Spencer nods, eyes scanning the rafters for the target. "Yeah. Thanks to you."

We weren't even supposed to be here. Spencer and I were walking into the FBI office when the tactical team was gearing up. Mark, the unit leader, asked if we wanted in on some fun.

I don't know if the searing pain and blood loss could be called fun, but here we are.

More shots fire, and I hear the heavy footsteps of someone in the rafters above. A sickening thud follows a final gunshot.

"Suspect down!"

* * *

"How are you holding up?"

It takes herculean effort to turn my head toward Spencer's voice. Something about his tone has me on alert, but it's hard to decipher with the pain medications dripping through the IV. "Been better."

"You took one for the team," he says somberly.

Unable to sit up, I glance around the room and search for another presence. It's only Spencer. I remember the searing pain spreading from my left shoulder, the ambulance ride to the hospital, the phone call Spencer made to Heather, the surgery to remove the bullet. "Heather here?"

Spencer shakes his head, then, in a tortured whisper, speaks the words I never thought I'd hear. "There's been an accident, Mav. Heather... she was on her way here... A truck ran a red light. She didn't make it. I'm sorry, brother."

I don't think I can process what he's saying. It's like my brain is stuck in a loop: She didn't make it, she didn't make it, she didn't make it.

His phone starts to ring, but he doesn't acknowledge it nor make any move to answer. Who keeps call—

The sound of my phone ringing snaps me awake. I'm disoriented—I haven't dreamed of that moment, of *her*, in a long time. Reaching blindly for my phone, my hand slaps around the nightstand until I find it. The illuminated screen makes me squint, but the name running across it sends a jolt to my heart.

She never calls. And it's the middle of the night.

"Clara?" I rush to answer and sit up, my voice scratchy with sleep. "What's going on?"

"Maverick. Someone's been in my apartment." She's whispering, but I can hear the fear in her tone. It makes all my protective instincts roar to life.

"Where are you?" I'm already moving, throwing on clothes, unlocking my weapon from its safe box, and tucking it into my waistband.

"I ran into the bathroom and blocked the door. I'm hiding in the shower stall."

"Good girl. I'm on my way. Don't open the door for anyone, you hear me? Stay right where you are."

"I'm scared, Maverick." Her voice trembles, and it's clear she's holding back tears.

I'm in my car less than a minute later, slamming the

door shut and peeling out of the driveway. "I'm on my way, sunshine. Stay on the phone with me. Tell me what happened."

Putting my phone on speaker, I listen to her breathing and break every traffic law in the book.

"I, uhm… I had a nightmare, and I couldn't… couldn't go back to sleep. I took a shower. When I walked b-back into my b-bedroom, the bed was m-made." It seems impossible for her voice to get any quieter, but it does when she says, "I didn't make the bed, Mav. I left the blankets on the floor."

A stream of curses fill the silence of my car. That motherfucker. "I'm almost there." Clara remains quiet—the sound of her sniffling and heavy breathing is all I hear.

I've spent the last seven years since Heather died focused entirely on work, throwing myself into cases whenever I can. On the occasions I needed a physical release, I'd go out and find someone—someone who knew it was only for one night. But that's all it's been. I haven't wanted to risk failing someone else the way I failed Heather. The reminder that her life was cut short because of me is a weight on the gas pedal, speeding me toward Clara.

I make it to Clara's apartment building in less than ten minutes, coming to a hard stop right in front of the entrance. "I'm here, sunshine. I'm on my way up. Don't leave the bathroom, okay? Stay there." I wait for her to confirm then hang up.

The slam of a car door snaps my attention sideways. I freeze before the building's front entrance when I spot a uniformed officer approaching. Must be Clara's protective detail. What good are they if this fucker can slip past them undetected?

I don't have time for this. Every instinct screams at me to reach Clara. Now.

I flash my badge without breaking stride. "Special Agent Maverick Rhodes."

The officer opens his mouth, but I'm already past him, pushing through the glass doors and heading straight toward the stairwell next to the elevator.

Shoving open the stairwell door, I race up the flights until I reach her floor. Her apartment is locked, but it takes zero effort to break the knob.

She won't be staying here, anyway.

Drawing my weapon, I leave the door open behind me —my only concern is making sure Clara is safe. The weight of the gun is comforting as I check each room, ensuring the apartment is clear before heading to the bedroom.

When I reach the bathroom door, I knock three times. "Clara? Sunshine, it's me. It's all clear. It's safe to open the door."

"Maverick?" I hear her call out from inside along with rustling against the door. A bang has my weapon up and a hand on the handle in a flash. Just as I'm about to break this one, too, the door swings open. I'm nearly thrown back when a small body collides with mine.

I quickly tuck my gun away then wrap both arms around Clara's shaking frame. "Shh, shh. You're safe now." I nestle my chin against the top of her head, running my hand in small circles along her shoulders. "You're safe, sunshine."

She pulls away much too soon, lifting her shirt to wipe her face. "I'm sorr—"

"Don't. Don't you dare apologize. You have nothing to apologize for, sunshine."

"I woke you up. And I soaked your shirt," she says, her tone rueful.

I don't even bother responding. I simply walk to her closet and search for a suitcase or duffle bag—anything she can use to put her things into because she sure as shit isn't staying here.

"Maverick? What are you doing?"

"You're not staying here."

"Wait. What do you mean I'm not staying here?" She watches me pull a suitcase from the top shelf and set it on her bed.

"You're not staying here," I restate. "You're staying with me. Pack your things."

She stares at me, brown eyes full of disbelief. Her jaw hangs open but no response comes out.

I point to her suitcase and repeat my demand. "Pack your shit, sunshine. I can pack for you, but I doubt you'll like how I do it."

Because at this point, I'll throw all the shit inside just so we can leave, and I'm not leaving without her. The sooner I get her away from this place, the better.

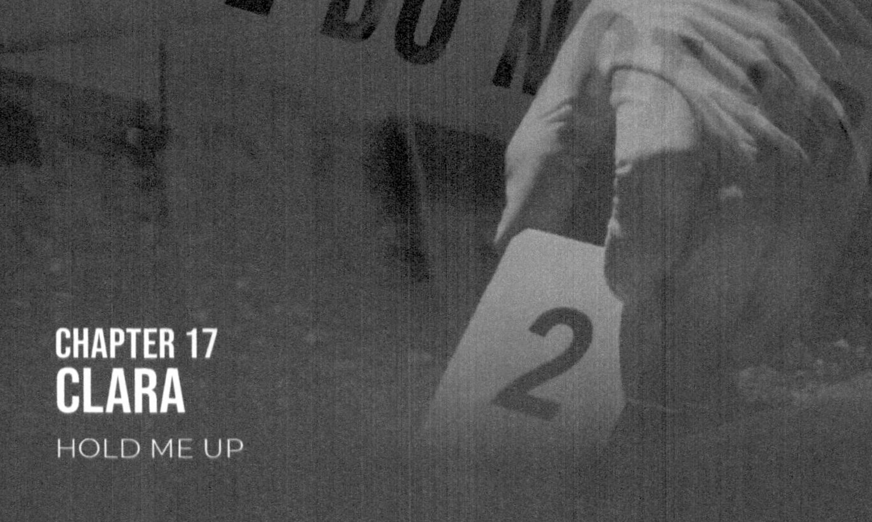

CHAPTER 17
CLARA

HOLD ME UP

"I WANT a unit at Clara's apartment ASAP … I don't care. Someone was in her apartment while she was in the shower. I didn't see anything out of place when I picked her up … Yes, I picked her up. She's staying with me … Don't give a fuck, Cruz. It's the safest place for her … It's not up for debate … Talk to her protective detail … Yeah, the bastard slipped past them … No, she won't need them anymore. I'll be her damned protective detail."

I lean my head against the car window and listen as Maverick speaks. He's positioned the phone between his ear and shoulder, muffling the sound of Cruz's responses. I don't think the good detective is particularly happy with Maverick at the moment, if his raised voice is any indication.

"I'm going to text Evie and Jesse, too. They'll meet your guys there." Some caveman grunt of acknowledgement is all Maverick supplies before hanging up and tossing his phone in the cup holder. He glances at me quickly, then averts his attention back to the road. "You okay, sunshine?"

"I'm tired." My whispered response intentionally avoids his question. If he notices, he's wise enough to not to comment.

"We're almost there, then you can get some sleep."

Yeah, that's not happening. I know I need the rest—my aching body and hollow eyes tell me so—but I mentally recoil at the thought of going to sleep. It's in the quiet hours when I spiral the farthest.

When we arrive at Maverick's modest, single story house, he leads me into the mudroom directly off of the garage. He refused to let me out of the SUV until he opened the door for me, and every time I tried to carry my own suitcase, he shot me a scorching look.

He's insufferable.

"How about I show you your room and put this down," he says over his shoulder as he lifts my belongings effortlessly and rounds the corner into the kitchen. "Then, I'll give you a tour. Want you to make yourself at home."

I follow Maverick without responding because, really, do I have a choice? I'm eternally grateful for him, and I can't deny the sense of safety that washes over me whenever I'm in his presence… I'm just frustrated. Not at him, but at the situation—at the fact that my choices have been taken from me. Again. Unfortunately for Maverick, I tend to lack a filter when my emotions run high. It's a good thing he can't see my face because, while I'm doing my best to keep the snarky comments to myself, the subtitles in my expression are crystal clear.

Before I can drown further in an ocean of self-pity, a bump against my thigh has me coming to a full stop next to the kitchen island. I let out a surprised squeak that draws Maverick's attention. He walks back toward me immediately, leaving my suitcase in the middle of the hallway.

"Juno! Here, boy."

I drop my gaze until I'm met with the sweetest face I've ever seen: deep, intelligent brown eyes framed by tall, alert ears, and a black-and-tan muzzle that's currently pressed against my thigh. His tail gives a hopeful wag as he astutely ignores his owner. Without a second thought, I drop to my knees and wrap my arms around his neck, pulling him close. This sweet dog. He saved my life. I mean, Maverick helped—of course—but if it weren't for Juno, I wouldn't be here.

My fingers sink into Juno's thick coat, warm and slightly coarse beneath my touch. Juno's body is solid and steady—an anchor against the chaos in my mind. I press my face into his fur as he stills for a moment, then lets out a soft, contented huff. Juno leans into the embrace, his breath fanning softly against my shoulder as he nudges closer, a low, happy rumble vibrating in his chest. I don't even realize I'm crying until he licks my cheek, his weight pressed against me like he understands exactly what I need.

Distantly, I hear Maverick call for Juno again, though it goes unanswered.

"He's fine," I whisper into Juno's fur, still unwilling to let go. "Aren't you, sweet boy?" I sit back on my haunches and gently maneuver his head to mine, pressing our foreheads together momentarily before delivering a kiss between his eyes. "Thank you. Thank you for saving me."

I'm distracted by another lick to my face, but I don't miss the way Maverick mutters under his breath—something about the "thank you" he got versus the one Juno just received.

"You've done it now, sunshine. He's going to follow you everywhere." Maverick shakes his head in amusement before waving me to follow him down the hall. "Come on, let me show you your room."

Placing one more kiss to my favorite canine's head, I stand and trail behind Maverick. Sure enough, Juno sticks by my side the entire way to my temporary bedroom. I pause at the door and take in the space that's a stark contrast from mine back at the apartment. It's nice and spacious, but it's cold and impersonal—like everything else I've seen so far in this house. A queen-sized bed rests against the far wall, centered in the middle of the room, covered in dark navy bedding. On either side, a bedside table holds a lamp and phone charger. Windows, draped in matching navy curtains, frame the desk along the left wall, letting in the soft glow of the streetlights outside.

"Don't mind all the blue—the FBI owns this house, and I'm guessing they didn't put much thought into interior decorating." Maverick has set my suitcase next to a door on the opposite side of the room. "This one's the closet," he points to the door beside him, "Feel free to put your things away. And this is the bathroom." He opens the bathroom door, revealing a standard shower stall with sliding glass doors, a vanity sink, and a toilet. "It has the basics. I know it's not much, but we can get you anything you need later today."

"I really appreciate it, Maverick. Thank you." I step further into the room, wishing there was something I could do that reflects just how grateful I am for him and everything he's done for me. He doesn't even know me, and he's invited me into his home. Well, his temporary home. I suppose the lack of personal items makes a lot more sense now.

"You don't have to thank me, sunshine. Are you hungry? It's late, but I can still give you that tour."

"Oh, I think I'm okay. I'll take a raincheck on the tour for now, if that's alright with you?"

"Of course. Sleep well. Let me know if you need anything." Maverick pauses at the threshold, holding the door open and signaling to his dog, who's still leaning against me. With a soft whine, Juno trots into the hall, then pauses to peek his head back inside before the door clicks shut.

By the time I finally managed to close my eyes—with every light on in the room—it was well after four in the morning. The time on my phone taunts me when I wake up, confirming what I already know: I've only gotten an additional two hours of sleep.

It takes several attempts to untangle my legs from the bedsheets before I stumble into the bathroom. This time, I don't avoid my reflection. I haven't wanted to see the physical evidence of what *he's* done to me—the things he's taken from me—but it's time to put my big-girl panties on. I can't hide from myself forever. And, quite frankly, I don't want to.

Pressing my palms down on the cold Formica countertop, I lean closer to the mirror, studying the stranger who looks back at me. The bruises on my face—the ones I earned through defiance—are nearly gone, fading into nothing. Soon, there won't be any evidence that I displeased him at all. My gaze drops to my wrists; the skin pink and tender where the coarse rope cut into me. I wonder if it'll scar, leaving me with a permanent reminder of my torment. I shift my focus back to the mirror and cringe at the dark puffy circles beneath my brown eyes. The shadows seem deeper, and with the weight I've lost, they exaggerate the hollow, lifeless look in my face. I look as though the life's been drained out of me—as though I'm just a shell of who I used to be.

I close my eyes and take a deep breath, attempting to center myself the way Tamara taught me. When I feel a little steadier, I push off the counter and head out of the bathroom. I grab my phone on the way out, only to freeze when I open the door and spot a black-and-tan bundle lying in front of my room. "Juno? What are you doing here, sweet boy?"

At the sound of my voice, the bundle rises and bumps against me. "Well, good morning to you, too. Let's go find your dad, because I smell bacon, and I hope he has some for me." Because if he doesn't… Well, Maverick will get a front-row seat to an exhausted and hangry Clara. Spoiler alert: it's not pretty.

Juno and I follow the sound of clanking pans and sizzling bacon into the kitchen. The sight that greets me sends a jolt to my heart: Maverick stands at the stove, wearing running shorts and a t-shirt, somehow managing to fry the bacon in one pan while scrambling eggs in the other. "Are you just going to stand there and watch, sunshine?"

Oops. Busted.

I clear my throat and slide onto a stool at the kitchen island. "Morning, Mav. It smells good. How can I help?" It's the polite thing to do, right? To ask how I can help? But, if I'm being honest, I just want to stay where I'm at and watch this man make breakfast. I don't really want to help.

"Good morning. It's about done, so you just stay right there." He glances at me over his shoulder with a smirk, like he knew I only offered to be nice. "You're up early. I figured you'd still be asleep."

"I, uh, I haven't been sleeping well."

Maverick turns off the stove and carries both pans over to the island counter where black silicone trivets await the scorching cookware. He sets them down and stares at me, his expression full of concern. "Will you be okay if I head into the office today? He doesn't know where you are; you're safe here, I promise. But I can stay if you want me to."

The full weight of his attention is unnerving—almost as if he can see right through me. I'm not sure how I feel about that. Still, I'm glad he didn't push when I said I haven't been sleeping well. "I'll be okay."

He makes a disbelieving sound before reaching for

plates and coffee mugs from the cabinet above the sink. After piling my plate with eggs, bacon, and buttered toast, he slides it in front of me. "Eat. Want coffee?"

"So bossy," I mumble before digging in. Maverick quirks a dark brow, and I recover quickly, offering him a sheepish smile. "Er, I mean… Thank you for breakfast. It's really good. And yes, please. I'd love coffee."

"You're welcome." He shakes his head, trying his best to hide a smirk before grabbing the coffee pot and filling both mugs to the brim. "Black, no cream or sugar."

He remembers. I don't know why that does something to me, but it does.

"Thank you. Truly." I carefully lift my mug and blow into it, watching the rising steam disappear. "When are you heading into work?"

"In about an hour. I'll bring dinner. And there's food in the fridge when you get hungry."

"Burgers?" I ask hopefully, unable to hide my little shoulder dance when he nods.

We finish breakfast in comfortable silence. Before Maverick can reach for my plate, I hop off the stool and make a beeline for the sink. "I'll wash the dishes." As expected, he starts to protest, but I cut him off with the same look my momma used to give me. "You cooked. I clean. It's only fair."

An exasperated sigh leaves him, but he doesn't argue. "Thanks, Clara. I'm going to get ready and put a call in for an unmarked car to sit outside while I'm gone."

"No," I rush out. "That's not necessary. I'll be okay, I

promise." It's not like *he* didn't get past the protective detail posted outside of my apartment last night, anyway.

Maverick gives me a long, searching look then nods. "Text me if you need anything today. Anything at all, you hear?"

"I will." Not.

I spend most of the day on the couch, curled up with my new best friend and binge-watching a TV series about a lone survivor of a race with black blood. The female lead is fierce—strong, independent, and takes zero shit. She makes me want to be more like her. Halfway through season one, my phone vibrates.

Tamara
Hey best friend. Want company?

Clara
I'd love some! But I'm at Maverick's.

Instead of responding to my text, Tamara immediately video calls me. I roll my eyes and hit accept. "What the hell are you doing at Maverick's?"

"Well, uhm... He came to get me last night. Or I guess it was early this morning."

"That's fucking obvious, sister. And you know it's not what I meant."

I sigh, dragging a hand down my face. I've been good today. I haven't thought too much about what happened. I haven't even checked the locks and windows obsessively—not with Juno next to me.

My voice is shaky and quiet as I walk Tamara through everything—from the moment I woke up to the second I stepped into Maverick's house. A few times, I have to pause when she shrieks, "Oh my god!"

"So, here I am," I finish, forcing a smile. But Tamara knows me too well; she knows it's fake as all get out.

"Why the fuck didn't you call me?!"

"I'm sorry, Tam. I panicked and called him."

"I meant today. You didn't call me today. How can I be there for you when you don't tell me this shit, Clara?"

A wave of guilt crashes into me, threatening to drag me under with its weight. The feeling is only amplified when I see her eyes glistening with unshed tears. "I'm so sorry, Tamara. I swear, from now on, I'll tell you everything right away."

"You better, damn it."

"I will. I love you, Tam."

"I love you, too, best friend. Call me later, okay? I work tonight, but I'll answer when I can."

Hanging up the phone, I set it on the armrest, then lean down to rest against Juno's warm body. Talking to Tamara always lifts my spirits, but I'd be lying if I said I wasn't a little envious that she's still herself—she's still free. I miss working and being around other people, but the thought of exposing myself to the outside world—knowing he's still out there—is utterly terrifying.

After dinner, I watch Maverick make his rounds through the house, ensuring the garage is closed and checking the locks on the doors. Once he heads into his room to shower, I move through the house to make my own rounds. The feel of my fingertips gliding over the locks and handles soothes the anxiety coiled tight in my chest. I know they're secure—I've already checked multiple times, and Maverick just did the same—but my brain won't let me stop. Not yet.

At the front door, I test the deadbolt, twisting it back and forth to be sure it's locked. Then I jiggle the handle once, twice, three times. It doesn't budge. The garage and back doors are next. I keep my breathing slow and measured, counting the seconds before forcing myself to step away and move on to the living room windows.

I pull back the curtain just enough to peek outside before running my fingers along the latch. Locked. I test it anyway, my stomach knotting at the thought of it some-how, impossibly, coming undone. It holds firm. I exhale, but the tension in my chest doesn't ease. It wasn't this bad earlier today—the darkness is making it worse.

I don't know how long I spend going through the motions, checking and rechecking every entry point, every possible vulnerability. The only room I leave untouched is Maverick's.

A sound behind me makes my pulse stutter. I whirl around, breath catching—only to find Maverick standing in the dim light of the hallway, arms crossed. He doesn't say anything at first; he just watches me, his expression unreadable.

"It's all locked up, sunshine," he finally says, voice low and even. "You're safe here."

I hold his gaze, his warm brown eyes steady on mine,

before I nod automatically. But I don't think he buys it. Hell, I don't even buy it. Because no matter how many times I check the locks, no matter how solid these walls feel around me, the fear lingers—curling in my chest, whispering that nowhere is truly safe.

CHAPTER 18
MAVERICK
NO PLAN

IT WAS hard as fuck putting on a normal facade when I got home this evening, especially throughout dinner.

I spent the day at the FBI resident agency office, combing through the photos and videos Evie took of Clara's apartment. We went over everything, searching for the smallest clue, but—of course—we came up empty-handed. This motherfucker is good; he left nothing behind.

Nothing except a single, deliberate message meant to instill fear.

A printed picture, tucked beneath Clara's comforter. He must have placed it there when he made the bed, hoping she'd find it. He wanted her to know she's still in his crosshairs.

It was a picture of Clara—asleep, curled into a ball, with only a thin blanket covering her. The shot was zoomed in, concealing any details about where she had been held, but the tear stains streaking her cheeks were unmistakable.

It hurt just to look at it. Still, hours later, it torments me.

Arlo and Spencer suspect the picture is a still from a video. The thought chills my fucking blood. That would mean he has a video—maybe multiple—of Clara in captivity. And if he has one of her, he has them of his other victims, too.

Now, from the dim hallway, I watch Clara in silence. She doesn't realize I've been standing here, observing as she moves from door to window, checking and rechecking every lock in the main house. She didn't go into my room —I would've known—but I'd bet she went everywhere else.

The anxiety is written in the tight set of her shoulders, the restless way her fingers linger on each lock. How did I miss this? I knew she wasn't okay, but she *really* isn't okay.

"It's all locked up, sunshine," I say finally, keeping my voice low, careful not to startle her. "You're safe here."

She meets my gaze, hesitating before offering a small nod. I wouldn't let anything happen to her. I hope she knows that. But I don't think she believes she's safe.

"Goodnight," she whispers as she passes me, heading straight for her bedroom.

Juno follows her, but a snap of my fingers has him returning to my side.

A blood-curdling scream shatters my sleep.

Within moments, I'm out of bed, gun in hand, sprinting toward Clara's room with Juno close behind. I shove the door open, momentarily blinded by the sudden flood of light. Blinking past it, I scan the room before rushing to her side. "Clara?"

She's still in bed, thrashing against the sheets, her face twisted in anguish and soaked with tears. Her chest rises and falls rapidly, ragged gasps escaping between the screams. She's trapped in a nightmare—drowning in it.

I don't want to startle her, but I can't just stand here and watch. Moving on instinct, I secure my gun in the firearm safe inside her nightstand, then reach out, running a soothing hand along her arm. "Clara. Sunshine, it's me."

She startles at my touch, her wide, terror-filled eyes locking onto mine. "Mav?"

"You're safe, sunshine. It was just a nightmare." As if to reinforce my words, Juno leaps onto the bed and curls up at her feet, his solid weight grounding her.

She scrubs at her face, but keeps her hands up to hide her eyes. "I'm sorry," she whispers, her voice small and fragile.

"Don't," I say firmly. "Nothing to be sorry for. Are you okay? Juno can stay with you if you want."

A beat of silence. Then, so softly I almost miss it, "Will you stay, too?"

I hesitate, but only for a second. "Yeah, sunshine. I'll stay. Do you want the light off?" The question is barely out of my mouth before Clara shakes her head profusely.

"Okay, okay. Lights on." I climb in beside her, staying above the comforter, careful to give her space.

Lying on my side, I study her face—the tightness around her eyes and mouth, the tears clinging to her lower lashes, the beads of sweat gathered around her hairline. My heart breaks for this woman and everything she's been through. The urge to hold her, to comfort her, is overwhelming. Damn near impossible to ignore.

"Is it okay if I hold you?" I watch her closely, waiting for permission. When she nods, I pull her gently into my chest, wrapping my arms around her. "Do you want to talk about it?"

Clara's silent long enough that I think she won't answer, but then, in a broken whisper, she recounts her nightmare—or fucked up memory. "Sometimes, on shower days, he wouldn't just watch me. He'd take the soap from me and wash my body and hair. When I didn't say 'thank you,' he told me he'd beat proper manners into me. And he did. That's where I was… One time, I made him so angry, he threw me across the room. Like a rag doll." She sniffles and exhales shakily. "He always tried to 'make it up to me' afterwards—being sweet, thinking that *touching* me would make it better. Every time I close my eyes, he's there. I can't escape him, Mav. I don't want to sleep. I'm constantly on edge, worried he'll come for me, so I check the locks and windows all the time. All the freaking time."

Fucking hell.

"I'm so fucking sorry, Clara." I press a kiss to her head and rub soothing circles on her upper arm. "You're not alone, you hear? I'll help you any and every way I can. I'll have a security system installed tomorrow."

"You don't hav—"

"I know I don't have to, sunshine, but I'm going to. I'm surprised this place doesn't have one already." I pause for a moment, wondering if the suggestion on the tip of my tongue might cross a line. "Have you, uh… Have you thought about talking to someone? You've been through a lot, and I can only imagine what you're going through now. I know a few therapists, and you could meet with them virtually."

Once again, Clara's silence is long, but eventually, I feel her nod against my arm. "Okay. I'll try."

"Good girl." I squeeze her tightly before loosening my hold, resisting the urge to nuzzle against her neck. "Sleep."

Sunshine,

I didn't want to wake you. Coffee's in the pot, just have to turn it on. I'll bring dinner home. Text if you need anything.

−Mav

Home.

It's been a long fucking time since I told someone I'd bring dinner home—since I walked through the door to find someone other than Juno waiting for me. Seven years, to be exact. But, for some reason, going home to Clara doesn't just feel different. It feels right.

I blink, shoving thoughts of her and last night aside. Shifting my focus to the present, I scan the conference room—the entire task force is here. It's time to concentrate on finding this son of a bitch before he finds her.

"Multiple jurisdictions are making this case difficult to solve and pin down," Cruz admits. "We're communicating with law enforcement in Illinois, Wisconsin, and Iowa, cross-referencing the evidence we have with theirs, but that's seven fucking police departments. It's messy."

"And a lot of surveillance to sift through, especially because we weren't able to nail down the exact time, date, and location for when some of the victims went missing," Arlo adds.

Clearing my throat, I tap my fingers against the table three times. "Clara told me something last night," I begin, locking eyes with Cruz—he's been the most vocal about how bad of an idea it is to have her with me—before surveying the rest of the team. "She said he would hurt her if she didn't say 'thank you,' that he'd beat 'proper manners' into her."

Spencer leans forward in his chair, fingers flying across his keyboard. "I'm going to add that to the report. I've been in touch with Special Agent Brenner at BAU; I'm sending a request for a criminal profile."

"Think he'd be willing to come down here?" Riley asks. "And how the hell can we get another whiteboard? This one's full." She points to the evidence board, overflowing with photos, maps, strings, and pins. "We're going to need another one to lay out the criminal profile."

"I'll go hunt one down!" Jesse's already halfway out of the room before any of us can say anything. He's never been one for long team meetings. His home is the lab, where he's on his feet and lost in his element. I'm not surprised he's the one who volunteered.

"I'll ask Brenner if he'll come down, but I don't know if he will." Spencer presses his lips together in thought before gesturing to the evidence board's timeline. "According to his established pattern, our unsub finds his next victim while he has the current one in captivity. He should've taken someone else by now. We have every police department on alert for missing persons reports fitting the victim profile, but none have come in."

"Clara's survival messed up his plans."

Spencer nods. "And he's methodical. He plans everything—the disguise he'll use for each victim, the traps he'll set, where he'll keep them, where he'll bury them. Every detail is calculated. But I don't think he's taken his next victim yet. And I don't think he will—not as long as Clara's alive."

"We need to lure him out."

HIM

DESIRE

"HAVE A GOOD DAY, SIR."

"Thank you. See you in the morning." My response is quick—clipped—as I quicken my pace, desperate to leave this building and hurry home.

The fingerprint reader beeps its acceptance, and not a second later, I throw open the front door, letting it shut behind me.

I don't stop.

I can't.

I'm already unzipping my slacks as I take the stairs toward *our* safe place.

I need this release. Fuck me, I need it.

The moment I'm in my chair, I release my aching cock, then press play on my favorite video.

My favorite girl.

I keep my eyes fixed on her beautiful face, remembering every detail of this moment.

The way she tried to hide how I made her feel.

My hips thrust in time with the rough fuck I gave her.

Does she still feel me?

The sound of our bodies coming together—her cries—has me working my dick so hard it bursts.

Fuck, fuck, fuck.

I smear my essence over my thighs, wishing it was her skin instead.

Goddamn, that felt good.

But it's not enough.

It's been too long since my monster has been sated.

He's raging, crawling beneath my skin.

He's only satisfied when he's dominating. Fucking.

He wants to bury himself inside of her.

Take her.

Ravage her.

Mark her with our seed.

Remind her that *he's* in control—*he's* the one who chooses if she lives or dies.

She's ruining everything.

She left her apartment. Didn't even find the gift I left for her. Didn't get to reminisce the way I did.

I watched her get in the car with that good-for-nothing special agent. Watched them from the shadows. Watched them pull into the garage. His garage.

He can't have her.

Can't touch her.

I need to get her away from him.

And I might have just the thing…

CHAPTER 20

CLARA
MAKE ME BELIEVE

I'M WATCHING the clock like a hawk, perched on the edge of Maverick's fancy office chair. I told him I'd try talking to someone—a therapist—and I'm a woman of my word. But I'd be lying to myself if I said I didn't want to walk out of this room right now and crawl under the blankets with Juno. That sounds like a much better plan than unpacking everything I've been through.

Maverick set me up in his home office, leaving me on my own after making sure I knew I could take as long as I needed before and after my appointment. His contact recommended Dr. Miller, a therapist who works almost exclusively with women who have experienced similar trauma.

Trauma.

It's funny how life shapes us through our experiences—the things we endure and survive. Are there levels of trauma? I thought I was handling the pain of losing my family pretty well; cutting them out of my life felt like amputating a limb. But does the trauma of the last few weeks compound that loss? Do I have multiple traumas now? How does this shit even work? Will the incessant need to check the doors and locks ever fade? Could I enjoy the darkness again and sleep with the lights off? That'd be freaking great.

I have questions. So many questions. I suppose that's what this session is for—and every one after.

I glance at the clock one more time. 11:34 a.m. My appointment is at 11:35 a.m., leaving me with exactly one minute to get my shit together.

I can do this.

Blowing out a deep breath, I click the link to start the secure video call. It connects instantly, and I'm greeted by a classically beautiful woman. Mid-twenties, blonde hair, and a gentle, warm smile. She looks approachable. Relatable. Safe. It's the first thought that comes to mind—the same one I had when I met Maverick.

"Hi, Clara," she says. "I'm so happy to meet you. My name is Ashley Miller, but please call me Ash." Her voice is soothing, welcoming. I find that I want to open myself up to her, to trust her.

I attempt a smile—at least I think I do. "Hi, Ash. Thank you for meeting with me on such short notice. I really appreciate it."

"Oh my goodness, that's what I'm here for! So, I know the basics of your case—Special Agent Rhodes gave me a brief run down—but I'd love to check in with you first. How are you feeling about today's meeting? Or just... today in general?"

"Uhm… I'm nervous," I answer, exhaling slowly. "I know this will be good for me. That I need it, but it's hard. I relive that nightmare every night, and I don't really want to relive it again."

"That's completely understandable." Her expression is kind, patient. "Do you need to address the trauma at some point? Yes, but I think you already know that. That doesn't mean you have to do it all right now. We do this at your pace—on your time and at your comfort level. If you'd rather focus on the present and revisit the past when you're ready, then we'll absolutely do that."

"Thank you, Ash," I whisper. I already feel overwhelmed, but in a good way. She won't push me, and I'm thankful for the grace.

"I want to ask.. Do you feel safe where you are?"

"Yes," I respond instantly, though I stare off into the distance and purse my lips. It isn't that I'm not being honest—because I am—it's just that, despite feeling safe with Maverick, I don't feel safe as a whole. After a pause, I continue, "It's… complicated. I feel safe with Maverick. There's something about him that's made me feel safe from the start, so whenever he's around, I'm okay. And Juno— Maverick's dog—has been with me every day. Having him here has been really helpful. But… I don't feel *safe* safe. There's a part of me that's convinced he'll find me again. Before I came here—to Maverick's—I checked my doors and windows at least fifty times a day, and that's not an exaggeration. I check them here, too, but not nearly as often. And I sleep with all the lights on; that helps."

"It makes sense that your sense of safety has been shattered. It might take some time before you feel completely safe, but even small steps are progress. Those small steps matter. And that you've already reduced how often you check the locks? That's progress, Clara." Ash shifts in her chair, leaning forward. "What's it like, sleeping with the lights on?"

"Real freaking shitty," I blurt, then slap my hand over my mouth. "Sorry! I don't know if I'm allowed to say that."

Ash laughs—a light, twinkling sound. "Say whatever you want. I have the mouth of a sailor. You're good."

Relief washes over me. "Oh, good. That makes me feel better. And sleeping with the lights on sucks—it's really freaking hard. Honestly, sleeping has been rough. But I'm too afraid to turn the lights off—it feels like every shadow is out to get me."

Ash hums, then asks, "Is there a bathroom in your room?"

"Yup. That light stays on, too."

"Have you tried turning off the main light but leaving the bathroom light on? Maybe using a lamp instead? This way your room isn't completely dark."

Why didn't I think of that? "Oh... I haven't tried that. There are two lamps in the room, but I just turn those on with everything else." I nod to myself. "I can try it."

"Have you been able to get any sleep at all?"

"The other night," I admit. "I had a nightmare, which isn't unusual, but I must've been screaming because Maverick came in. Juno, too. I asked him to stay. It was probably the best sleep I've had since... well, since everything."

"I'm glad you have him," Ash says gently. "You need a strong support system."

I hesitate, then ask, "Would it be... weird or inappropriate if I asked him to stay again tonight? I'm just so freaking tired."

"I don't know about 'appropriate,' but you do whatever you need to do to make it through the night. Don't worry about what other people think. Take it one day at a time and fuck everyone else."

Oh, I really, really like her. I let out a fake gasp, then offer her a genuine smile. "Thank you. I needed to hear that."

"I'll always be honest with you." She tilts her head. "How's it been going outside?"

I scrunch my nose and clear my throat. "It... hasn't. Unless you count walking from Maverick's car to the house."

"That doesn't count," she says, amused. "Does he have a backyard?"

I dip my chin.

"Would you consider sitting out there with Juno? Just for a little while? You can tell me all about it next time. Maybe ask Maverick to sit with you."

All I can do is nod while tears prick my eyes. Have I really let him control me like this? Let my fear take over to where I haven't even stepped outside unless absolutely necessary? I don't want to live like this anymore.

For the rest of our session, we shift to lighter topics, and I relax. My first impression of her was right; she's easy to talk to. As we schedule our next appointment for the same time next week, I feel something I haven't felt in a long time.

Relief.

I have someone to talk to. Someone who won't judge me.

I give myself ten minutes to decompress before stepping into the living room. Maverick is on the couch, laptop on his lap. He abandons it the second he hears me. "Hey, how did it go?"

"It went really well," I answer. The truth in that statement surprises me. I wasn't sure how I'd feel about therapy, but talking with Ash felt right—I feel lighter. After claiming the corner of the couch, Juno wastes no time meandering over and curling up at my feet. "I like her. Thank you so much for finding her for me."

"Of course, sunshine. I'm just glad you have someone to talk to."

"Yeah, me too. She makes me feel comfortable." I lift my gaze to his, running my hands nervously along the armrest.

Maverick watches me closely. "What is it?"

I wet my lips, my pulse thrumming. "I want to ask you something." I pause, meeting his eyes as my fingers press into the couch, the deepening indentations evidence of my nerves. "Would you... Would you be okay sleeping with me again? I slept so much better with you there." Before he even has a chance to respond, I hastily add, "But you don't have to. Please don't feel like you have to say yes. I don't want to make this weird, I just... Ash said it wouldn't hurt to ask."

His soft brown eyes widen slightly, and for a long

moment, he's silent. Like he's contemplating my ridiculous, needy request. My heartbeat pounds in my ears as I wait. When I think he's going to say no, he nods.

"Ash is right," he murmurs. "And yes, sunshine. I can. For as long as you need me to."

My hands tremble as I turn off the bedroom light, dimming the room. The bathroom light and both bedside lamps are the only things warding off the darkness.

"You can keep the light on, sunshine."

"No," I exclaim, then wince. "Sorry. I mean… Ash suggested turning off the overhead light but keeping the lamps and bathroom light on."

I glance at Maverick, leaning against the desk. He's been watching me closely all night. It's unnerving but comforting. Exhaling, I shake my head and whisper, "I need to do this."

"Okay, sunshine. But if you need all the lights on, just say the word, and I'll take care of it."

I offer him a small, grateful smile before walking toward the bed and lifting the comforter. Hesitation stops me, and it takes more effort than I'd like to admit to slip beneath the covers.

It isn't completely dark—the soft glow from the lamps and the bright bathroom light illuminate every inch of the room.

I can do this.

The moment I pull the blanket up to my face, Juno

jumps onto the bed, settling at my feet. His weight is a balm to my nerves.

Maverick moves to lie on top of the comforter—like last time—but I quirk an eyebrow at him. "I'm not going to bite, Mav. You can get under the blankets."

A chuckle rumbles in his chest. He slides beneath the covers, shifting onto his side—his front to my back. Inches separate us, but I need him closer. I scoot back, silently hoping he gets the hint.

He does.

The tension in my body unravels as his arms wrap around me, pulling me against him. Between Juno's warmth and Maverick's solid presence, I've never felt safer—even with the low lighting.

"Thank you for this, Mav."

"You don't have to thank me, sunshine." He presses a soft kiss to the back of my head, then runs his hand down my arm three times before tracing slow, soothing circles.

"You do that a lot."

"Do what?"

"Things in threes. You tap three times, knock three times… it's always in threes."

"Huh." He's quiet for a moment, and I revel in the feel of his fingers continuing their gentle pattern on my skin. "My mom… She used to say the number three is a symbol of completeness. I guess it helps me feel balanced when I'm feeling unsteady. Didn't realize I did it enough for you to notice."

I notice everything about him. It's hard not to. But I don't tell him that.

"Are you feeling unsteady now?"

"I'm… uneasy. Knowing he's still out there puts me on edge. I need to keep you safe."

"You do." I adjust my head on his arm. "I hope you know that."

Finding myself curious about his family, I ask, "Are you close with your mom?"

"I was." His voice tightens with emotion, and I immediately regret asking. "She passed away a few years ago."

I suck in a breath. "I'm so sorry, Mav. That must've been hard."

He nods against me. "It was. My parents had me later in life—I was their only child. My dad passed away about two years before her, but they were both in their eighties. They died in their sleep."

The pain of losing a parent—both parents—is a pain I wouldn't wish on anyone. I say nothing, just reach up until I find his hand, intertwining our fingers and resting them on my shoulder.

"What about your family?" he asks after a beat. "Tamara mentioned you're estranged. Do you have any siblings?"

I stiffen. I knew this was coming. I didn't want to talk about my family with Ash, but I opened this can of worms by asking about his.

"You don't have to answer," he adds, sensing my hesitation.

"No, it's okay." I clear my throat and swallow hard. "I don't have any siblings. It was just me. My mom and my stepdad. My dad, too."

I haven't talked about my family since I told Tamara a

couple of years ago. It's a crushing weight, bearing down on me, threatening to pull me under. I have good days and bad days. On good days, I can think of my mom without an overwhelming sense of sadness—I can acknowledge that I miss her, then continue with my day. But when those bad days hit? I feel as though I'm drowning. Images of my mom and the sound of her voice fill my head, making my heart ache—all the memories of what was and the longing for what could've been. On those days, I can't shake the sadness.

I start to think that maybe I can talk about it without crying, but the moment I feel the sting behind my eyes, I know it's a lost cause. Clearing my throat, I continue in barely a whisper, "I miss them, you know? Especially my mom. I have to tell myself she's dead because it's the only way I can cope."

A tear escapes before I can stop it. I cover my eyes, taking a shaky breath. "Crap."

"It's all right, sunshine. I have you." Maverick squeezes my hand.

"It's been years since we've spoken—I don't think the grief ever goes away, you know?" And I know he does; I know he understands how I'm feeling because we share a similar loss. "But I do miss her. I miss her lumpia," I confess with a rueful chuckle. "They're these Filipino egg rolls, and they were my favorite. She'd cook any Filipino dish I asked for. I can never make them as good as she can; it just doesn't taste the same. And I miss the way she smelled. Is that weird?"

"No, not weird at all. I miss the way my mom smelled,

too." He pauses, then, with a soft voice, he asks, "Can I ask what happened between you?"

Dampness gathers where my cheek rests against his arm. I start to shift, intending to wipe it away, but Maverick only holds me tighter.

"I didn't always agree with their beliefs—religious or political," I start, voice unsteady. "I usually nodded and smiled any time they said something I disagreed with; we didn't always have to agree, you know? But my stepdad... He found God later in life, and that became his entire identity. There's nothing wrong with that, of course—to each their own—but he had a hard time accepting when other people viewed things differently. I think he thought it was a challenge—a challenge to his faith, even though it wasn't. He kept pushing and pushing... pushing his faith onto me. When he told me I'd go to hell because I don't believe in God, I couldn't take it anymore." I take a breath, steadying myself. "And my mom... she supported him. Once, she would've fought for me. She used to say nothing mattered more than blood. But I guess that's changed. So when it became too much, I cut ties with them. I walked away," I finish sadly.

Maverick exhales sharply. "That's fucked up. I'm so sorry."

"It is," I sigh. "But I've learned that family isn't just about blood. Sometimes, blood ties are toxic—unhealthy— and you have to let them go."

"And your dad?"

"God, I haven't seen him in... thirteen, maybe fourteen years? He lives on the East Coast. We don't talk much.

Mostly because of me." I pause, then correct myself. "No, it's all because of me. It's not that we weren't close—we were, a long time ago. But after so much time apart, he's practically a stranger. I don't know how to bridge that gap."

I release a breath. "I'm so thankful for Tamara. She's like the sister I never had. Hell, she's all I have."

Sleep tugs at me, sadness settling into something quieter—something bearable in Maverick's embrace. And just before I drift off, I swear I hear him whisper, "You have me now too, sunshine."

But maybe it's just a dream.

CHAPTER 21
MAVERICK

FOR THIS YOU WERE BORN

CLARA'S UNEASY. It's in the stiffness of her movements as she lifts her coffee to her lips, in the way her eyes dart across the backyard, searching for an intruder who isn't there.

Navigating new fears after the trauma that fucker put her through isn't easy, but her will to heal and move forward continues to amaze me. I saw her strength back in the hospital, and I admired her then, but now? Her determination calls to me like a tide to the shore—pulled by an unseen force in her direction, inevitable and unrelenting.

This morning, while I was making breakfast, she walked into the kitchen and asked if we could eat outside. Said it was something on her list—something she needed to do.

Now, her plate sits untouched, and she hasn't stopped stroking Juno's head in her lap.

"Clara," I say, keeping my voice low. "We don't have to eat out here. We can go back inside."

"Nope. I'm doing this, Maverick." She sounds so sure, but her expression betrays her.

"Then you better eat, woman." I give her a hard look. I'd bet good money she's lost weight since the abduction, and I don't fucking like it.

"Grr. Fine."

"Did you growl at me, sunshine?"

She ignores me, suddenly interested in her food. Lifting a forkful of eggs to her mouth, she pretends not to hear the question. I shake my head and let it slide, turning my focus to my own breakfast before I have to head into the office.

***

"Maverick," Spencer greets me as soon as I walk into the conference room. "Brenner isn't able to make it from Quantico, but he sent over the criminal profile report."

"Good. Let's pull it up," I say as I take a seat, eager to hunt this guy down.

"Riley set up the profile board so we can fill it in as we go." He nods toward the second whiteboard positioned next to the evidence map. Right now, it's mostly blank, except for the "What?" column.

An arrow, courtesy of Riley, connects this column to the main investigation board. The "What" consists of eight rapes, seven murders—each victim buried alive—and one attempted murder, leaving the only known witness to the unsub's face: Clara.

I guess Riley figured it spoke for itself.

"Given the evidence and additional information from

Clara Santos," Spencer begins, "Brenner says our unsub is a white man in his late forties. He's someone we wouldn't expect. Someone who has a high-profile position, possibly in politics."

"Well, that's just fucking dandy," Jesse says with an exaggerated sigh.

I don't disagree. If our unsub is in a high-profile position, that presents an enormous fucking hurdle for the team.

"According to Brenner, the violent nature of the crimes suggests a history of abuse—likely maternal. It's possible his father abandoned him at a young age."

Rapping my knuckles three times on the table, I straighten and lean forward. "That makes sense. Remember how Clara said he'd punish her if she didn't use proper manners? He could be enacting similar punishments that were done to him. And, historically, it's the mother—or maternal figure—that enforces proper etiquette."

"And," Riley chimes in, "that matches Brenner's description of a high-profile position. That would mean our guy came from a family with money, especially considering a political background."

"So, etiquette lessons gone bad." Evie rolls her eyes and leans back in her chair. "This fucking guy is unreal. He strikes me as a narcissist. He knows he's smart. He dresses well. And he's a cocky son of a bitch."

"Brenner thinks the same. He said a psychological evaluation would show a history of social camouflaging and narcissism. We're dealing with a guy who understands that he has to wear a different face in public to conceal the 'true' side of himself." Spencer clears his throat and lifts the report. "Brenner wrote, and I quote, 'He's meticulous. When you find him, you'll likely find detailed journal entries. He reads these during his 'off' weeks when he's gotten rid of one victim and is waiting for the right time to abduct another. He uses this to relive the fantasy.'"

Arlo lifts a finger, waiting until Spencer finishes before he speaks. "I ran the timeline through our program. He travels far but always keeps his victims in the same city where he stalks them. Catherine Bennett was an anomaly —she was taken across state lines, unlike the others. There was something about Clara that made him act sooner."

A loud ringing cuts through our conversation. I pull out my phone, Cruz's name flashing on the screen. "Rhodes."

"We think we found the warehouse."

"Hold on," I say with urgency, immediately tapping the phone. "I'm putting you on speaker. What's going on?"

"Officer Martinez radioed in a few minutes ago. They were sweeping the warehouse district and found an office space in a warehouse about three miles in. He said it looks like a prison cell. I'm headed there now."

"Did he touch anything?" Evie and Jessie ask simultaneously, their voices rising like a synchronized echo.

"Just the doorknob. He said he backed out when he opened the door and saw the bed."

"What's the address?"

"It's the old milk processing plant off Broadway and 5th."

"We're on our way."

Tires screech against the cracked asphalt as the SUV comes to a sudden halt. The vibration of the vehicle stopping barely registers before I'm already out and heading toward the entrance, Spencer and Arlo right behind me.

"Jesus. You're not allowed to drive anymore, Rhodes," Arlo chides.

"Next time, ride in the van. I drive how I drive."

I watch as said van sharply turns into the parking lot. As soon as it stops, Riley, Evie, and Jesse leap out and head straight for us.

Police tape cordons off every entry point, surrounding the milk factory like a warning. The weathered brick of the building stands stark against the chaos, its surface bathed in the flickering red and blue lights from several police vehicles.

"Rhodes!" I hear Cruz before I see him. He cuts through the throng of officers, brushing past our small group as he ducks under the tape. "It's been cleared."

He doesn't need to tell us to follow him. Without a word, we instinctively turn on our heels and fall in line.

The double doors leading into the building are heavy, requiring effort to push open. Inside, the space is vast and open—an eerie emptiness hanging in the air. A small office is oddly placed in the middle of the room. I glance around, taking in the sealed windows, industrial equipment piled in front of another set of doors, and an alcove that likely leads deeper into the factory. This place hasn't seen use in years. Rochester's Warehouse District is a mix of new, unfinished buildings and old, dilapidated structures that desperately need to be gutted. The milk processing plant falls squarely into the latter category.

Dust coats the concrete floor, disturbed only by a series of footprints leading from the entrance to the office.

"We'll get started here," Evie says, stopping to survey the floor. "Try not to make any new footprints, please." Without glancing at us, she and Jesse begin unpacking their equipment.

Leaving them to do what they do best, the rest of us cross the space toward the interior office, carefully stepping in the old prints.

The office door has a deadbolt on the outside. Next to the doorframe, a small, rectangular window catches my eye —the same one Clara described. I roll my shoulders and straighten my spine, then step into the room to face Clara's prison.

A bed, stripped down to the bare mattress, is shoved against the far wall. An iron ankle cuff lies haphazardly on the ground, attached to a chain welded to the metal bedpost. The room is small, lacking any dust from the main area. The scent of cleaning supplies is strong and lingers in the air—bleach and pine. It's been scrubbed clean.

We canvass the space in silence. I linger in front of the barren shower stall, imagining Clara, terrified, showering while the bastard waited right here, his eyes locked on her every move.

"Hey, Mav." I breathe deeply and turn toward Arlo. He's

standing by the door, inspecting the wooden doorframe. "I found something."

"What is it?"

"See this hole in the frame?"

My brows furrow as I walk over, leaning in to examine the spot he pointed out. The hole is small, barely noticeable unless you know where to look. It's wide enough to conceal a tiny lens, the edges sharp and clean.

"Fuck. I see it. Camera?"

"Yes. I noticed the same holes—all barely noticeable—around the room. There's one in the windowsill over there," he says, pointing to the window next to the door. "Another in the wall facing the toilet and shower, and then this one—right by the bed. The cameras are gone."

"Didn't you say the photo Samson left in Clara's apartment looked like it came from a video still?" Cruz asks, glancing between Arlo and Spencer.

"Yes, and I'd say it came from the camera embedded in the door."

"We know he travels far to find his victims, and he doesn't bring them to Rochester," Spencer muses aloud, pacing between the spots Arlo identified. "He's not a man who can come and go freely—not if he has a high-profile career. So he sets up the cameras where he keeps his victims. He watches them from his house, on his phone whenever he can't be there in person."

"To relive the fantasy," I murmur, recalling Brenner's criminal profile report. We may not have found journals here—though that doesn't mean they don't exist—but the videos are another memento, providing him with the same twisted pleasure at the expense of his victims.

My hands tense at my sides, fingers curling into fists to stop them from trembling. The weight of Clara's imprisonment hits me harder than I expected. The thought of the unsub watching those videos of her, replaying his sick fantasy again and again, gnaws at my insides. A cold sweat pricks at the back of my neck. I try to steady myself, but the fear sinks deeper—a familiar knot tightening in my chest.

And I know, without a doubt, that I'm going to fail Clara the same way I failed Heather.

CHAPTER 22
HIM

JUDITH

FUCK, how I've missed her.

Missed devouring her with my eyes as she trembled—her fear so potent, I could taste it on my tongue. Watching the water sluice down her body, knowing what I'd do to her the moment she stepped out of the shower.

Into my waiting hands.

It has my monster impatient, restless and rattling deep inside my chest.

He wanted her gone—buried beneath the earth, his essence dripping out of her—but now he wants her back.

Wants inside her.

To sink his teeth into her flesh.

Taste her skin.

Breathe her in.

I want that, too.

Adjusting the binoculars, I press myself against the attic window, as close as I can get without touching her. This house has the perfect view of her bedroom; it's become the only place I can watch my obsession in real time. I have an hour before the owners come home from their overnight shift.

Plenty of time.

She doesn't know I'm watching, doesn't know I'm panting after her—each hot breath fogging the glass. She's not in the shower this time. No, this time she's undressing. Teasing me.

My eyes lock onto her as she removes her shirt, revealing perfect tits behind a thin sports bra. She wouldn't be wearing a bra—or panties—if she were still with me.

My monster seethes as she pulls on more clothes. She should be wearing ours. Our shirt. Our boxers.

Ours.

Even with his anger thrumming through me, I take out my cock and stroke hard, the anticipation building, a groan tearing from my throat—

I stop.

I'm on a mission.

This will have to wait.

I'll celebrate at home, fucking myself to her video. To the sounds of us.

Standing in front of the door, I'm tempted to force my way in. To take her with me.

I wouldn't keep her in that office again. No. This time, she'd be in my room. Tied to my bed. Mine to use whenever I want.

Maybe I'll ignore my monster this time.

Maybe I'll keep her forever.

Mmm, I like the sound of that.

But not yet. The time isn't right.

A grin spreads beneath the black ski mask and balaclava. I can already picture the look on her face when she sees the contents of the envelope.

She's too close to him. I need to rip her away.

My leather gloves creak as I pull the envelope from my coat pocket and tape it to the door. Sweat builds beneath the layers of fabric, but it doesn't matter.

She needs to see me.

She needs to know she isn't safe.

Stepping back, I lift my gaze to the camera above the door and wave.

It's time to come out, Clar.

CHAPTER 23

CLARA

NOW THAT WE'RE ALONE

MAVERICK HAS BEEN distant since he came home from work last night. He still held me in bed, chasing away my nightmares with the security of his arms, but it felt different. Distant.

It fills me with restlessness, a coiling knot that refuses to unravel.

Determined to break the tension, I plan to make him breakfast and ask about the distance. I sift through the dresser for my comfort outfit—leggings and a worn, over-sized shirt. My chosen armor for the day. Confrontation never fails to spike my anxiety, but I'm learning. Learning to communicate instead of bottling up my emotions—a habit that's hard to break.

As I pull on my clothes, an eerie sensation prickles down my spine. A feeling of being watched. It sinks its claws into me, making my skin erupt in goosebumps.

The feeling doesn't fade as I hurry downstairs, hoping to beat Maverick to the kitchen.

I should start breakfast, but unease grips me, driving me to check the doors and locks instead. Only after I've reassured myself do I grab a glass of water and pull up the security app on my phone—Maverick had the system installed a few days ago, just like he promised. I scan the feed from the exterior cameras, hoping to quiet the gnawing in my gut.

Then I see it.

The glass slips from my fingers, shattering at my feet.

Juno rounds the corner seconds before Maverick, barking and heading straight for me. Maverick holds him back, his sharp gaze flicking from the broken glass to my frozen stance. I feel the blood drain from my face, my body locked in terror.

My eyes burn with unshed tears, and I grip the phone until my knuckles whiten.

"Fuck, sunshine. Hold on. Don't move."

Distantly, I hear Maverick open the entry hall closet, then slam it shut. Before I can fully register what's happening, I'm lifted into his arms. The heavy cadence of his footsteps echoes through the house as he carries me into the living room, lowering me onto the couch before kneeling at my feet. His arms encircle my legs, a silent attempt to ground me, but the comfort feels just out of reach; I'm too shaken.

"He's found me," I whisper. The image burns in my mind—a figure cloaked in black, waving at me, letting me know he's come for me. The Grim Reaper's come to collect his due. "He's found me. He's found me."

Juno shoves his way through Maverick's hold and

presses his head against my thigh, urging me to run my fingers through his fur.

With a gentle touch, Maverick pries the phone from my grip.

"Fuck." His voice is tight as he glances at the screen. Then he pulls out his own phone, barking orders before turning back to me.

"You're safe, Clara. I promise. You're safe."

Am I?

Are we ever truly safe, or do we simply live under a false sense of security?

Something tells me there is only one truth. No one is ever truly safe—there is only the illusion of safety. And mine has shattered, scattered like the shards of glass on the cold kitchen floor.

Without responding, I wipe the tears from my face and push to my feet. No. I will not let him do this to me again.

He turned me into a shell of myself once, stripped me of everything until I was nothing but a hollow echo. Unrecognizable. It's taken everything—everything—to claw my way out of that black abyss.

Never again.

The fear pulsing through my veins ignites into something hotter, sharper, until I'm set ablaze with rage.

Maverick calls my name, but I don't stop. I rip open the front door, ignoring his protests.

There.

A single white envelope—addressed to me—is taped to the door, swaying slightly in the breeze.

He wants to taunt me? To control me with fear? Fine.

I snatch the envelope down, slam the door shut, and march back into the living room. Maverick watches me, silent but wary. He doesn't try to stop me as I sit, my fingers tightening around the envelope.

My name is scrawled across it in black ink. With a heart.

A fucking heart.

Maverick exhales sharply. "Clara—"

"No." My voice is steel. "I won't let him win, Maverick. Not this time."

I tear open the envelope, my pulse hammering in my ears.

I almost regret it.

Inside is a single photo—one that will haunt me forever.

A woman. Slumped against the steering wheel of a car, her body trapped in the twisted metal. Blood stains her face, but it's her eyes that consume me.

Lifeless. Staring into nothing.

A chill skates down my spine. I flip over the picture, noticing the message he's left for me.

A taunt. A promise.

A warning.

Still think you're safe, Clar?

Maverick takes one look at the photo, and his face blanches. His jaw tightens, muscles flexing beneath his trimmed beard as his grip on the couch cushions turns his fingertips red and knuckles white. In his other hand, he barely restrains himself from crumpling the photograph. His breathing is slow, controlled—too controlled—as if he's trying to keep himself from reacting, to keep his emotions in check.

But his eyes betray him.

They darken with something raw, something dangerous, thickening the air between us until it feels suffocating.

I'm silent as I watch his chest rise and fall—the deep, measured breaths doing nothing to calm the tremor in his hands. His nostrils flare as he reads the message scrawled on the back.

Then, slowly, he exhales through his nose, dropping the picture and dragging a hand through his silver-streaked hair. His usual composure—his steady, unwavering strength—feels like it's on the verge of snapping.

When he finally speaks, his voice is low. Tight. Lethal.

"That son of a bitch."

His tone sends a shiver through me. Because for the first time since this nightmare began, Maverick looks truly shaken. Not just angry, but thoroughly rattled.

I've never seen Maverick like this.

It should frighten me, but it doesn't.

I don't know who this woman was, but she meant something to Maverick. Her death shook him.

He left this message for me, but he fucked up. He made this personal for the one person who has the means to tear him down.

Now that I know he's out there—waiting for me—I'm ready for this battle.

And I'm not alone.

MAVERICK

JUST PRETEND

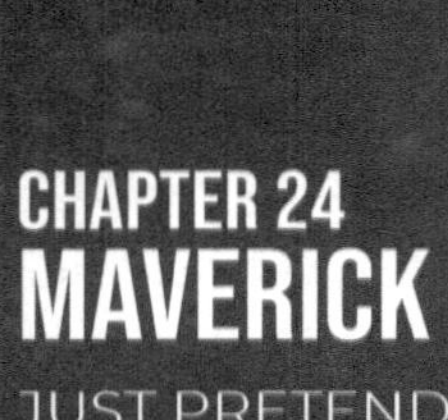

THE DRIVE to Minneapolis is tense. There's a lot unsaid between Clara and me, but I need time to process. I don't want to lose my shit on her—she doesn't deserve that.

This isn't her fault. It's his.

He has no idea what he's done by bringing Heather into this. And to what end? To frighten Clara? To make her think she'll end up like Heather—alone, broken, dead? He's already fucking tried.

I glance in the rearview, watching Clara stare out the window. She chose to sit in the backseat with Juno. I don't know if it's because he comforts her, or if she's distancing herself from me. Maybe both. I wouldn't blame her—not after the way I ordered her to pack her things and get in the car. I've barely spoken to her since.

We left Rochester as soon as the forensics team collected everything they needed, including the envelope and the photo. I sent a copy of the security footage to Arlo, hoping he'll be able to retrieve something useful. But given how careful this guy has been, it's unlikely.

How the fuck did he even get that picture? It's from Heather's police file—from her fatal accident the night she was on her way to see me. If he has access to accident reports, that means he's either inside the department or has ties to someone who is. It makes me wonder what else he has access to.

Sighing, I refocus on the road. I'm taking Clara to my house in Minneapolis—it's the safest place for her now, and I refuse to leave her side. My team will hold down the fort in Rochester. The commute isn't unreasonable if I'm needed on the ground.

A call comes through the speakers, and I quickly transfer it to my Bluetooth earpiece. "Talk to me, Arlo."

"I don't have anything from the security feed yet. It's clear he's wearing extra layers, likely to bulk up his figure and obscure his identity. But I looked into the milk processing plant. It was recently purchased by a corporation for renovations."

"How recent?"

"Within the last two years. Around the time the City of Rochester opened bids for the existing warehouses in the district. But the company that purchased the plant is ASE Anvils Corp. No other businesses in its profile. And when I dug deeper, I found that ASE is a shell corporation. I'll keep digging to find the owner."

"Thanks, Arlo. Appreciate it."

"It's what I do. And hey—before you go, Jesse's here."

Before I have the chance to respond, Jesse's voice infiltrates the line. "Boss man. The office space was relatively clean, but the unsub missed a few spots."

"Tell me you found something good."

"I'll do you one better. There were strands of light brown hair between the bed frame and the mattress. The analysis is still running, but I'd bet money it'll match the DNA profile from Clara's forensic exam."

"Call me as soon as the analysis is complete. We need to release his sketch to the public."

"That reminds me," Jesse says. "Cruz wants to do another press conference. Said we might be able to lure him out. And you two think alike because he said he wants to release the forensic sketch, too…"

"What else did he say?" I can hear the hesitation in Jesse's voice.

"He wants to say there was a witness at Silver Lake Park… and he wants to release Clara's name."

Shit.

I've been fighting to keep her name out of the media, giving her as much privacy as possible to heal without reporters swarming her. It was only a matter of time, but damn it. I didn't want it to come to this.

"I'll talk to her and call you back."

"You got it, boss man."

The moment the call ends, Clara's eyes meet mine in the rearview. "Talk to me about what?"

"We can talk about it later, sunshine."

"No, we can't."

Her dark brown eyes narrow, sharp and unyielding. If death could be dealt with a glance, I'd be a dead man.

I grind my teeth and dip my chin. No matter how much I want to shelter her from this, I can't. Clearing my throat, I give her what she wants.

"Cruz wants to hold another press conference. He wants to release the forensic sketch, tell the public there was a witness at Silver Lake Park… and he wants to release your name."

Clara is silent for so long, I almost regret saying anything. But when she finally speaks, I realize I've underestimated her.

"Good. He should do it."

"Are you sure? This will unleash a media shitstorm."

"We should've released my name before now. I'm done hiding, Maverick. Besides, where are they going to find me? I doubt reporters are going to camp out on your lawn. Hell, they won't even know I'm there. I haven't worked at The Pour House since that night, and I haven't been back to my apartment. I can handle it."

"I know you can. I just want to make sure you're prepared. You'll be all over the news."

"Tell him to do it."

I hold her gaze for a beat before nodding. "Okay. I'll tell him."

Back in the hospital, I told Clara she was a fighter. I meant it. But somewhere along the line, my own fear—of failing her, of losing her—made me forget that. She's shown me she won't back down.

And this bastard has no idea what's coming for him.

THE BEACH

DÉJÀ VU WASHES over me as Maverick pulls into the driveway of a dark gray two-story house, coming to a smooth stop in front of the garage. It's quiet. Still. Safe. But that does nothing to ease the tension stretching between us like a live wire.

Juno lets out an eager bark, likely excited to be home, and is the first to move, hopping down from the backseat the second Maverick opens his door. I stay put, gripping the strap of my bag like it's a lifeline, staring at the house as if stepping inside will change something—what, I don't know.

Maverick doesn't rush me, but I feel his eyes on me through the rearview mirror. Waiting.

With a steadying breath, I push open the door and step out, the cool evening air biting at my skin. Maverick retrieves the rest of our bags, then slams the trunk shut, brushing past me toward the small front porch tucked beneath a slanted roof. I wait at the bottom of the steps—a false barrier between us—as he unlocks the front door.

When he steps inside, the house swallows him whole, the darkness stretching deep into the silent space. He flicks a switch, flooding the entryway with warm light. It casts long shadows against the walls, making everything feel smaller. More suffocating.

"Come on, sunshine," he says, his voice softer now, lacking the sharp edge it held back in Rochester.

I follow him in. The space is clean but lived-in—his personality stitched into every detail in a way it wasn't at the rental. Dark hardwood floors stretch beneath neutral walls, a charcoal-gray sectional anchoring one side of the living room, while built-in bookshelves line the other. The door to the adjacent office is ajar, showcasing the case files scattered across a heavy wooden desk—proof that, even at home, Maverick never truly clocks out.

He drops his keys on the entry table and heads straight for the kitchen, raking a hand through his hair before bracing both palms against the counter. His back is rigid, his shoulders tight. He's still wound up from the drive, from the call, from everything.

I should say something. Instead, I just stand there, gripping my bag.

"The bedroom's down the hall," he says after a long beat, still facing away from me. "Bathroom's across from it. If you need anything, just—" He lets out a sharp breath and finally turns to face me. His expression is unreadable. I don't like it. "Just let me know."

"And the other room?" I ask, more for something to fill the silence than anything else.

"My office."

I nod, shifting on my feet, but neither of us move. I can't stand the weight that hangs between us, and I don't think I can get settled without addressing it. It's not just today—it's the distance since last night.

Finally, I clear my throat. "Maverick."

He doesn't move as I step closer, stopping just shy of touching him. "This," I say, gesturing between the two of us, "feels heavy. I don't like it. It doesn't feel right."

Maverick's jaw tenses as he stares past me, his gaze unfocused. Then he sighs, leaning back against the counter, rubbing an eyebrow with his forefinger. Exhaustion drags at his features. He looks utterly drained—mentally, emotionally.

"I'm sorry, sunshine."

When he doesn't continue, I arch a brow. I'm not walking away without resolving this, and I'm sure as hell not letting him off the hook that easily.

"Come here."

He doesn't wait for me to move. He simply grips my hips and pulls me into him, wrapping me in the solid warmth of his arms. It takes me a beat to respond, but then I'm holding onto him just as tightly, resting my cheek against his chest. It's different from how he holds me at night—this is grounding, steady, a silent reassurance that neither of us is alone in this.

"It isn't you, Clara. I need you to know you've done nothing wrong." His breath is warm against my temple, his voice thick with emotion. "I just... We found the warehouse yesterday."

I stiffen, but he tightens his hold.

"I've been on edge ever since," he continues. "I'm sorry for pulling away. And this morning, with that photo... I needed time to process, but I shouldn't have barked orders at you or ignored you. That wasn't fair to you."

I pull back enough to meet his gaze. "You don't have to be sorry, but I need you to talk to me. If you need space, tell me. I can handle that. What I can't handle is feeling like I'm tiptoeing around you. It's hard enough knowing I've taken over your space, okay?"

"Stop. You're not taking over anything. You're here because I want you to be."

I want to ask: In what way? As someone he's bound to protect? A victim? Or something more? I might be working on my communication, but in this, I'll own the fact that I'm too chickenshit to voice the question.

"I can sleep in the living room with Juno," I say, my eyes darting to the floor. "I don't want to take your bedroom."

"Sunshine." Maverick's voice is firm but gentle. His brows knit together as he gently grips my chin between his thumb and forefinger, tilting my head back until I have no choice but to look at him. "You're sleeping in the bed. And I already told you—I'll sleep next to you for as long as you need me to. That doesn't change because of today, you hear me?"

"I hear you," I whisper.

"Good." He leans forward and presses his soft lips to my forehead. "Go get settled in my room. It's the last door at the end of the hall. I'm going to let Juno out and call Arlo. I'll have a security system installed as soon as possible."

"Okay." I give him one more squeeze before slipping away, making my way down the hall.

Maverick's bedroom is exactly what I expected—dark, minimal, and distinctly his. The walls are painted a deep charcoal, nearly black. I turn on the bedside lamp, the soft glow cutting through the darkness. A massive king-sized bed dominates the space, dressed in black sheets and a thick, dark gray comforter. No frills. No unnecessary decor. Just function.

The air carries a faint mix of cedarwood and something undeniably him—clean, masculine, steady. It's comforting. It's a space designed for practicality, and standing here, I can't help but think it fits him perfectly.

Running my hands over the soft comforter, I release a weary exhale. I need a shower. I need to wash away the day clinging to my skin.

By the time I crawl into bed, exhaustion weighs heavy on my limbs, and I leave only the bathroom light on.

I wake to the feel of the mattress dipping, warmth at my back. A low murmur calms my racing heart.

"Shh, it's just me. Go back to sleep, sunshine."

I barely manage to lift my head. "What time is it?"

"Only ten."

God, it feels so much later.

Turning on my side, I tuck my head beneath his chin. It's more intimate than before, but it feels right.

"Mav?"

"Yeah, sunshine?"

"Will you tell me about her?"

"Yeah, sunshine," he repeats with an acquiescing sigh. "I will." He presses a kiss to the top of my head and traces his fingers in slow circles along my back. I wait a few beats of silence before he tells me about his past, breathing in his scent to relax my nerves.

"Her name was Heather. That picture… it was from the night she died seven years ago." His throat bobs. "It was my fault."

"How so?"

I listen as he tells me about the raid. The call. The crash.

The guilt of it all is evident in the tightness of his voice—the sorrow unmistakable. "If I hadn't gone on that raid, if they hadn't called her… she'd still be alive."

"I'm so sorry, Mav." A pause, then, "Was she your wife?"

"No," he sighs, the word heavy with an unspoken ache. "Heather and I were together for about three years. I don't know if I would've proposed, but… I loved her."

I tighten my hold around him, offering silent comfort where words feel inadequate.

"I failed her." His voice is barely above a whisper. "I'm afraid I'm going to fail you, too. And I can't, Clara. You hear? I can't fail you."

"You won't, Maverick." The promise feels small, but I mean it.

Tilting my head, I press a light kiss to his cheek, brushing the corner of his mouth in the process. The faint contact sends my heart galloping, and I feel it with intensity when he flattens his hand against the small of my back.

He's just as affected as I am—lifting a hand to cup my cheek, his breath catches. We're so close, and the heated look in his eyes charges the space between us.

"Please say I can kiss you, sunshine."

The need in his voice steals my words, but I don't need them. My slight, barely discernible nod is all it takes. The second our lips touch, I forget how to breathe. The world tilts, and a low groan rumbles from his chest, sending warmth spiraling through my veins. I feel the exact moment his restraint frays—his mouth moves against mine, tender yet desperate. It's a kiss that's both a question and an answer.

When he shifts closer, I gasp, my awareness narrowing to the solid press of his body. He takes the opportunity to flick his tongue along my upper lip, coaxing a response that comes instinctively. My fingers fist the front of his shirt, clinging to him as heat coils low in my stomach.

And then, all too soon, he pulls away. His breath is ragged, skating over my skin when his forehead touches mine.

"Damn, sunshine."

He places a soft, slow kiss on my lips before easing back completely, not pushing for more.

I don't know whether to be relieved or disappointed. A riot of emotions leaves my head a mess, my body humming with something I haven't felt in too long. I swallow hard and settle against his chest, pressing my ear to the steady rhythm of his heartbeat.

The desire he's stirred in me battles against everything else—the past, the uncertainty, the fear. Is it too soon? Am I wrong for wanting this? For wanting him?

I don't have the answers, but that's a problem for tomorrow.

Tonight, I let the sound of his heartbeat lull me to sleep.

CHAPTER 26
CLARA

LIFTS

I STRETCH out on the couch, repositioning as Juno settles in front of me. Thank goodness Maverick's sectional is deep—this dog has no concept of personal space. Shaking my head, I pull a throw blanket over my legs and refocus on the show I've been binge-watching all day while Maverick works in his office.

"When's your appointment with Ash?"

Maverick's voice startles me, and I snap my head up from the TV, shooting him a half-hearted glare.

"Uhm… 11:35. What time is it?"

"11:35," he says, amusement lacing his tone.

"Oh, crap!" I scramble upright, accidentally shoving Juno to the floor in my haste. "Sorry, sweet boy!"

I'm halfway to his office before I realize I didn't ask if I could use his space. Spinning on my heel, I find Maverick still standing by the couch, arms crossed with a smirk on his face.

"Do you mind if I use your office? And your computer?"

"Have at it, sunshine. I'll be here when you're done."

"You're the best," I exclaim, hustling into the cozy room and closing the door behind me.

As soon as I click the secure link, Ash's face appears on the screen, her warm smile easing some of my tension. She can't be mad that I'm late if she's smiling, right? That's what I'm going with.

"Hi, Ash. Sorry I'm late!"

"Hi, Clara! No worries at all. How've you been?"

The warmth of her voice reels me in again, coaxing me to open up—to say the things I avoided last time.

"It's, uhm, it's been a little rough."

The second the words leave my lips, tears well up, and I don't have the strength to hold them back.

I drop my face into my hands, elbows braced against the oak desk. I inhale deeply—a failed attempt to steady myself. When I finally look up, Ash's expression is soft. Patient. Waiting.

"I was starting to feel more like myself these last few days. Maverick and I had breakfast outside the other morning," I say, smiling through the tears, recalling how he was willing to bring everything back inside when he sensed my discomfort. "It wasn't as easy as I thought it'd be. Maverick could tell—he asked if I wanted to go back inside. But I was determined to stay. I felt like if I went inside, I'd be giving up and letting him win, you know?

At my pause, Ash nods, but she doesn't speak—she holds space for me without pressing.

"I was proud of myself," I continue, speaking softer, "even though I couldn't let go of Juno."

"You should be proud of yourself, Clara. That's incredible progress."

"Thank you." My head cants, and I stare off into the distance. "But when Maverick came home that night, he was… different. Distant. There was a tension that wasn't there before, and it made me feel like I'd done something wrong."

"Did you ask him about it?"

My chin dips, and tears fall from my cheeks to my collarbone. "I wanted to. I had it all planned out: I was going to beat him to the kitchen and make him breakfast. But something didn't feel right. I had this… feeling, like I was being watched. I couldn't focus. I had to check the doors and locks. Then I looked at the security camera feed… and I just lost it."

Ash leans forward, her brows knitting in concern. "What did you see?"

"I saw him, Ash. He was right there, waving at me through the camera, taunting me." My voice trembles as I wipe my face with my sleeve, inhaling a shaky breath. "He wanted me to know he found me—wanted to scare me. And he did. At first, I was terrified. I was frozen, but then all I felt was rage. At him. At myself."

"What made you angry at yourself?"

"Because," I emphasize, the word clipped and raw. "It's been fucking hell living with this fear, and I was finally doing better. But the second I saw him, my first instinct was to retreat back into the person he turned me into."

"That's a natural reaction, Clara."

"I know," I whisper. "I know, but I didn't want it to be

my first reaction." I bury my hands in my hair, gripping until the sting in my scalp becomes too much. "I was angrier at him, though, for coming after me—for leaving me a message."

"Do you want to tell me more about the message?" Ash's voice is calm, soothing the torrential waves of my emotions.

"It was a picture." I look up, locking eyes with her through the camera. "A fucking picture of Maverick's girlfriend after her car accident. And on the back, he asked me if I still thought I was safe."

Ash's expression tightens and her eyes widen in shock.

"Maverick packed us up immediately and drove us to Minneapolis. I've never seen him like that, Ash. He hardly said a word to me. It wasn't until we got to his house that I had the nerves to confront him. We talked about it… the photo, the distance. He thinks he's going to fail me."

"Did he say why?"

"He blames himself for Heather's death. She was on her way to see him at the hospital when the accident happened. He said he's afraid he's going to lose me, too. He's even working from home now, just to stay close."

"How do you feel about that?"

I hesitate, then admit, "Would it make me a bad person if I said I was thankful that he made the decision, so I didn't have to beg him to stay?"

"Not at all. From what you've shared, it's clear you feel safest when Maverick is close to you. That's completely valid and it makes sense to want to be near him."

"I suppose so." I trail off, letting the silence fill the

room. My pulse pounds in my ears, my palms sweaty against my neck as I brace myself for what comes next.

Ash waits—never rushing me, content to give me the time to breathe and gather my thoughts.

"Did Maverick share with you what happened while I was missing?"

"He told me enough to understand how best to help you," she answers gently.

I hum, tipping my head slowly. "I was locked in that room for a couple of weeks, I think. It's hard to say; time there was blurry. He didn't touch me that first week, but the second week..." My teeth sink into my lower lip, hard enough to draw blood. "That's when it started. He raped me."

Ash doesn't flinch, only nods—the only indication she already knew.

"I kissed Maverick last night," I confess, the words rushing out in a breath. "And I feel like something is wrong with me. I shouldn't want him, right? It's too soon, isn't it? After what *he* did to me?"

"Oh, Clara," Ash says, voice soft with compassion. "There's no timeline for healing. Everyone's journey is different. There's no rule book that says you have to wait a certain amount of time before you feel ready for intimacy. The only thing that matters is that you feel safe with him— and you do. That much is clear. What's important now is that you take things at your pace."

"So I'm not wrong for wanting more with him?"

"No, you're not wrong at all. How did you feel after the kiss?"

Remembering the feel of his lips on mine sends goosebumps rippling across my skin. "Like I wanted more. But when he pulled away, I didn't know if I should be relieved or disappointed. Relieved that he didn't push me, disappointed because I think I wanted him to."

"Have you thought about telling him? About how you feel?

"Oh, god." I groan softly and hide my face in my hands, my cheeks flushing in embarrassment. "Do I have to? I mean—that's a dumb question; I know I should."

"There's no requirement," Ash responds with a smile. "But communication is going to be paramount for your healing and your connection with him. If he knows how you're feeling, he'll be better equipped to support you. You need to be able to check in with yourself to make sure you're okay as things progress, and he needs to be able to check in with you, too. That conversation could be a powerful first step toward something more. Do what feels right, Clara."

"Do what feels right," I repeat quietly, nodding to myself more than to her.

"Always. Only you know when you're ready. But I want to prepare you—some women who've experienced sexual trauma move forward without flashbacks or triggers, while others don't. There's no way to know in advance, so both you and Maverick need to be ready for that possibility."

"That's what I'm worried about. But you're right. I'll talk with him." I wince just thinking about initiating the conversation, but I know it has to happen. If I want more, I have to take that step. And I do want more.

Ash beams, her smile kind and full of pride. "Good. I'm really proud of the progress you've made, Clara. You should be proud, too. Same time next week?"

"That sounds great. Thank you so much, Ash—for everything."

"I'm always here for you. And if you need me before then, just reach out."

The session ends, and I slump against Maverick's desk, pressing my forehead to the cool wood as I try to slow the wild beat of my heart.

I can do this.

With a deep breath, I push to my feet and go to find him.

The living room is quiet when I finally emerge from the office. Maverick is stretched out on the sectional, one arm propped behind his head, the other lazily draped across Juno's back. The dog is curled up beside him, snoring softly and clearly living his best life. Maverick's gaze is fixed on the TV screen, but his posture is loose—relaxed in a way that tells me he was waiting for me without making it obvious.

I linger in the doorway, content with just watching them. And maybe to give myself a few moments to rein in my fraying nerves.

He glances over, catching sight of me, no doubt noticing the way my eyes are still red and puffy. His expression shifts—gentle, concerned—and he pats the spot beside him. "Hey."

I cross the room and settle next to him without a word. The second I sit, Juno readjusts to rest his head in my lap with a sleepy huff. I run my fingers through his fur, grounding myself in the silence.

Maverick reaches over, brushing a knuckle along my jaw before slipping an arm around me and pulling me close. "You okay, sunshine?"

"I think so," I whisper, leaning into his touch. "Are there any updates on the case? Do you know when the press conference will be?"

His fingers lightly brush the hair from my face, tilting his head to study me. I'm not sure what he's looking for, but when he finds it, he shakes his head. "Tomorrow. Cruz and everyone else will be there. We can watch it from here."

"Don't you need to be there?"

"I'm where I'm supposed to be," Maverick says without hesitation.

"Smooth talker." I release a breath and rest my head on his broad shoulder, letting the stillness settle around us.

After a few minutes, I decide to break the silence.

"Mav? Can I ask you a question?"

"You don't have to ask—just ask me."

I shift in his arms, turning my body and bringing up a leg so I can face him. My knee rests over his thigh, his arm brushing against my shoulder.

"Why do you think he chose me?"

Surprise flickers across Maverick's face before he smooths his expression. His hand finds the nape of my neck, applying the lightest, most comforting pressure.

"We don't know why he chose anyone, if I'm being

honest. You fit the profile of the other women, but that's all we know."

"What profile?"

"Do you really want to know?"

"Yes," I assert, leaning into his hand.

He sighs.

"All of the women had three things in common: the type of job they held—all customer-facing roles, like bartending—no family in the area, and similar physical features."

My brows draw together as I think about the other women—the ones who didn't make it. I've been so caught up in my own trauma that I haven't let myself consider theirs. An ache settles in my chest, a crack I didn't know was there, deepening with the knowledge that I get to be here and they don't.

"What are you thinking about?"

I must've gone quiet too long because Maverick's hand gently lifts my chin, guiding my gaze to his.

"I just… It just hit me that I'm the only survivor. Why do I get to live and not them?"

"Clara, baby… You can't think like that. He followed a pattern with the others, but he broke it for you. We don't know why—and maybe I don't want to know. Because if he hadn't… you might not be here. And I can't think about that, either. It was sheer luck that Juno and I were out for a run on the trail. Sheer fucking luck that he heard you."

"I can't help but wonder," I whisper, "if it's my fault for catching his attention. If I hadn't worked that night, none of this would've happened. If I hadn't flirted with him… let him drive me home…"

"Hey—no." His voice turns firm, brooking no argument. "None of this is your fault. You hear me? None of it. He would've found a way. He set his sights on you, and nothing you did or didn't do would've changed that."

"I just need this to be over. I need him to leave me alone. Why won't he leave me alone?"

"We're going to find him, sunshine," he says, his tone low and sure. "And when we do, he's going to wish it wasn't me."

"Thank you," I say softly, lifting a hand to stroke his cheek. "For being here. For making me feel safe."

"You don't have to thank me."

I press my lips together in contemplation, then shift the mood—the subject. "Last night… when I kissed you—"

"Do you regret it?"

"What? No, of course not!"

"Good. Because I don't, either."

I draw in a breath. "I talked to Ash about it today… I don't regret kissing you. I wanted to kiss you. But when you pulled away, there was a part of me that was relieved because you didn't press me for more… and another part of me that was disappointed because I wanted you to. I couldn't help but think… Maybe I'm wrong for feeling that way about you. Especially after what he did."

Maverick's jaw tightens slightly, but his hand stays gentle where it rests on my neck.

"You're not wrong." A heavy emotion laces his tone, and the weight of it sends a shiver down my spine.

"What he did doesn't get to define what you want. He doesn't get to take that from you. You're allowed to feel whatever you feel, Clara. Wanting me—wanting this— means one thing: you're alive. You're living, baby."

The words land with a soft, earth-shaking thud inside me. There's so much to unpack in what he just said—so much I'm not sure how to process yet—but one truth stands out: he never said he didn't want me. And that matters more than I thought it would.

Still, I need to hear it. I need the reassurance.

"Are you saying… I mean, do you want this, too?"

In one smooth movement, Maverick lifts me into his lap, his hands strong but careful. Poor Juno lets out an indignant huff as he's displaced from his spot. My legs straddle Maverick's thighs, his chest rising and falling beneath my palms where my hands settled. He leans in until his mouth brushes mine—close enough to feel the heat of his breath, but not quite a kiss.

"Sunshine," he murmurs, an effusive whisper into my mouth. "I haven't let myself get close to a woman in seven years. But here you are, so deep in my skin you could never get out. I don't know that I could let you go even if you wanted me to. And I'd wait forever for you, if that's what you need. You lead this. Always. You tell me what you need, and I'll give it to you."

My breath catches, a soft inhale that sticks in my throat. My fingers curl into the fabric of his navy tee as I search his face—every word, every look, every heartbeat, anchoring me to this moment.

"I'm scared," I whisper, glancing away as my gaze fixes

on his throat. "I want this, but I'm afraid something is going to trigger me and ruin it."

His arms tighten around me, one hand cradling the back of my head like I'm something precious.

"Then we take it one breath at a time, sunshine." His lips brush the corner of my mouth, featherlight, not demanding—just a promise. "And if something does trigger you, I'll be right here—reminding you that it's me holding you, touching you, worshipping you."

I close my eyes and relax into him, into the steadiness of his words and the warmth of his hold. I wouldn't wish what I've been through on anyone, but I can't deny that every broken, harrowing step somehow led me here. To him. And for the first time, my heart feels lighter—as though I've set down a weight I hadn't even realized I was carrying.

CHAPTER 27
HIM

I'M GONNA GET WHAT'S MINE

HE WASN'T SUPPOSED to take her out of the fucking city.

She's ours.

A low growl builds deep in my chest. My monster rages, surging like a storm that refuses to be contained.

Closing my eyes, I inhale deeply and press my palms flat against the desk. We can't lose our shit here. No. No one can see us—not the real us. I have to stay diligent, keep this facade in place until I get home. Until I'm back in our safe place.

When I'm confident the hurricane inside me won't bleed into my voice, I pick up the phone and dial the one person who can get me what I want.

"Good evening, sir. How can I help you?"

"I need an address." I pull the letter opener from its gilded holder and press my thumb against the blade, watching as crimson pools at the tip.

"Yes, of course, sir. For whom?"

"Maverick Rhodes. He's part of the RPD-FBI Task Force."

And he's in my goddamned way.

"An official request, sir?"

"No," I snap, setting the letter opener down and sucking the blood from my skin. "I need to speak with him regarding a different matter."

It's taking everything I have not to unleash my fury. How dare he question me? He's beneath me. He does what I ask—when I ask. Without question.

"Understood, sir. I'll have it on your desk by tomorrow morning." His voice quavers, but he recovers, waiting for me to end the call.

"Make it your priority," I command before slamming the phone down.

Playing this role is exhausting. I'm surrounded by peasants. Gullible peasants who are all too easy to manipulate —too blind to see me.

I stand and straighten my tie. It's been too long since we've had a release. We waited. Wanted to save ourselves for her again. To revel in the warmth of her skin.

But we can't wait anymore.

Slipping on my suit jacket, I adjust my Rolex and leave the office, walking with purpose to the elevator.

It's when I step outside that I see her. Dark hair swaying behind her in the wind, her face glued to her phone. From her profile, she could satisfy us. Her beauty is close enough to Clara's—not quite, but close.

We can't afford to be too choosy tonight.

I let the glass doors close behind me and follow this new beauty to her destination.

Ducking into the coffee shop behind her, I quicken my pace until I'm just ahead—close enough for her to run into me.

"Oh! I'm so sorry!" Beauty nearly drops her phone as she stumbles back. Her dark brown eyes meet mine and widen with recognition, sending a chill down my spine—and blood to my cock.

I reach out and steady her by the waist, my touch light—for now. Reluctantly, I let go.

"Oh my goodness. I am so, so sorry," she repeats.

Mmm. That voice. Sweet as sugar.

Does she taste sweet, too?

I flash my famous smile and extend my arm, gesturing for her to take her place in line ahead of me. "It's quite all right. Are you okay?"

She shakes her head, stepping behind me as we inch toward the counter. "No, no. You were here first," she says shyly. "And I'm okay. Thank you."

"No thanks needed," I respond, winking before turning toward the menu.

I wait for it.

It always comes.

Three.

Two.

One.

"Getting your caffeine fix before you head home?" she asks. "I need one, too. It's been a long day."

There it is.

I turn just enough to meet her gaze, offering her another well-practiced smile. We know how to play this game.

"A long day, indeed. Sadly, mine's not over quite yet. The caffeine's to get me through a few more hours."

"Oh, that sucks. I'm Marie, by the way." She offers her hand.

"Nice to meet you, Marie," I say, gently encasing her hand in mine.

"Can I buy your drink? It's the least I can do for bumping into you."

"What kind of gentleman would I be if I let you pay for my coffee?"

At the counter, I place my order. When the barista asks if that's all, I nod toward Marie. "Add hers to my tab."

By the time I reach the Pick Up counter, Marie has followed. I want to watch her hips sway, but I force myself to wait. To be patient.

"You didn't have to do that, you know."

Her voice.

I want to hear how she sounds when she screams.

"I didn't have to. I wanted to. Headed home now, Marie?"

"Sure am, thank God. The caffeine will keep me company on my walk."

"You're walking?"

"Well, to the bus stop first. Then I'll walk the rest of the way. It's not too far."

"No family to give you a ride?"

"Oh, no. I just moved here not too long ago. Fresh start, you know?"

"That I do."

Our drinks are called. I grab them both, handing hers over with just enough of a touch to make our fingers meet.

"I was planning to work from home the rest of the evening," I say casually. "I'd be happy to give you a ride, if you'd like."

"I wouldn't want to impose." She shifts on her feet, hesitant. Tempted.

"I wouldn't have offered if it were an imposition, Marie."

"Well," she says, eyes lifting to meet mine before flicking toward the window and the downtown chaos outside, "only if it wouldn't be out of your way."

Sometimes, it pays to be known in the city.

They think they can trust me.

But this one won't realize her mistake until it's far too late.

And tonight, my monster has plans—a message to send.

CHAPTER 28
HIM

THE DRAIN

THE DIRT IS SOFTER near the water. Damp. Easy to move with each thrust of the shovel. It gives beneath me, as if it's eager for the gift it's about to receive.

I lost track of how long I've been digging. The moon hangs low now, shards of light casting a silver sheen over her pale body, curled on a bed of twigs and dried leaves.

I drop to my haunches beside her and the shallow hole I've carved, wiping a sheen of sweat from my brow. I reach out and brush her dark hair away from her face. Her skin is still warm, reminding me of how sweet she tasted. How beautiful her screams were.

"You were almost perfect," I murmur, voice soft enough to blend with the rustle of leaves. "So close to her."

A trail of mud follows my fingertips as I run them along her jaw. "You were almost enough."

My monster stirs again, but he's no longer frantic. The rage that gnawed at my insides has dimmed to a hum—a satisfied purr. We took what we needed.

I lift her body and ease her into the grave. There's no box for her, not like the others. The earth settles, curving around her like a cradle. Her head tilts slightly to the side, lips parted as if she were asleep.

A pang of disappointment coils in my gut. We would have preferred she suffered: to know that she screamed and cried. To know she attempted to claw her way out of the grave I so painstakingly dug for her.

But time is of the essence. And the message she carries... Well, that's more important.

With a few handfuls of dirt, I begin covering her. The soil—soft like powder—scatters across her body, clinging to her lashes, her collarbone, filling the hollow beneath her chin.

I pause and peel off my gloves, replacing the mud-covered vinyl for a fresh pair.

The Polaroid camera waits on the portable table beside the box of gloves and the rest of my tools—set up out of habit, though I didn't need them tonight.

Picking up the camera, I snap two pictures of my latest conquest, lying deathly still in her earthly bed—one for us to remember her by, and one for our message.

I stare down at the photos, then slip them into my suit pocket and resume shoveling.

The hole isn't deep, but it doesn't need to be.

When I finish, I place a few fallen leaves over the disturbed ground. Not too much. Just enough to keep her hidden until I'm ready for her to be found.

I lift the camera once more and take one final shot—

this time of the grave, framed by the still water, marking its location.

This task is complete.

But I'm not done.

Not yet.

CHAPTER 29

MAVERICK
HEART SHAPED BOX

"HE SENT US ANOTHER MESSAGE. We're postponing the press conference until after we assess the crime scene."

My pacing halts mid-stride in the living room. I pull the phone from my ear and stare at the screen in disbelief, as if Cruz's words didn't register.

"What was the message? How did he send it? What's the crime scene?" I fire off questions in rapid succession, not waiting for answers.

I should be in Rochester. On the ground. Helping. Cruz and the team have kept me in the loop, and I've been doing what I can from here, but this turn of events is unsettling. It changes everything. If "message" and "crime scene" mean what I think they do—another body—then our unsub is escalating.

"Slow down, Rhodes," Cruz chides with a sigh.

I can already see him rolling his eyes, an insufferable smirk on his face. He knows dragging this shit out pisses me off. If you're going to give me information, give me the fucking information.

"Cruz, get the fuck on with it."

His tone shifts. "We received an envelope at the station around four this morning. It was sent to me but addressed to you. Inside were two Polaroids. One was of the victim in a grave; the other, a wider shot of the grave fully covered. He wanted us to see the location—she was buried along Silver Creek Lake."

"Goddamn it." I pivot toward the sliding doors, eyes locking on Clara as she tosses a ball for Juno in the backyard. She's made so much progress. Since coming to Minneapolis—since our talk—she's been lighter. Braver. Letting herself exist again. Eating breakfast outside, spending time out there with Juno. The thought of shattering her newfound peace makes my chest ache, and fuck if I don't want to protect her from that.

"There's more," Cruz says. "I dispatched units to secure the crime scene while I was on my way and called your team to meet me there. That was about three hours ago." He's silent for a beat before he adds, "This murder was different from the others. He didn't stalk the victim; didn't abduct her or hold her captive. Sammie's preliminary report puts the time of death around eleven last night."

"Shit. Cause?"

"Snapped neck. She wasn't buried alive like the others. The victim's purse was buried with her, too—license ID'd her as Marie Ann Douglas. Rochester local. Background's running now. Physically, she matches the victim profile.

Dark hair, brown eyes. But everything else? Doesn't match his signature."

"He's unraveling," I mutter. "Clara's survival threw him off—we knew this. But he's been without a victim for too long, and he hasn't been able to get to Clara. I'd bet he saw Marie yesterday and made a split decision. This wasn't a planned attack."

"Spencer said the same. But listen—the body wasn't just a message for us. He wrote on the back of both Polaroids… He meant them for Clara."

My hand tightens around the phone, the plastic creaking in protest against my death grip.

"Tell me."

Cruz's voice is low. "He wrote: 'You're mine, Clara. Come back to me and this will stop. Your FBI friend can't save you, just like he couldn't save her.'"

I clench my teeth so hard my jaw aches. "Jesse and Evie been on the scene?"

"They just wrapped up. Heading back to the FBI office now."

"Good. I'll call them. And Cruz?" I hesitate. "I want his composite released at the press conference. It needs to go wide. Tell me when; I want to watch it. And keep me posted. If you need me, you say the word."

"Focus on protecting Clara. That's your job right now. We'll take care of it here."

As soon as I hit 'End Call,' I send a text to the team. I hate being this far away, but Cruz is right about needing to keep Clara safe. And there isn't anyone else I'd trust to do it.

Maverick
Heard about the crime scene and vic.
Keep me updated on everything.

Jesse
You got it, boss.

Riley
I'll video conference you in this
afternoon. Evie's sorting through the
evidence photos and videos now.

I'm staring at my phone, the text lingering on the screen, when I hear the sliding door open. Juno trots in first, tail wagging. Clara follows behind him, but she pauses when she sees me—sees my expression.

"Mav?" Clara steps in front of me. Her deep brown eyes are full of concern. "What's wrong?"

Rage and guilt war within me, and I can barely speak. Can barely move. After a long pause, I finally meet her gaze.

"He's killed again."

The blood drains from her face, paling her golden complexion. I watch as she regains composure, straightening her spine and pulling her shoulders back—like steel forged under fire.

"What happened?"

I tell her everything. All of it. Her eyes glisten, but she doesn't cry. She dips her chin and swallows hard, closing her eyes. The minute action is a beacon, a silent call for Juno as he nestles into her side like a shield.

And the sight of it breaks something in me, sending waves of inadequacy through my body.

I spin and hurl my phone at the wall. It hits with a heavy thud, cracking the drywall and bouncing to the floor, the screen still glowing.

Regret slams into me instantly. I'm a fucking fool.

I move toward her, hands raised. "I'm sorry, sunshine—"

She flinches. She doesn't back away. But she flinches.

Fuck.

Slowly, I pull her into my arms, giving her every second she needs to pull away.

She doesn't.

She melts into me, and I bury my face in the crook of her neck, breathing her in like she's the only thing keeping me upright. "I'm sorry, baby," I whisper. "I didn't mean to scare you. I'm just—fuck—I'm so angry. At myself. If I'd caught him, Marie would still be alive."

Clara pulls back, her touch featherlight as she cups my face. The way her fingers stroke my beard with affection makes my throat tighten.

"Maverick Rhodes," she says, voice fierce despite the softness of her touch. "Don't you dare."

I start to speak but she silences me with a finger pressed firmly to my lips.

"No. I'm talking. You're listening. You haven't failed anyone. Do you understand me?"

I can't look her in the eye. I stare at her throat instead and nod, obliging her request—her demand—that I let her speak, even if I don't believe a damn word she's saying.

"Hey. Look at me." She waits until our eyes lock before continuing. "You are the reason I'm not drowning in that dark abyss I woke up in. I don't want to imagine where I'd be—who I'd be—if you hadn't been there. You saved me, Maverick Rhodes. Over and over. You're the steady presence that keeps me grounded, keeps me safe. You are not a failure. Marie's death is not your fault. That's on him. Heather's death is not your fault; it's the bastard's who hit her and ran. I need you to understand that. Tell me you understand."

My chest caves in under the weight of her words. Her belief in me. Tears threaten, burning behind my eyes. I blink fast in a poor attempt to will them away.

When her fingers swipe beneath my eyes, something inside me snaps—an overwhelming urge to feel her in my arms. It's like a siren's call I can't resist. Instinct takes over, and I pull her in, one hand on her hip, the other sliding in her hair. With a tenderness I didn't know I possessed, I tug gently, guiding her face to mine.

There's no hesitation when I claim her mouth, no room for doubt—just certainty and the undeniable need to feel connected to this woman. Her lips part for me, soft and yielding, and the kiss deepens—turning desperate and all-consuming.

When she moves against me with matched urgency, I tighten my grip in her hair, holding her steady as I slide my tongue into her mouth. The taste of her undoes me. I don't know if I've ever wanted—needed—anyone like this. Not ever.

She lifts a leg around my hip, and I take the cue without

question. I hoist her up, pressing her body flush to mine. Her arms wrap around my neck, her legs around my waist, locking in place as I grip beneath her thighs. The position aligns us perfectly—her warmth against the ache I've been carrying. For her.

I nip at her bottom lip before softening the kiss, our breath mingling, heavy with want and unspoken promises.

"Mav," she breathes, resting her forehead against mine.

"I know, sunshine." My voice is thick and hoarse, barely audible through the loud beating of my heart.

"No," she says with more certainty. I start to lower her, but she tightens her legs around me and shakes her head. "Bedroom. Take me to the bedroom."

I lean back just enough to meet her gaze, to read her—to really read her. "Are you sure?"

Her eyes don't waver, her voice conveys her strength and confidence. "Take me to the damn bedroom, Maverick Rhodes."

I told her she'd always know it was me—holding her, touching her, worshiping her.

Who the hell am I to say no now?

CHAPTER 30

CLARA
RED VELVET

MAVERICK DOESN'T ASK me twice. He adjusts his hands on my thighs, holding me in a bruising grip, and starts down the hall without a word, carrying me as though I weigh nothing.

I bury my face in the curve of his neck, breathing him in. My lips find his pulse, leaving featherlight kisses against his warm skin. His beard brushes against my cheek as I nuzzle higher, nipping his earlobe—soft, deliberate.

A low growl rumbles from his chest, sending a thrill straight through me. "Fuck, sunshine," he mutters, voice rough and even. "Keep doing that, and we're not gonna make it to the bedroom."

I'm not opposed to that idea. Every inch of me aches for him, and this hallway feels like the longest stretch in the world. I open my mouth to tell him so, but before the words come, we reach the bedroom door.

Thank god.

He nudges it open with his shoulder and strides inside.

As soon as we reach the bed, he lowers me, dragging my body against the hardness of his during the descent. His gaze roves over every part of me, as if he's trying to memorize it—the hunger in his eyes matching mine.

I reach for the waistband of my leggings, but his palms press down my wrists, stilling me.

"Let me," he says in an almost reverent tone. "I want to undress you. I want to take my time worshipping you until you forget everything but my name."

He lifts one of my wrists, pressing a tender kiss to the inside. My breath catches at the gentleness of it, the contrast between his rough hands and his soft mouth.

"Will you let me do that, baby?" he whispers.

God, why is that so sexy?

"Please," I breathe. I stare up at him, letting my eyes soak in every detail of his face. The morning light spills through the window—the soft glow highlights the sharp cut of his cheekbones and the strong line of his jaw. The soft specks of gray in his beard catch the light, and God, all I can think about is how I crave to feel that coarseness against my thighs.

His lips quirk into something between a smile and a promise as he hooks his fingers into the waistband of my leggings. With reverence, Maverick slides them down my hips. His eyes never leave mine—not even when he leans in and trails open-mouthed kisses along my calf, each press of his lips making me ache more.

A soft whimper escapes me when he nips the sensitive skin on my inner thigh. But he doesn't move higher.

Doesn't give me what I need. My hips lift off the mattress, chasing contact.

"You can't rush me, sunshine." His voice is a low growl, thick with restraint. He gives my other thigh the same teasing attention while my core throbs with neglect. "I told you I want to take my time."

"Take your time later," I plead. "I need you."

"You need me?"

"I need you."

"You have me." His words are a vow, and I feel them in my bones.

He leans forward, nuzzling the damp fabric covering me before dragging his nose along my soaked sex. The groan he lets out is guttural. "You're fucking soaked, baby."

I sit up long enough for him to pull my sweater over my head and toss it aside. His hand slides behind me, deft fingers unclasping my bra. With a gentle push to the center of my chest, he lays me back down.

"Fuck. You're the sexiest thing I've ever seen," he murmurs, cupping my breast. His palm is calloused, rough against my sensitive skin.

A cry escapes my lips when his thumb and forefinger roll and pinch my nipple, the sharp pleasure making me arch into him. His tongue flicks out right before his mouth envelops me. I rake my fingers through his dark hair, holding him to me as he gives each nipple the same devoted attention. He alternates between sucking and tugging my nipple between his teeth, threatening to send me over the edge.

My legs wrap around his waist, and I grind my hips against the hard planes of his stomach.

"Maverick, please."

He trails kisses up my chest, capturing my lips with a hunger that knocks the air from my lungs. His tongue sweeps across the seam of my mouth, and I open for him, moaning when he deepens the kiss. He grips my neck, devouring me like a man starved.

I fumble for the hem of his shirt, desperate to feel his skin. "Take it off," I pant.

He obliges, reaching one hand behind his back and yanking off his shirt in one smooth motion. My eyes roam over his chest—broad, muscled, and dusted in dark hair, with a trail leading south into his jeans. He's everything. And I want all of him.

His hands stroke my thighs, tapping them in a silent request. When I release him, he shifts down, kissing my stomach as he goes. He pulls my panties off with aching slowness and spreads my legs wide, resting them over his shoulders.

I should feel exposed. Embarrassed. But all I feel is want. I've never felt this intense need before—this aching desperation.

"Stay still for me, baby," is all the warning I get before his mouth is on me.

I cry out, my body curving as his tongue flicks my clit, sucking it between his teeth. One of his hands splays across my stomach, pinning me to the bed, while the other slides between my legs—two thick fingers plunging inside me. He curls them just right and groans against me like I'm the one unraveling him.

He adds a third finger when he feels me tightening. "That's it, sunshine. Come for me."

The orgasm rips through me. I shake beneath him, crying out his name.

He kisses my thighs, then locks eyes with me as he brings his soaked fingers to his mouth and sucks them clean. "Fucking delicious."

Jesus.

"Taste yourself, baby," he growls, crawling up to claim my mouth. I moan into him, tasting myself on his tongue.

"Please, Maverick. I need to feel you inside me."

His jeans can't come off fast enough. He strips, kicking them aside with his boxers, and I nearly whimper at the sight of him. Thick. Hard. Veined. A drop of precum glistening at the tip.

I reach for him, wanting to taste him, but he shakes his head. "No, this is about you."

He steps between my legs, our lips colliding while his cock presses against my clit. My hips roll, grinding against him, and he groans—a feral, rumbling sound.

He wraps my hand around his length, guiding me to stroke him. "You have no idea how hard it is not to bury myself inside you right now. Want to feel you wrapped around me, feel you come around my cock."

God, yes.

"Condom?" I ask, breathless.

"I have one," he says, resting his forehead to mine, "but fuck, I want to feel you."

"I'm clean. And I'm on birth control," I whisper. The memory of the STD test and forensic exam assaults me, but I shove it away. There's no room for that here, not with him, not in this moment.

"I'm clean, too," he says, his lips brushing against mine with each word.

"Don't make me beg again, please."

"You don't have to beg, sunshine. I'm yours."

Gripping my hips, he positions himself and presses the head of his cock at my entrance.

Then I freeze.

He feels the instantaneous change—feels the tension, the hesitation.

"Hey," he whispers, his brows knitted in concern. "You okay, baby?"

I nod, but my body doesn't relax.

"It's me, sunshine. Holding you, touching you." He gazes down at me, taking one of my hands and flattening it against his chest. "Just me."

I feel the rhythmic, rapid beat of his heart—the steady pounding anchoring me in the moment.

And then he flips us. I'm straddling his lap, his back against the headboard.

"You're in control," he whispers against my lips, brushing my hair from my face. "One breath at a time."

I inhale. Exhale. I lock eyes with him, focusing on the warmth in his espresso gaze.

This is Maverick. I'm safe.

He doesn't rush me. Doesn't push me. He waits, allowing me to take this at my pace.

And I love him for it.

When I'm ready, I lift and guide him to my entrance, slowly sinking down on him. His breath catches. My pussy stretches. My body trembles. And when he's fully sheathed, it's like something clicks into place.

His hands find my hips, helping me move—slow, rolling thrusts. I tilt my head back and start to close my eyes, reveling in the waves of pleasure he creates.

"Don't." A pleading whisper. "Don't close your eyes. Keep them on me. Know that it's me inside of you."

Tears prick my eyes, but I ride him harder, chasing the high.

"You're doing so good, baby," he praises, his fingers digging into my hips. "Fuck, you feel…"

His voice trails off as he leans in and sucks my nipple into his mouth, never breaking eye contact. It's slow, sensual, causing goosebumps to ripple across my skin.

"That's it. Who's inside you, baby?"

"You," I cry.

"Say it."

"You! Maverick."

That's all it takes. He bucks up, thrusting deep—and I shatter around him.

"Fuck, fuck, fuck," he groans, holding me down as he thrusts into me. "So fucking tight. Oh, fuck, Clara." He comes with a roar, spilling inside me.

We collapse together, a tangle of limbs and heartbeats.

He trails kisses across my jaw and whispers into my mouth, "You're perfect, sunshine. And just so you know, I'll last longer next time."

I laugh, curling into him as he wraps me in his arms and shifts us onto our sides, his warm body pressed to my back. I drift off like that—safe, held, at peace.

The smell of bacon wakes me.

I slide out of bed and pull on Maverick's shirt, the hem brushing mid-thigh. Padding barefoot down the hall, I find him in the kitchen. He moves with easy confidence as he flips pancakes and sips coffee.

I wrap my arms around him from behind, bestowing a kiss to the center of his back. He stills, then turns. A smile tugs at his lips as he sweeps me up and sets me on the counter.

"I was going to bring you breakfast."

"Mmm. That sounds nice," I murmur as my arms drape over his shoulders, fingers trailing the nape of his neck.

"And my breakfast is right here," he says, peering at me with mischievous eyes while placing a hand between my thighs. "Now that I've had you, I'm going to have a real hard time keeping my hands off you."

A shiver runs through me—just before his phone vibrates on the counter.

Maverick groans and rests his forehead on my shoulder. I brush my lips over his hairline before reaching for his phone, tilting it so we can both see the screen.

An incoming video call.

Riley.

We both look at the screen, then at each other.

"Do you want to take that in the office?" I ask, keeping my voice light.

Part of me wants him to say yes—to not hear what Riley has to say about the investigation. But the stronger part of me—the part willing to claw and fight—wants to stay, wants to know what's coming.

He shakes his head. "No. You can listen."

"I'll go get dressed," I say, hopping off the counter. "Answer it."

CHAPTER 31
MAVERICK

TOMORROW WE FIGHT

"THE PRESS CONFERENCE is in two hours. We'll release the sketch and a few details about the crime scene from this morning." Riley rubs her temples as she speaks, the exhaustion evident in her voice.

Guilt is a persistent itch, burrowing beneath my skin. I should be out there with them. I hate the feeling of being sidelined—even when I know I'm not. I've never wanted to be in two places more than I do now.

Riley opens her mouth to say something else when her eyes catch on movement behind me. I turn and find Clara entering the kitchen, heading straight for the table. Juno trails close behind, her little shadow.

I gesture to the seat beside me, where I've already laid out her breakfast and coffee. She slides into the seat without hesitation, drawing her chair closer to the table. Her determined gaze settles on the phone propped up against a bottle of orange juice. Juno huffs and drops to the floor with a soft thud, curling up against Clara's feet.

"Hi, everyone. I'm Clara," she says with a steady, clear voice.

When I glance at the screen, I see a silent question in Riley's eyes, and I respond with a subtle nod. Clara's here on her own terms. She's ready to be a part of the conversation.

"It's good to finally put a face to the name, Clara," Evie says warmly, a genuine smile gracing her face. "This one here is Riley," she adds, a thumb pointing to her left. "She's the one who thought of the fuzzy slippers, by the way."

Clara beams. "Thank you so much for those! And the rest of the clothes. You two were lifesavers."

She picks up her coffee mug, and I notice the way her fingers flex. She's holding it like an anchor.

"And these three unintimidating gentlemen are Jesse, Arlo, and Spencer," Cruz says, flashing a grin as he gestures to each man.

Clara shakes her head in amusement, waving at them politely. Her fingers tighten on her mug again as she assesses the room through the screen.

"Have we gotten anything back from the ME?" I ask, pulling the focus back to the case.

Jesse raises his hand and leans toward the camera. "I found semen on the victim's body. Ran the DNA as soon as I got back to the lab." He pauses to open the file in front of him. "One hundred percent match to the other samples, boss. It was him. No doubt about it."

Beside me, Clara doesn't flinch, but I see it—the way her jaw tenses ever so slightly. Her expression remains stoic, but her dark brown eyes appear even darker.

Spencer clears his throat. "Sammie conducted a rushed autopsy. She hasn't completed the final report, but she called to share information she thought was time-sensitive. No semen internally. No defensive wounds. No skin beneath the victim's fingernails. No restraint marks. Cause of death was cervical fracture."

"So far, everything points to consensual sex," Riley notes. "My guess? He snapped her neck at the end of the act—or just after."

Clara inhales deeply, her exhale barely audible. Her shoulders rise and fall with each slow, measured breath. She doesn't look away. Doesn't shut down. But her fingers curl tighter around the ceramic mug, like it's the only thing tethering her to the moment.

I slide my hand under the table and gently clutch her thigh, offering silent support. She turns her head just slightly, giving me a sidelong glance. Her mouth twitches, and her chin dips in a small, almost imperceptible nod, letting me know she's okay.

"What do we know about Marie?" I ask, keeping my voice level.

"Marie Ann Douglas. Thirty-two. Moved to Rochester six months ago from Wichita, Kansas," Arlo replies. "No family nearby, no car in her name. She worked as a receptionist at the art gallery downtown—same block as the mayor's office."

Clara's eyes narrow a fraction, her brows knitting together as if in thought. She doesn't speak, but I can tell she's absorbing everything—connecting dots I can't see.

"I've got a team helping Arlo and Spence review exterior surveillance footage from businesses within a mile of the art gallery," Cruz says.

Arlo nods. "We hope to spot her, maybe with our guy."

"And I sent uniforms to her place on Rolland Street." Cruz sighs and shakes his head. "Might be nothing, but if this started as a consensual encounter, maybe she brought him back there."

Clara shifts beside me, her body angling slightly forward as if leaning into the conversation. She wants to understand. Wants to face this.

"Keep me in the loop," I say. "Let me know if you need me down there, yeah?"

"We will, boss," Jesse replies. A chorus of agreement follows, firm and familiar.

I glance at Clara again. Her mug is still in her hands, untouched. But she hasn't looked away from the screen once.

As soon as the call ends, I pull Clara into my lap. She doesn't resist—just shifts until she's settled. She's tense but leans into me. I tilt her chin, locking eyes with her.

"You okay, sunshine?"

She blows out a sharp breath, cheeks puffed before the exhale. "Honestly? I don't know."

She finally lifts the coffee mug to her lips, taking a tentative sip. Her eyes remain distant, brows drawn as her thoughts churn.

"That poor girl didn't die the way the others did," she murmurs. "And he didn't do the same things to her. Why not? What changed?"

"That's what we're trying to figure out," I say, though my answer feels thin.

Clara's gaze drops to the mug, her finger tracing the rim. Then, quietly, she says, "The girl... Marie. She died because of me, Maverick."

I open my mouth to protest, but she cuts me off with a scathing glare. Message received; I close my mouth.

"She did," Clara asserts, voice unwavering. "You said he sent a message. He said if I come back to him, he'll stop."

"You're not going back to him."

She inhales slowly, closing her eyes for a beat. But when she opens them again, they're fierce—burning with anger, and all of it aimed at me.

"I'm not an idiot," she says. Her voice has a sharp edge— cold and clipped. She starts to shift off my lap, trying to create space between us. I stop her with a steady grip on her thighs, keeping her in place—keeping her grounded.

"I'm not stupid enough to say I'll go back to him just to make it stop. To stop him from killing anyone else," she continues, voice rising slightly, the words tumbling out faster now. "But that doesn't change the fact that he killed her because of me. If he kills someone else, it'll be because of me, and that's blood on my hands."

"No," I say in a firm tone. I lift one hand, curling it around the back of her neck. My thumb brushes just beneath her ear as I guide her face back to mine. "Look at me."

She does.

"He will kill again whether you went back to him or

not. That's what monsters do. You didn't start this. You didn't choose it. He did."

She holds my gaze, breathing hard, and I see the battle playing out behind her eyes: guilt battling logic, trauma strangling reason. And underneath it all, fury. Not at me. Not entirely. At him. At herself. At everything she's lost. At this whole fucked-up situation.

"I should've died in that hole." Her voice cracks on a broken whisper. "If I had, maybe he'd be done by now. And Marie would still be here."

My grip tightens just slightly, not enough to hurt, but enough to anchor her.

"Don't say that," I growl. "Don't ever say that. You hear me? Don't ever fucking say that. You're where you're supposed to be. Right here with me."

She doesn't cry. Her body is rigid, but she doesn't pull away again. She leans in, bringing her forehead to rest on my cheekbone.

He's not fucking getting her back.

An hour later, we're on the couch, the tenseness in her body quieted but not gone. Clara's curled into my side with her head resting against my shoulder, legs folded beneath her. Juno's at her feet—apparently his permanent spot.

The TV is a quiet hum in front of us; the news anchor droning on and on through the lead-up to the press conference. A banner at the bottom of the screen flashes:

BREAKING: Rochester PD and FBI Task Force to Release Suspect Sketch in Recent Homicide.

Her fingers are laced loosely with mine, her thumb moving in slow, absent circles over my knees. Clara hasn't said much since the conference call earlier. She hasn't had to. She's here. Still fighting.

She doesn't need me to be proud of her, but I am. Fuck, I am.

I glance down at her, brushing a strand of hair away from her face. She doesn't look away from the screen, but her hand tightens around mine ever so slightly.

"You ready for this?" I ask.

"As I'll ever be," she breathes.

The screen shifts, cutting to a live feed of the podium outside the precinct, reporters already jockeying for position.

The countdown begins.

We both watch in silence, waiting for the world to learn what we already know.

CHAPTER 32
CLARA

SECRETS AND LIES

"I'M Detective Jonathan Cruz with the FBI-Rochester Police Department Task Force, working to identify and apprehend the man the media has dubbed The Chameleon. This individual is responsible for the murders of seven women across four states: Minnesota, Wisconsin, Iowa, and Illinois."

Cruz pauses, allowing the gravity of the statement to settle over the room. The press is silent, every eye on him.

"This morning, the body of Marie Ann Douglas was discovered in a shallow grave near Silver Creek Lake. We believe her death is linked to the same suspect."

A murmur ripples through the crowd, and Cruz lifts his voice to cut through it.

"Surveillance footage shows the suspect wearing a different disguise with each victim. But his eighth target was found alive here in Rochester. Clara Santos is the only known survivor. She was discovered buried alive in Silver Lake Park. Based on her account and a corroborating eyewitness, she worked closely with our forensic artist to create a composite sketch."

The screen to the left changes, displaying the sketch in high resolution: sharp cheekbones, a neutral expression, the haunting stare of a man capable of erasing his identity as easily as changing a shirt.

"If you recognize this individual," Cruz continues, "please call the task force hotline. Any information, no matter how small, could be vital."

He steps back from the podium, and the chief of police takes his place briefly to introduce the next speaker.

"Thank you, Detective Cruz. And now, a few words from Mayor James Evans."

He strides up confidently, his posture straight, his expression solemn and statesmanlike. The cameras adjust their focus, and the room quiets again.

"People of Rochester," the mayor begins with a calm, well-practiced voice, "we are devastated by this morning's discovery. Another young woman lost her life, and we grieve with her family. I want to reassure you that we are working closely with the FBI and the Rochester Police Department to keep our community safe."

He pauses and stares into the camera. "If you have any information about the individual shown, I encourage you to come forward."

He continues speaking, but I don't hear the words.

All I can focus on is that voice.

God.

My stomach turns to ice.

My lungs seize.

I struggle to inhale my next breath.

A sharp chill slides down my spine.

No. No, no, no.

It can't be.

How can this be possible? It can't be him. He's the mayor.

The fucking mayor.

But I know that voice. I would know it anywhere. It taunted me in my prison. I hear it in my nightmares—soft, cruel, dripping with false comfort, while I lay in the dark with dirt beneath my fingernails.

He doesn't look the same. The hair is wrong. It's shorter now. Darker. His nose is wrong. Thinner? I can't tell, but I know it's wrong. And his eyes. His empty brown eyes are hidden behind glasses. He always wore contacts with me— I remember wondering what he'd look like in glasses.

Now I know.

And I wish I didn't.

My whole body locks. My throat tightens.

Oh, god. I'm going to be sick.

"Turn it off," I manage to say in a barely audible whisper.

Maverick stiffens beside me. "What?"

"Turn it off," I repeat. Louder. Sharper. Demanding.

He fumbles for the remote, eyes still on me as he kills the TV.

Silence drops over the room like a bomb.

I stare at the dark screen. My hands are shaking, and my heart is pounding as if it's trying to claw out of my chest.

Juno lets out a whimper by my feet and nudges my hand, but I can't move.

"It's him," I breathe. "It's him." The words scrape my throat like broken glass.

Maverick turns to me, eyes narrowing, brows knitting in confusion. "Who's him?"

"The mayor, Maverick." My voice is suddenly steady; all the fear giving way to fire. I meet his warm brown eyes—a contrast to *his*—when I say, "Samson is the fucking mayor."

CHAPTER 33
HIM

HIT YOU WHERE IT HURTS

THAT FUCKING COMPOSITE SKETCH.

Doesn't even look like us.

Which, I suppose, was the point.

But they won't find us. They never will. We're too careful. Too clever. Too many steps ahead.

I tamp down a wince as my monster thrashes beneath my ribs—claws like knives pounding against bone. He's furious. Screaming. Seething. That fucking detective said her name. Her name.

No one else is allowed to say it.

Only us.

"Thank you, Detective Cruz. And now, a few words from Mayor James Evans," the chief of police announces as that smug bastard steps away from the podium.

"Sir, you're up," my assistant whispers, leaning in discreetly.

I nod, adjust my suit, and ensure the mask is in place.

Duplicity concealed. A slight tightening of my jaw, a slow breath, and there it is—composure.

As I approach the podium with a confident stride, I meet the cameras with a solemn expression. My voice is steady. Calm and well-practiced. Every word measured, delivered like a man who cares. Like a man who protects.

And they're eating it up. Imbeciles, the lot of them.

The moment the speech ends, I turn from the flashing lights and empty praise and walk straight toward the car. My assistant tries to get my attention—something about a meeting.

I don't care.

I don't have time for their mundane routines.

Don't have the patience for them.

All I can think about is her.

My Clara.

She's in my head, in my blood.

She's taken over my brain, filling every quiet second with noise.

And now I know where that special agent has taken her. Where he's keeping her captive. Keeping her away from us.

My monster regrets burying her. She belongs to us.

And it's time she remembered that.

We'll write her a letter.

A proper one.

CHAPTER 34
MAVERICK

I DON'T MOVE. Don't blink. I stare at Clara like I didn't hear what she said—like my brain misfired and needs a second to reboot.

But then it hits me.

And it hits hard.

I jerk to my feet, the motion sudden, like I've just been sucker-punched. "No—" I mutter, my voice flat and hollow. "No. That's not—"

I rake both hands through my hair, pacing a short, agitated loop across the room before whipping back around to face her. Her eyes are wide, glassy. Red-rimmed. She's not lying. She can't be lying.

"You're sure?" I ask, even though I already know the answer. It's written all over her face.

"I'm sure." Her voice scrapes through the air, like it took everything she had to force the words out. "I'd know his voice anywhere."

My eyes snap to the blank TV screen. The silence in the room feels suffocating.

"Jesus Christ."

She nods slowly, hands shaking. Her chest rises and falls too fast, telling me she's barely holding herself together.

My stomach twists. My pulse hammers in my throat. I can't breathe past the rage burning beneath my skin.

"He's not just close to the case," I say in disbelief, barely recognizing my own voice. "He's in it. The press conferences. The updates. The concern. All of it—he's been hiding in plain sight. Watching everything."

I curse under my breath and ball my fist, the sting of my nails digging into my palm anchoring me.

"This whole time… This whole fucking time."

Juno lets out a soft whine, pulling my attention back to the couch. He climbs onto Clara's lap without hesitation, nuzzling into her chest. That's when I notice the rivulets of tears streaming down her face. One hand covers her mouth as though she's trying to contain the flood while the other absently strokes Juno's fur.

The sight is enough to snap me out of it, punching the air from my lungs.

Shit.

I exhale sharply and drag a hand down my face.

Crossing the room, I kneel in front of her and tap Juno's hind legs, guiding him off her lap. Her hands drop to her thighs.

"Hey," I say softly, placing my hands over hers. "I'm here, baby. I've got you, okay?"

For a moment, she doesn't move—doesn't even blink. But then her gaze finds mine, and I see the shift. The fire catching hold beneath the grief.

"I'm angry, Maverick," she says. She wipes at her face with her palms. "God, I wish I could just be angry without fucking crying."

"I know, sunshine." I press a kiss to both cheeks, then swipe the tears away with my thumbs. "We need to call Cruz. Let the team know. You're not alone in this. Not for a second."

I reach for my phone on the coffee table. The press conference should be over by now. My fingers tremble as I unlock the screen and scroll to Cruz's number.

He answers on the second ring.

"We've got a fucking problem," I cut in before he can speak. "Clara just ID'd Samson. He's the goddamn mayor. She recognized his voice during the press conference. Round up the team and get to Minneapolis. Meet me at my place. We need to move fast."

There's a beat of stunned silence, then, "We're on our way."

The line goes dead.

I lower the phone slowly and stare at it for a second, like the weight of what I just said hasn't fully settled yet. The mayor. The motherfucking mayor. He inserted himself into the investigation just enough to seem involved but not enough to raise suspicion. He was monitoring us. Manipulating us.

No fucking wonder he was able to access Heather's

police file. And it wouldn't have been difficult for him to find the location of my rental.

All this time…

If Clara hadn't watched the press conference, hadn't heard his voice…

Fucking hell.

I suck in a breath and let it out through my nose, trying to keep my emotions in check. I push my frustrations aside, focusing on Clara.

Still kneeling on the floor by her feet, I adjust my position, crouching in front of her. "Sunshine," I murmur, reaching for her hand. "They'll be here soon. About an hour and a half. Let's get you something to eat, yeah? Maybe even pretend we're normal for five minutes?"

Her lips twitch, just barely. "Normal's overrated."

"Yeah, but I'll take boring and safe over this nightmare any day."

I help her off the couch and guide her into the kitchen, keeping things simple—grilled cheese and tomato soup. Comfort food. She doesn't eat much, but she lets me sit beside her while she picks at her food. I don't push. I just stay close.

"Mav?"

"Yeah, sunshine?"

"Do you mind if I go into your office and call Tamara? I haven't talked to her in a few days. She's going to kill me."

Clara leans back in her chair and nudges her plate away, but I don't miss the slight tremble in her voice. She needs someone to talk to. Someone who isn't me. Someone who isn't wrapped up in all this fuckery. I get it. I don't like it, but I get it.

"You never have to ask. The office is yours."

I stand and offer her my hand, pulling her gently to her feet and into my space. "You tell me if you need anything, okay?"

"Okay," she whispers.

She rises on her toes and presses her soft, full lips to mine. I wrap my arms around her waist and pull her in closer, deepening the kiss. My tongue traces the seam of her lips, and she parts them for me with a quiet sigh. I nip her bottom lip and suck gently before easing back.

Her breathing's shallow when she opens her eyes. "What was that for?"

"Because I wanted to. Because I can. Now go call Tamara before she gets mad. She's scary."

I turn her toward the office with a gentle nudge, swatting her ass as she walks away. She tosses me a look over her shoulder, half a smile playing on her lips. I watch her until she disappears into the room, closing the door behind her.

I let out a deep, heavy sigh and lean back against the counter before burying my face in my hands. I don't move. I can't.

Goddamn it. What a clusterfuck. I need to think. Need to process what just happened.

We need to be careful. Can't have any missteps. We don't know who he's got in his pocket, and we can't let anything get back to him; a leak could compromise everything. Getting a warrant is going to be a fucking nightmare. The evidence has to be ironclad—indisputable. One wrong move, and he'll vanish… Or worse, take someone else and then vanish.

An hour and a half later, headlights sweep across the living room wall, alerting me to the team's arrival.

Clara's still in the office. She's been talking to Tamara this whole time. Her voice has been a constant soundtrack —soft, sometimes laughing, sometimes quiet. Once or twice, I heard her crying, and each time, it made my chest tighten. I didn't listen to her words, just the sound of her voice. The rhythm. Like a heartbeat. Like home.

I knock once on the door.

"They're here, sunshine," I say. "Take your time. Just wanted to let you know."

We're all gathered in the kitchen.

Arlo and Spencer are set up at the counter, fingers flying across their keyboards. Cruz, Evie, Jesse, and Riley occupy the table, surrounded by notepads, open files, evidence photos, and half-drunk mugs of coffee. I sit close to Clara, having pulled her chair just a little nearer to mine. If anyone notices, no one says a word.

"Wait," Evie says suddenly, sitting up straighter. "Arlo. Didn't you say the art gallery was on the same block as the mayor's office?"

"Yeah," he replies, eyes still locked his screen. He glances over his shoulder. "Why?"

I already know what she's thinking. "I want exterior

camera footage from the mayor's office the day Marie was taken," I say. "Don't focus on Marie. Look for him."

"Smart," Evie murmurs.

"We need to come up with a plan," Cruz says, arms folded, eyes flicking between all of us.

"A meeting," Spencer offers. "Ask him for a sit-down with the task force. He's manipulative, but he's also a narcissist. He won't be able to resist an opportunity to be the center of attention."

"Smug son of a bitch." Jesse scrubs a hand down his face, glaring at the table as if it's personally offended him. "He'll sit there, thinking he's got one over on us, knowing he's the fucker we're looking for."

"We could pitch it as a third press conference," I suggest, "but this time, he takes the lead. A direct appeal to the city of Rochester."

"To stir the public. Say we're desperate for a break because the hotline's been dead," Riley adds. "That's brilliant."

Clara speaks up then, tentative but steady. "How difficult would it be to get a warrant?" There's curiosity in her voice, and maybe a touch of guilt for asking.

"We'd need hard, physical evidence," Evie says. "Something tangible. If we can get him to touch a glass or bottle —anything—we might be able to pull DNA."

"But we have to do it without him knowing," I add, acknowledging the hardest part. "And when we get the warrant, we don't announce it. We move the second it hits. He can't know."

"I found something," Arlo exclaims, his voice sharp and urgent.

We all freeze.

He unplugs his laptop and brings it over to the table, setting it in front of me. "Here. Look." He rewinds the video and hits play.

The mayor steps out of his office and casually turns down the street at the same moment Marie appears in the frame. He keeps pace behind her, looking like any other businessman walking down the street. A few beats later, they both disappear inside Revolution Coffee.

Spencer leans over the screen. "I'll pull the surveillance feed from the coffee shop."

"If we can catch them walking out together," Cruz says, "and the DNA comes back as a match to our crime scene? That's concrete evidence. That's game over."

I can feel Clara's eyes on me. I turn to her.

She leans in, voice low. "You want to go to Rochester, don't you?"

"I'm not leaving you, sunshine."

"That's not what I asked." She arches a brow, silently challenging me. "Do you want to go?"

I hesitate, then concede. "...Yes. But—"

"No buts." Her voice is soft, but fierce. "You should go. I'll be fine here. You need to do this. We all need you to do this. Would it be okay if Tamara stayed with me?"

"You're positive?"

She rolls her eyes, crossing her arms below her chest. "I just told you to go, didn't I?"

"Pretty sure she did, boss," Jesse mutters, casually looking through files.

"No one was talking to you," I chide, shooting him a glare. Turning my attention back to Clara, I offer her a small smile. "I'll be back tonight. I won't stay in Rochester. I can commute until this shitshow is over."

There's no way I'm leaving her to sleep alone. She's made so much progress, and who knows how today's revelation will affect her?

She nods once. "And Tamara? She can come by while you're gone?"

"Of course," I say gently. "You don't even have to ask. It'll make me feel better if you aren't alone."

Clara smiles at me—a full smile this time—and stands. "I'm going to call her."

I track her as she heads off to make the call, then look to Cruz. "Set up the meeting with the mayor."

CHAPTER 35

CLARA

IF YOU LET ME

"YOU HAVE no idea how happy I am that you're here," I tell Tamara, taking the pot of chicken adobo off the stove and setting it on the trivet with a sigh.

"We're bonded for life, best friend. You're stuck with me," she replies, flipping off the rice maker before grabbing two bowls and placing them on the kitchen counter.

Maverick left for Rochester a few hours ago. He sent the team ahead, but waited until Tamara arrived before following them. When he opened the door for her, she was armed with a bottle of Cabernet Sauvignon, a grocery bag, and a non-negotiable demand to cook my favorite Filipino comfort dish.

Now, the rich aroma of soy sauce, vinegar, and garlic permeate the kitchen. I plate the food, giving Tamara extra potatoes and piling extra rice into mine—like always.

I carry both bowls to the table, carefully stepping around Juno, who's weaving between my legs like a little shadow. Tamara grabs the wine and two glasses before sitting down, filling them to the absolute brim.

"I'm pretty sure you're not supposed to pour that much," I say, eyeing the deep red liquid sloshing precariously close to the rim.

"Girl, I'm not bougie. Why the hell would I pour half a glass just to refill it two minutes later? That shit makes no sense."

"You're crazy." I laugh, shaking my head. With delicate movements, I bring the glass to my lips, sipping slowly and praying I don't spill it all over myself.

Tamara lifts one shoulder and blows on a steaming spoonful of food with little effect. "What's actually crazy is that I haven't had this in... I don't even know how long. You know it's my favorite."

"I taught you how to make it," I remind her, raising a brow.

"Yeah, but it never tastes the same."

I hum, knowing exactly what she means. My mom taught me how to cook a handful of Filipino dishes, but they never tasted like hers. And hers never quite tasted like grandma's. There was always something missing.

Dinner passes in comfortable, familiar conversation. Tamara fills me in on the latest gossip at The Pour House—regulars who come in and ask her to "teach" them yoga—and how she's garnered a decent clientele for her in-home yoga studio.

It's impossible not to feel a twist in my chest. I'm proud of her—so damn proud. She's chasing her dreams, living her life. But I'm envious, too. She's doing all the things I can't: chasing my dreams, living my life.

Juno must sense the shift in my mood. He lifts his head from where he's been curled up beneath the table and rests it gently on my lap. He emits a soft whine until I automatically run my hand over his head, grounding myself in his steady comfort.

"You ever call that nurse from the hospital?" Tamara asks suddenly, setting her spoon down and reaching for her wine—the second one… also filled to the brim.

I freeze, my spoon halfway to my mouth. "Rosie?" I murmur. Lowering the spoon, I sit back in my chair. "No, I've thought about it. A lot. But everything's just so chaotic. I'm scared I'll somehow drag her into it, and I couldn't live with myself if something happened to her because of me, you know?"

I swirl the wine in my glass, watching it catch the light. "But when this is over… I'd like to. She reminded me of my mom." I pause, letting the ache settle in my chest. "It probably sounds weird, right? I barely knew her, and here I am saying she felt like my mom."

Tamara's lips pull into a soft smile, and she reaches across the table to squeeze my hand. "It's not weird at all, sister. She felt something too, or she wouldn't have given you her number. You should call her. I wanna meet her."

"Yeah," I say, almost to myself. "That'd be nice."

A beat passes, and then Tamara's smile shifts into a grin —mischief blooming on her face. "So. You and Maverick."

I laugh, then look down into my bowl. I can feel the blood rush to my cheeks. "He's… I don't even know how to explain it. It's like he's my rock. He keeps me grounded. I feel safe with him, like I can breathe again. Like I'm not broken." I hesitate, my voice softening. "I think I love him, Tam. But that's insane, isn't it? It's too soon."

"Best friend. Love doesn't wait for permission. That shit doesn't follow a calendar. And, last I checked, there isn't a rule saying you have to wait months—or years—to fall in love."

"I know. I just don't know what happens after all this. What if he wants me gone? What if I only feel this way because we've been together constantly since the night my apartment was broken into? We haven't even been on a real date. I can't even leave the freaking house."

Tamara shakes her head. "Well, that's just not true because, first of all, y'all had breakfast outside. That's basically a date. Like a romantic, rustic kinda date."

"You know what I mean, Tam," I say, rolling my eyes as I swat her hand.

"I do," she says, her voice softer. "But you've been through hell. You deserve to be happy. And, best friend, he makes you happy—I can tell."

"He does." I rub my brow and sigh. "I just hate that I'm stuck. Remember all those romantic suspense books I read?"

"Girl, do I ever." She wiggles her brows dramatically, pursing her lips in a kiss.

I ignore her and give her a pointed look. "Those books always have that moment where the female main character does something simple, like step outside to grab a coffee or take a walk, and then the next thing she knows, she's been kidnapped. Again. And I know it's fiction, but it's stuck in my head. I can't bring myself to leave the house."

"You'll step outside when you're ready."

"These walls…" I gesture around us. "They're oppressive. But… weirdly comforting. Like a safety net."

Tamara squeezes my hand again. "That's not stupid. If the walls are what help you feel okay, then let them. And nobody wants you endin' up like them girls in the books."

She pauses dramatically, glancing at the ceiling as if she's weighing something important. "Well… except when they get railed ten ways from Sunday."

I should've known better. I should've known not to sip wine right then. I clamp a hand over my mouth, trying not to spray it everywhere. Laughing through my nose, I force the wine down, wincing as it burns my throat.

"Oh my god," I cough, wiping a tear from my eye. "I freaking missed you."

The soft *snick* of the locks snatch my attention from the TV to the front door. My heart gives a little jump, the flicker of fear shifting seamlessly into relief when the deadbolt slides back, and Maverick steps inside.

I watch silently as he tosses his keys and wallet onto the entry table. When his eyes find me curled up on the couch, a blanket draped over my legs, and Juno snoozing heavily against my side, his entire face transforms with a smile.

"It's late, sunshine," Maverick says, his voice low and worn. "You're still up?"

I glance at my watch. Nearly midnight. I lost track of time once Tamara left, and I started binge watching TV. Again.

I shift to sit up a little straighter, careful not to disturb Juno too much. "Yeah," I whisper, "I didn't want to lay down without you." My fingers fidget with the edge of the blanket, and I duck my head, turning my attention back to the episode playing quietly in the background. "That makes me sound needy. I'm sorry."

Maverick crosses the room in a few easy strides, stopping just in front of me. Mindful of Juno, he leans down, bracing his hands on either side of me, caging me in. His eyes study my face before softening.

"Don't ever apologize for that," he murmurs.

He lifts a hand, curling his finger beneath my chin and tilting my head up before pressing a lingering kiss to my lips. I lean into him, savoring the moment—the soft comb of his fingers through my hair grounding me in a way nothing else can. "I like that you waited for me," he says, his lips brushing against mine with each spoken word.

Maverick places a kiss on my forehead before straightening, leaving me bereft without his warmth. "I'm gonna grab a quick shower, sunshine. Be right back, okay?"

My chin dips, a small smile tugging at my lips as I watch him turn toward the hallway. But a thought catches in my chest, tightening there until I can't keep it inside.

"Mav?" I call softly before he gets too far.

He stops and turns back, pausing at the hallway entrance. "Yeah, sunshine?"

"Do you, uhm…" I trail off, gathering my courage. *Live,*

Clara. With nerves fluttering in my stomach, I meet his gaze and push through the lump in my throat. "Would you like some company?"

His lips quirk, that familiar, heart-stealing smile pulling at his mouth. "You're always welcome to join me, baby. You don't need to ask."

With that, he disappears down the hallway.

Steam curls around me as I step into the bathroom, my heart thundering. The air is thick and warm, the glass fogged. Maverick stands beneath the spray, water coursing down his back, his shoulders loose with exhaustion. He hasn't noticed me yet. Or if he has, he doesn't show it.

My stomach twists with nerves.

The last time I showered with a man in the same room, it was under watchful, controlling eyes. Eyes that violated. I squeeze my eyes shut for a second, inhaling deeply and shoving the memory away before it can dig its claws in deeper. I won't let it take this from me.

This is different. This is Maverick.

I exhale a shaky breath, willing my heartbeat to steady. I *want* this. I *need* this. I need to rewrite those dark memories and replace them with something real, something safe.

I take my time undressing, letting each unwanted memory—each unwanted touch—fall away as my clothes pile around my bare feet. When I finally open the shower door, a fresh wave of steam billows out.

Maverick turns, a soapy washcloth in his hand. His eyes find mine, asking without words if I'm sure about this.

I don't have to think.

I've never been so sure of anything in my life.

The door closes behind me as I step inside, the heat wrapping around me instantly. The sight of him standing there waiting for me without pressure, without expectation, nearly undoes me.

"Hi," I say, my voice barely louder than the water hitting the tile.

A slow, warm smile spreads across his face. "Hi, sunshine."

I step closer to him, my eyes roving over every inch of his skin. I catch sight of the small, circular scar near his shoulder—silvery and raised against his warm olive tone. It draws me in like a magnet.

I reach out, tracing the mark with the tips of my fingers. "Does it hurt?" I ask softly.

He shakes his head, a shiver running through him, goosebumps breaking out across his skin under my touch.

"Aches sometimes," he rasps, "but it doesn't hurt."

I watch him for a while, just breathing and drinking him in. The way he runs his hands through his hair. The calm, unhurried way he moves. His skin slick with water as he rinses, the muscles in his back flexing. I squeeze my thighs together, heat blooming low in my belly.

"Can I wash you?" His voice is gentle, steady, yet rough around the edges.

I swallow hard. "Yes."

He steps closer and turns me with a gentle touch, settling my back to his chest. I can feel his heart beating against mine.

"Are you sure, sunshine?" he murmurs near my ear. "You feel tense."

I nod, voice catching in my throat. "I'm sure, Maverick." Lifting a hand behind me, I stroke his cheek, reveling in the feel of his beard against my fingers. "The last time someone was there… while I was in the shower… it was in that prison. I don't want to think about that anymore. I want you to replace those memories. I want to think of *this* —of *you*—instead."

Maverick exhales, pressing a kiss to my temple. He takes my hand and brings my wrist to his mouth, resting his lips on my pulse point for a beat. "Well, then. Let me rewrite your memories, sunshine."

He guides me beneath the stream until my hair is drenched, warm water cascading down my back. He reaches for the shampoo, lathering it between his hands before massaging it into my scalp. His fingers are firm but gentle, and I can't help the moan that slips from my lips.

"Feel good?" he murmurs.

"Like you wouldn't believe."

He rinses the suds away and repeats the process with conditioner, his fingers gliding through my hair. Then he reaches for a soft cloth, lathering it with soap and starting at my shoulders. He moves slow, rubbing the fabric against me in small circles—down my arms, across my stomach.

He lingers at my breasts, between my thighs—everywhere but where I'm aching. I can't withhold the whimper that escapes me. "Please."

"Shh," he whispers. "Let me worship you."

Maverick takes his time rinsing my skin, and I watch the suds swirl and spiral down the drain like ghosts.

"I need you," I breathe.

"This is about you," he says. "I want to give you what you deserve. Want to rewrite your memories, just like you said. Want you to remember the way I touch you."

He tilts my chin, kissing me softly, reverently, before trailing his lips along my jaw, stopping at my ear.

"Tell me what else I need to rewrite."

My breath hitches. I don't want to say it. *I don't.* But if anyone can take my pain and hold it gently, it's him.

On a broken whisper, I say, "He used to dry me off with a towel."

Maverick bites his bottom lip, breath stuttering. Then he nods. "Be right back, baby."

He steps out of the shower, leaving the door ajar. I watch as he dries off quickly, wraps a towel around his waist, and then reaches back in to shut off the water. He holds out a hand to me.

I take it and step out, letting this moment—this tenderness—swallow me whole.

He grabs two towels from the rack. With one, he gently wipes my face and neck, then carefully squeezes the water from my hair.

"Want you to keep your eyes on me. You hear, sunshine?"

"Yes," I breathe.

After a beat, a harsh breath falls from my parted lips. Samson was always silent when he dried me off, amplifying my fear in anticipation of what would come next. "Talk to me, please."

He nods, dropping the wet towel and picking up the fresh one. As he dries my body—slowly, thoroughly—he never looks away. His voice is soft and low, words brushing over my skin like his hands.

"You're so strong, Clara. And so damn beautiful. Brave. Need you to know you aren't broken. You're here. With me."

His words, his touch, *all of him*, unravels me, filling my eyes with tears. I'm unable to will them away, and he pauses when he notices the rivulets running down my cheeks. The towel in his hand joins the one on the floor, and he brings his thumb to my face, wiping the tears as they fall.

His eyes—those rich, dark chocolate eyes—search mine, heavy with an unspoken question. I offer him a trembling, watery smile. I'm okay. More than okay.

He moves to the sink where I keep my toiletries, pumps lotion into his hands, and begins smoothing it over my skin. His touch is reverent. Healing. Softening something sharp inside me—rending through the darkness.

Brushing his soft lips against mine, he whispers into my mouth, "What else?"

I draw in a shaky breath. "He'd take me to the bed."

Maverick says nothing. Just takes my hand and leads me toward the bedroom.

He stops at the foot of the bed, and I freeze. The position. The angle. The memory. There's no way he'd know that our current stance—me between the bed and his warm body—is the same position Samson locked me in.

I tremble, the air catching in my lungs.

He doesn't miss it.

He presses a kiss to my shoulder, then grazes his lips across my skin. Turning me, he cups my face in his hands.

"He doesn't belong in these moments. He has no power over you, sunshine." He pauses, tilting my head until I meet his eyes. "It's you and me."

It's in this moment that clarity washes over me. I feel it in my bones; an undeniable truth settling inside me like a warm embrace.

I love him.

And I would endure it all over again, just to be here—right here, right now—with him. A thousand times over.

CHAPTER 36
MAVERICK

RIVER

SHE'S STILL ASLEEP when I wake. The sun hasn't risen yet, but I can see her clearly—soft, peaceful, and so fucking beautiful. Her dark brown hair is a mess around the pillow, and her lips are pursed slightly as if she's in the middle of a dream.

I can't look away.

I study every inch of her face, memorizing every detail as if I'll need to recall it in perfect clarity one day. Because I will. I've never felt this way about anyone before. I loved Heather, but this feeling? Nothing comes close. And I haven't let myself think too hard about what happens when this is over. When the case ends. When she regains her freedom. Will she decide to continue her life in Rochester? Where would that leave me?

Coming home last night and finding her waiting up for me made me realize exactly what I want. *Her*. I want to come home to her every night. Just the thought of not waking up next to her, of not falling asleep with her in my arms, knocks the air from my lungs.

"I feel you watching me," she murmurs, her voice small, sleepy, and impossibly sweet. She doesn't even open her eyes.

I lean in, nuzzling her cheek and pressing a soft kiss to her forehead. "You're beautiful," I whisper. "Good morning, sunshine."

She blinks at me, the corners of her lips tugging into a smile. "Mmm, good morning. What time is it?"

"Early. We don't have to get out of bed yet."

"Oh, good." She nestles closer, tucking herself into my side, fitting against me perfectly.

Draping an arm over her waist, I soak in the heat from her bare body. In this comfortable silence, I can feel her chest rise and fall with each breath—the concerto of our heartbeats in perfect symphony.

"Tell me about your dreams. The coffee shop with a bar," I say after a minute.

She looks up at me, brows furrowed. "How did you know about that?"

"Tamara mentioned it. Will you tell me?"

"I pretty much live for coffee," she starts, a soft smile gracing her lips. Her gaze drifts to my shoulder, settling on the scar. She traces absent circles with her fingertips before continuing, "I've always wanted my own coffee shop. When I started bartending at The Pour House, I realized how much I loved it—getting to know the customers, the music, the liveliness…"

Her voice trails off as though she's envisioning the scene. I wait.

"Coffee shops always close early—at least, the ones I like, anyway. So, I thought it'd be nice to have a coffee shop that's open late, with a bar on one end. I imagine a cozy area with bookshelves and couches… and a stage on the other side. Live music. Poetry nights."

She smiles up at me then, full of wonder and hope, and my heart squeezes. I want her to have everything.

"Tamara and I talked about yoga nights. She'd lead the classes, then top up with some stiff drinks." She nuzzles her face into my chest. "It's a pipe dream."

Before I can respond—before I can tell her it's not a pipe dream—she asks, "Did you always want to be an FBI agent?"

I pause, considering my words. "I knew I wanted to be in law enforcement… I spent years as a police officer. When I became a detective, I worked closely with the FBI to solve a few cases. A spot opened up at the Minneapolis field office, and I took it. I don't regret it."

What I don't tell her is that, while I don't regret this path I've chosen, I'm not sure how much longer I can walk it. The death. The darkness. The danger. If Clara were taken from me because of this career, it would destroy me—reduce me to dust, swept away by the weight of her loss, the weight of my failure.

Right here, right now, if she asked me to toss my badge aside and help her chase her dream… I'd do it in a fucking heartbeat.

She hums, then leans back just enough to look up at me.

"What is it?" I ask, keeping my voice quiet.

"I… I have something to tell you."

I meet her eyes. "Then tell me."

She swallows and holds my gaze, her voice barely above a whisper. "I don't know if it's too soon, but… All I know is… I love you, Maverick Rhodes."

For a second, all I can do is look at her, stunned by the force of those words.

I lift my hand, catching her chin between my thumb and forefinger. "Do you know why I call you *sunshine?*"

She shakes her head, a slight furrow in her brows, the edges of her pouty lips turning down.

"In that hospital, despite everything you'd been through, you shined so damn bright. You didn't even know it. Your strength. Your fire. The way you kept fighting." I brush my thumb against her lower lip. "You are the only light in my darkness, Clara. I love you."

She leans in and kisses the corner of my mouth, then wraps herself around me—her arm around my waist, her leg tangled with mine, her head tucked beneath my chin.

In this moment, my universe narrows to a single point of light, and nothing else exists. Just her. Just us.

***

Early morning air fills my lungs and cools my sweat-soaked skin. My feet strike the concrete in a steady rhythm; Juno effortlessly keeps pace beside me.

God, I needed this run. Needed to burn through the endless frustrations of this case and the looming meeting with the mayor. I'm on edge—every fiber of my body is strung tight, threatening to snap. Nothing can go wrong.

I savor the fire in my muscles, letting it fuel me and push me closer to home. By the time Juno and I make it back, the sun's climbing, and each breath I take burns something fierce. Juno trots in front of me, tongue lolling, tail wagging like he knows exactly what's waiting inside. *Who's* waiting inside.

The scent hits me as soon as I open the front door— eggs, bacon, and toast. I step into the kitchen and find Clara at the stove, looking like a damn vision. Barefoot with her hair thrown in a small, messy bun. She's wearing one of my sweatshirts, and suddenly, I don't want to see her wearing anything else.

She glances over her shoulder and smiles, bright and soft and *home* all at once.

"Perfect timing," she says. "Breakfast's almost ready. And your water is right there." She nods toward the tall glass on the island, filled with ice and beaded with condensation.

"Thank you, sunshine," I breathe, pulling in a slow inhale through my nose to settle the post-run adrenaline. I stop at the counter, grab the glass, and down it in one go. "Smells good. Where do you want to eat?"

Some mornings we eat inside. Others, we take it out to the patio. I always let her choose—whatever makes her feel most at ease.

"Outside," she responds, tilting her chin and pursing her lips in that silent, unmistakable request for a kiss.

I'm more than happy to oblige.

In two strides, I reach her and press my mouth to hers—gentle but lingering. "I'm going to grab a quick shower," I murmur against her lips. "Then I'll help bring everything out."

"I can handle it. Worry about your shower, my love. You stink," she teases, a playful grin overtaking her face.

I don't miss the way she called me *my love*, or the way it wraps around my heart. Unable to help myself, I lean in, grazing my lips along the nape of her neck.

"You mean I smell like a man," I growl near her ear.

Then, I give her ass a quick swat and head for the bathroom, grinning as she squeals and calls after me.

True to her word, Clara had breakfast ready on the patio table.

We eat in a comfortable quiet. Juno sprawls in the grass nearby, belly-up and useless after the run.

The weather is starting to turn as we head deeper into fall, but the crisp air is refreshing, and the heat of the sun offers just enough warmth to keep the chill at bay.

Clara's sock-adorned feet rest in my lap beneath the table, her toes occasionally brushing against me. She cradles her cup of coffee like it's something sacred, holding it close with both hands.

Halfway through my second cup, my phone buzzes on the table.

I glance at the screen. Arlo. I swipe to answer and bring it to my ear. "What's up?"

His voice cuts through the morning calm. "Finally got a hit on the shell corporation that owns the warehouse. ASE Anvils Corp. Don't know what made me think of it, but I ran the name through a scrambler. It's an anagram, Maverick."

I sit up straighter, my brows pinching together. "An anagram for what?"

"ASE Anvils… Lisa Evans."

"You've got to be shitting me."

"Nope. Lisa Evans was the mayor's aunt. She died about twenty years ago. Came from money; her husband was a politician who passed a few years before her."

I exhale, running a hand down my face. "Why the hell would he name a shell corp after his dead aunt?"

"Good question. I'll keep digging. Something's off."

"Yeah, I feel it, too. Thanks, Arlo. See you at the office."

I end the call and set my phone down, finishing the last of my coffee.

Clara watches me carefully. "Everything okay?"

"Yeah," I sigh. "The warehouse you were kept in… It's owned by a shell corporation." I reach down, curling my hand around her foot and gently squeezing. "Arlo got a lead, but it's raised more questions than answers."

My thumb glides along the arch of her foot, repeating the motion to soothe both her and myself. I won't keep anything from Clara, but the mention of the warehouse, the mayor, any of it… it weighs heavy. Especially when I have to leave her again.

She doesn't respond, but the scowl on her face says enough.

"Tamara coming over today?"

"She is," Clara says with a nod. "She should be here soon."

"You want me to wait until she gets here?" I ask. The idea of her being alone in Minneapolis while I'm two hours away makes me uneasy.

She shakes her head. "No, it's okay. You need to get to work. I'll be fine, my love."

I squeeze her foot one last time, then ease her legs off my lap and stand. Leaning down, I press a kiss to her forehead, then to her lips, lingering just a second longer.

Together, we clear the patio table, carrying the dishes and leftovers inside.

"Weekend patterns make sense now," Spencer mutters, staring at the calendar and timeline projected on the wall. "His position as mayor doesn't exactly afford him free time during the week. But the weekends? That's when he can disappear."

We're looking at everything—each piece of evidence, each crime scene—with a new lens.

The warehouse. The timelines. The gaps. The victims.

All of it shifts into grim clarity, with the mayor at the center.

"He had the time to make the commute to his victims. Hours in either direction," I add, jaw tight. "He had the resources. He just had to make it back by Monday morning."

Arlo clears his throat, typing rapidly. "Pulled footage from Revolution Coffee the day Marie vanished. Mayor walked out with her at 4:28 in the afternoon."

"This is what we need," Riley says, her voice carrying a hint of excitement. "We can place the mayor with the victim. Place him leaving with her. Now, we just need to get his DNA to confirm he killed her."

The door swings open, and Cruz storms in, his face as dark as a thundercloud. He lifts an evidence bag containing a sheet of paper, walks up to the table, and throws it down.

Hard.

"Fucking message," he spits.

We all freeze.

Cruz locks eyes with me, voice sharp and low. "It's a letter. For Clara. He sent it to the precinct."

I swear under my breath and reach for the letter, sealed in the bag. My blood percolates as I take in each word.

"Any prints?" I ask, voice gruff.

"None," Cruz says.

I stare at the letter for a beat before tossing it onto the table as though it held something toxic.

"Fuck. How long until the meeting?"

"Two days," Spencer answers.

Too fucking long.

The second I walk through the door, I know something's wrong.

The house is quiet. Too quiet.

Clara's on the couch, exactly where she was when I came home last night—but she's not watching TV. She's not reading.

She's not even moving.

She looks like a statue. Frozen. Still. Staring blankly ahead.

Juno is curled in her lap. His ears flick once in my direction, but he doesn't move either.

"Sunshine?"

Nothing.

I round the couch slowly, and that's when I see it.

An unfolded letter sits on the cushion next to her. Black ink scrawled across white paper in familiar writing.

Fuck.

THE LETTER

My perfect Clara,

Do you remember the first night I saw you?

You were behind the bar, moving with such grace. So beautiful. So perfect. You smiled at me. Your smile was always so warm and inviting. You even remembered my drink when I came back the very next night.

That's when I knew you were special.

Do you remember the things you told me? You don't have to pretend you forgot. I remember everything. Your dreams... the little coffee shop with a bar. Do you still want that? Because I can give it to you, Clar.

I'll take better care of you this time. I promise.

I miss you. I miss the way it felt to be inside you.

Did you get my message? I tried to save myself for you again. I really did. But I just couldn't help myself. You don't understand how much I need you. My body craves you. I crave you. So I thought maybe Marie could be like you. Thought she could be enough. But she wasn't you. She didn't feel like you.

She didn't like it when I called her your name.

Maybe the next one will be better. It's just until I get you back.

Once I have you, I won't need them anymore.

I'll be waiting.

Don't make me wait too long.

    —Samson

CHAPTER 37
MAVERICK

12 ROUNDS

I HAVEN'T LEFT Clara's side in two days.

Not since I found her on the couch, that goddamn letter beside her as if it had hollowed her out from the inside. It took hours to bring her back to herself that night.

We've fallen back into our familiar routine, but she's subdued. I don't like it. And now, I'm supposed to leave her and head into work. It's the last thing I want to do, but I don't have a choice.

The meeting with the mayor is in three hours.

Three damn hours.

I rub the back of my neck and glance at the clock. 10:00 a.m. Tamara should be here soon. I can't bring myself to leave until I know Clara isn't alone.

She's curled up in the corner of the sectional, Juno lying across her feet, her fingers idly stroking his ears. Her expression is softer this morning, more present. She glances up at me as though she knows I'm watching her—

as though she knows what I'm thinking. "You can go, Mav. I'll be okay."

She's trying to reassure me, but I can hear the hesitation in her voice.

"I'm not walking out that door until Tamara gets here, sunshine," I say gently but firmly, walking over to crouch beside her. "I just—" I exhale, shaking my head. "I need to know you're not alone."

Her hand cups my jaw, thumbs brushing my cheek. "You stayed for me. Two full days. You have work to do, my love, and I'm okay now. I promise."

The knock at the door slices through the room. I rise instantly, crossing the floor in three strides and opening it.

Tamara steps in, a tote bag slung over her shoulder and a determined look on her face. "I brought snacks, chocolate, and a bad rom-com. I'm not leaving her side. You don't have to worry."

I nod and proffer a tight smile. "Thank you."

I turn back to Clara. She's standing now, her eyes locked on mine. I close the space between us and wrap my arms around her.

"I'll be back tonight," I murmur against her hair. "I'll call you when it's over."

She nods against my chest. "I love you."

I capture her chin and tilt her head up, kissing her slow and deep. Pulling back just enough to look at her face, I brush my lips across her forehead. "I love you, sunshine."

Then I leave—clenching my hands and holding my breath. I won't be able to breathe until this fucker is gone. Behind bars or six feet under.

Preferably the latter.

"Thank you for meeting with us, Mr. Evans," Cruz says as the mayor unbuttons his suit jacket and settles into the leather seat at the head of the conference table.

We left that seat open on purpose. He needs to feel as though he's in control. As though he's the one holding the reins in this room. I sit to his left, Cruz to his right, a series of files and news articles spread out in front of us.

"Please, call me James," the bastard smiles, flashing a polished politician's smile. "I'm willing to do whatever I can to help."

"We appreciate that," I say with a curt nod. "The media's been spinning some wild theories about The Chameleon. It's stirring panic in Rochester."

"Our tip line's been flooded," Cruz adds. "People are scared. Asking if they're safe, if we're close to finding him. Unfortunately, we haven't received any credible leads. We're hoping that, with your involvement, we can reassure the public."

James leans forward, elbows on the table. Eager. Hungry to play the hero. "What would you like me to do?"

He needs to feel as though we need him, as though we're desperate to catch this motherfucker and can only do it with his help. As though he's the lynchpin in solving this case.

Cruz takes the lead, voice steady. "The chief was here earlier. We discussed a third press conference."

"But this time, we want you to lead it," I chime in. "The public trusts you. Probably more than they trust the rest of us."

The mayor's eyes gleam behind his glasses as he leans back in his chair—a false king on a borrowed throne.

The door creaks open before he can respond, and Jesse sticks his head in. "Coffee run. You guys want anything?"

"Thanks, man," I say. "Black coffee."

"Americano for me," Cruz adds.

James pauses just long enough to seem gracious. "Oat milk latte, extra shot. Please."

Jesse disappears with a nod.

Fifteen minutes later, he's back with a tray of drinks. "Got your orders, gentlemen."

He passes them out, but when I take a sip of mine, it's not black coffee that hits my tongue. It's oat milk and espresso. Thick and bitter. I school my face, hiding a grimace. Jesse catches my eye for a split second.

Showtime.

As Cruz and the mayor start discussing public messaging strategies, I match James sip for sip, waiting a few beats in between to make it appear natural. He doesn't notice. Why would he? He thinks we're the ones in the dark.

"We could drip-feed some details," I muse. "Maybe a partial timeline."

"Well, let's take a look at it," Cruz says, standing and rounding the table.

I rise, coffee in hand, and make my way around the

table. The mayor follows, distracted by the evidence board. He sets his cup on the table behind him.

I loop around subtly, swapping our cups in one fluid motion, then glance at the timeline Spencer mocked up this morning. Two fake crime scenes at the top.

"We have to be careful." With the hand holding the coffee, I gesture to the top of the board. "What do you think about releasing these?"

The mayor's eyes narrow at the unfamiliar cases. "I wasn't made aware of these two."

"We were alerted to those recently," Cruz explains smoothly.

While they talk, I pull out my phone and shoot off a text.

Maverick
Go.

A minute later, Jesse reappears. "Everyone good in here? I'm heading out."

"We're good," I reply. "You can take this. I'm done." I hold out the nearly empty cup—the one the mayor's mouth was all over.

Jesse raises a brow. "I'm not the errand boy, boss man. Trash is over there," he says, pointing lazily to the receptacle.

"And you're closer," I counter flatly.

He rolls his eyes, takes the cup, and disappears without another word.

The meeting drags on for another hour. We finalize plans: a third press conference in three days and a public statement to be released by the mayor in the morning. He thinks he's tightening the noose around the case.

But really, it's his neck the noose is around.

Thirty minutes later, Cruz and I are in the lab, pacing like caged animals and under strict orders from Jesse to keep quiet.

When a series of beeps breaks the tense silence, the three of us descend toward the screen. The results are in.

Jesse stares at the monitor, blinking. "It's a match."

Time stops.

The DNA on the coffee lid matches the semen found on the victims. A conclusive, undeniable match.

Enough probable cause for a warrant. Enough to bring the walls down.

"Speak nothing of this outside of the team. We can't risk letting this get back to the mayor." I glance at Cruz. "Not even the chief."

I exhale slowly, my heart thudding in my chest.

The monster wears a mayor's smile.

But not for much longer.

CHAPTER 38
MAVERICK

PLAY THE PART

"THIS IS A FUCKING DISASTER." Judge McClannan sighs heavily and removes his glasses, letting them hang around his neck. He swipes a thick hand down his face and stares at the evidence.

The DNA report and case files are spread out before him, the surveillance footage paused on the laptop to his right, showing the mayor and Marie walking out of the coffee shop together.

Judge McClannan is a seventy-something, heavyset man—his coily silver hair a contrast to his dark skin. His demeanor is light, but I've heard enough about him to know that he takes no shit in the courtroom. He's worked closely with Cruz for at least a decade, and Cruz trusted him enough to confide in him. Not wanting the evidence to travel, he agreed to meet us at the FBI resident agency office.

"I'd ask if you were sure, but…" His voice trails off as he gestures to everything in front of him.

The evidence speaks for itself.

"Yeah, I know." Cruz shakes his head, keeping his eyes locked on the judge.

The entire task force waits on pins and needles, eager for the signature to appear on the warrant. We briefed everyone at the same time, needing to ensure our circle was small.

"All right." Judge McClannan's deep, raspy voice severs the quiet. He pulls a ballpoint pen from his chest pocket, cursing under his breath as he signs his name on the solid line.

The moment he signs the warrant, it feels as though the air shifts. It hasn't felt real until this second.

We let out a collective breath and thank the good judge. We've been chasing a ghost for months. Now, we're walking into the monster's lair with a key in hand.

Cruz and I are the first to arrive on scene. The mayor's house is befitting of a man who built a reputation on charm and control—grand, polished, and meant to impress.

The house is a colonial revival—three stories of symmetrical perfection, with white columns, dark shutters, and stone steps leading to an arched front door. The setting sun washes the place in warm gold and blood-orange light, highlighting its beauty. It looks like a picturesque landscape on a magazine cover. Classy and timeless without being ostentatious.

But it's a pretty facade, hiding something rotten behind the walls.

Cruz lets out a low whistle. "Fucker's got taste, I'll give him that," he mutters.

I grunt, eyes sweeping over the property. "Fucker's got secrets."

We make our way up the steps, pausing at the door.

"A fingerprint scanner? Really?" Cruz asks, disbelief coating his voice.

Cruz knocks—or rather, pounds—on the door. "Mr. Evans," he yells. "It's Detective Cruz."

No one answers.

After a few more loud knocks, it's clear the mayor isn't home.

"Arlo," I call. "You're up!"

I hear a shift of bodies behind me before Arlo appears at my side. He takes one look at the electronic door handle and shakes his head. "Just a minute."

Two minutes later, the handle is in Arlo's hand and the front door is pushed open.

Cruz and I are the first to enter, followed by my team and a few trusted RPD officers on the task force.

The inside is just as pristine as the outside. Not a single thing out of place. This is the home of a man who controls his environment, down to the last inch.

But monsters don't always live in haunted houses. They live in places just like this, using their charm and riches to cover their tracks.

"Search everything," I tell the team. "Attic, basement, crawlspaces. Lift the fucking floorboards if you have to."

We split up. The team fans out, Cruz takes the study, and I head up the stairs toward the master bedroom.

It's as polished as the rest of the house. A king-sized bed with ironed sheets. Ornate, heavy, wooden furniture. A large bay window.

I stride into the attached bathroom—equally extravagant—and sift through drawers and cabinets. Finding nothing remarkable, I make my way back into the bedroom.

I step inside the closet. It's so organized, it looks like a display room. Rows of crisp suits, all lined up by color. A pendant light fixture hangs from the middle of the space.

My fingers trail along the back walls, hoping to find a seam or a loose panel, but I come up empty.

Something feels off.

Swallowing down my frustration, I turn and study the wall closest to the door frame. It's lined with shelves full of designer dress shoes, but the white cornice molding seems thicker here.

I trail my fingers down the wall, close to the molding. And there it is. It blends in so naturally, I almost miss it.

I press against the panel. It shifts.

"Got something!" I holler. "Hidden entrance in the master closet!"

Cruz is at my side in seconds. Footsteps in the hallway alert me to the rest of the team heading our way.

I tug the panel open, revealing a narrow, well-lit, spiral staircase leading upward.

We ascend slowly, guns drawn. When we breach the space, it confirms every nightmare Clara ever had.

A workstation takes up half the attic. Three large monitors glow faintly, casting shadows on a row of external hard drives. A worn leather chair sits neatly in front of a keyboard and mouse.

"Rhodes, come look at this shit."

I turn to find Cruz standing in front of a clothing rack filled with various uniforms and lower quality suits.

My attention is drawn to the tall dresser next to the rack. I pull latex gloves from my pocket and slip them on. Opening the top drawer, I'm greeted with dozens of fake IDs and bundles of bills.

"Un-fucking-believable," I mutter as I open the rest of the drawers, finding high-end wigs, a variety of glasses, different shades of contact lenses—the whole fucking gamut. He has everything he needs to blend in, to camouflage himself. Like a true goddamn chameleon.

"Rhodes. Cruz," Riley beckons.

Jesse and Evie have already started setting up their equipment, securing the scene for photos, videos, and evidence collection.

Cruz and I weave around them to the other side of the attic where Riley is, flipping through the pages of a book.

Three bookshelves line the back wall. My brows furrow as I take them in, each shelf full of the same style of books. I move closer and pull one off the shelf at random.

No. Not books.

Journals.

Dozens of them. Leather-bound. Numbered.

I inspect the journal in my hand—number thirty-nine—then flip it open. The handwriting is neat. Familiar. Obsessive. Pages filled with photos and scrupulous details—license plates, routines, favorite coffee orders. His victims. His hunts. His fantasies. His truths.

"Box all these up," I order.

Exhaling loudly, I take in the scene before me. I don't know what I expected to find, but this level of obsession and sophistication wasn't it.

Glancing toward the workstation, I spy Arlo and Spencer setting up their laptops. They'll be bringing the external hard drives and computers back to the office, but they're no doubt getting a head start on cataloguing everything.

The RPD officers follow Jesse's lead, carefully boxing and bagging evidence.

Cruz has a crowbar in his hand.

I raise a brow, starting for the back corner where he's staring at an oversized trunk as if it insulted his leather shoes. "What are you doing, Cruz?"

"About to open this fucking trunk. What's it look like?"

"Evie! You get a photo of this yet?" I question before Cruz takes the crowbar to task.

"Yup! All good," she responds, the camera viewfinder pressed to her eye and fixated on the dresser.

Cruz doesn't wait any longer to pry the trunk open. The lock snaps with the force of a bone breaking—sharp and sudden.

The hinges groan in protest when Cruz opens the lid.

"This ain't storage," he says.

"Trophies?" I ask, even though I already know the answer.

"Trophies."

Personal belongings. A locket. A keychain. Torn pieces of clothing. A ring I recognize from one of the early victim photos.

Cruz doesn't say anything. He doesn't need to.

I stare at the contents of the trunk, heart pounding like a war drum in my chest.

This is it. This is everything we need.

CHAPTER 39
CLARA

TWISTED

EVERY TIME I think I've found a sliver of normal, *he* finds some way to shatter it. To rip apart the progress I've made—the life I'm trying to rebuild.

When I found that letter on the front porch, I knew it was from him before I even opened it.

And then I opened it.

Everything inside me recoiled as I read his words; a reminder that I'm still living in the shadow of what he did to me.

I don't know how long I sat frozen on the couch, the letter left open next to me and Juno curled in my lap, before Maverick came home and found me like that.

Lost.

Again.

It makes me angry to admit that I let Samson—James, whatever-the-fuck his name is—drag me back to that place. That dark, dangerous corner of my mind where my fear runs rampant.

Where I'm still buried.

But Maverick brought me back, like he always does. My protector, never leaving my side. God, the love I feel for him is overwhelming. He's my tether; my anchor when the past tries to swallow me whole.

"Hey, best friend. You okay?" Tamara's voice pulls me back, soft but pointed as she bumps her shoulder into mine. Her brows draw together, etched with concern.

The kitchen smells like garlic and rosemary, warm and inviting. Tamara and I have made a quiet routine out of cooking dinner together when she visits while Maverick's working.

"I'm okay," I say, blinking and shifting my gaze to the window. Juno's outside, living the high life, sunbathing in the grass. Shaking my head at his antics, I return to the simmering sauce on the stove. "I was just thinking."

"About what?"

I glance at my phone on the counter for what must be the hundredth time. The screen is still dark.

"He hasn't called yet," I admit.

Maverick texted me after the meeting with the mayor. *DNA match. We've got him. Might be home later than I thought. Love you.*

That was hours ago.

"He'll call," Tamara says gently. "That man is gone for you."

I let out a quiet laugh and shake my head. "You should probably watch your fingers," I tease.

Tamara's chopping romaine lettuce, cucumbers, and

grape tomatoes for the salad. She makes me nervous whenever she handles a chef's knife. To be fair, she's improved. But we've had too many bloody incidents in the kitchen to last me a lifetime.

"Rude," she chides, rolling her eyes before focusing on the knife in her hand.

It takes everything in me not to pick up my phone. There's a tightness in my chest, a visceral unease that lingers. I try not to read into it. I tell myself he's just busy. This is how it goes when they're close to something big. And with the DNA coming back as a match, he's likely on his way to get a warrant.

That was the plan, anyway. But it doesn't stop me from worrying.

The doorbell rings.

"That would be the groceries," I say, wiping my hands on a towel as I head toward the front door. We needed a few missing items, including dessert, and neither of us felt like leaving the house. An Italian dinner without tiramisu felt blasphemous. And I'm pretty sure Tamara would throw the salad bowl at me if I tried to serve her my preferred salad dressing—squeezed lemon juice and salt—instead of Olive Garden's.

I open the door, a light smile already forming. "Thank y—"

But the half-formed smile falls, and the words die in my throat.

It's not the delivery driver.

A man stands on the porch, bathed in the warmth of the

setting sun. His features are too familiar. His expression too calm.

My blood runs cold.

"Hello, Clara."

CHAPTER 40
HIM

BLOOD ON YOUR HANDS

IT TOOK every ounce of control I had to rein in my monster when I saw the additional crime scenes at the top of their stupid fucking timeline. I wanted to snap that idiot detective's neck when he droned on and on about releasing information from them.

Where the fuck did those come from? Those girls were never ours.

Something is wrong.

Off.

And we don't fucking like it.

The itch beneath our skin is incessant, unbearable. It's screaming at us—telling us that we're wasting time. We can't wait any longer. We need to get to Clara.

I slam the car door shut so hard the frame shudders. Staring up at the FBI resident agency building, I calculate the quickest route to Minneapolis. Rhodes will be on his way soon, but we can beat him there. There's more than enough time.

And I know just where we're taking her.

Somewhere special.

Somewhere I've never taken anyone else before.

The closer we get to Clara, the easier it is to breathe. With each mile burned away, that relentless itch lessens, and our heart races faster. All that's left now is the moment. The taking.

As I pull into the driveway, my eyes lock on an unfamiliar car parked in front of the garage. She has company.

Who the hell is here with her? It doesn't matter. Rhodes isn't here, and he's the one we need out of our way.

With a deep inhale, I lift the center console lid and retrieve the small lock box tucked beneath a panel. Clara won't come easily, but we don't mind. We can make it easy. I select one of the pre-filled syringes before stowing the box away and getting out of the car.

Excitement runs like fire through our veins. Every movement brings us closer to our prize. I pause in front of the front door and knock, loud and firm—a storm announcing its presence.

She makes us wait a minute before opening the door. Our Clara looks like she's expecting someone else, a small smile blooming on her lips. The second her eyes meet mine, it dies.

"Hello, Clara," I say, keeping my voice low.

Her eyes widen, and I watch as the blood drains from her face.

Clara's body jolts like it wants to run, but I shake my head slowly and cluck my tongue. "You shouldn't be here, Clar. It's time to come with me."

She opens her mouth to scream, but I'm already there, plunging the needle into her neck. She crumples in my arms with barely a sound, and I lay her at my feet before pocketing the syringe.

"Clara?" An unfamiliar, feminine voice calls from somewhere in the house. "What the hell is taking so long? I need the salad dressing!"

I look up just as the waitress from The Pour House rounds the corner. She stops abruptly, her eyes flicking from me to Clara, then back to me. I see the moment recognition hits, followed by fear.

"No!"

The woman charges forward, a twisted, determined look etched on her face.

I step over our Clara and meet her halfway. One backhand, coupled with her own momentum, sends her flying into the wall. She crashes onto the floor with a satisfying *thud*. Her body lies in a heap, still and unmoving.

My monster wants to make sure the woman won't be an issue—wants to make sure she's dead.

But we don't have time.

"This wasn't supposed to happen like this," I mutter through clenched teeth, turning back to Clara.

This is why we plan, why we wait. It's too late now.

I hoist her body up and throw her over my shoulder, fitting my arm snugly beneath the curve of her ass. My fingers twitch with longing.

God, we missed this.

I kick the door shut behind me and head for the car.

It's time to go.

The drive is a blur, forty-five minutes passing in the blink of an eye.

Tires crunch the deteriorating concrete as I stop in front of the large colonial house we never wanted to see again. But admittedly, it's perfect for what we have in mind.

I step out of the vehicle—the sharp, damp air cooling our heated skin—and open the trunk. Clara's still out cold, limbs limp and peaceful.

Good. It'll make this faster.

I lift her again, savoring the weight of her body against mine, and carry her through the front door without a glance at the dust or peeling wallpaper. I move through the dark kitchen and stop at the cellar entrance. Finding the old latch, I pull until the hatch creaks open, exhaling years of stale air and damp earth.

I descend into the darkness and lay her gently on the dirt floor before pulling the light string above us. The lone bulb flickers—buzzing awake after years of slumber—until it brightens the dark space just enough to see the shadows in the corners.

We promised we would take better care of her this time. My monster yearns to keep her, to end our hunt with the only prey who embodied true perfection. If only he listened to me the first time.

We told her we'd bring her home, but Clara needs to atone for making this difficult on us. For living with another man. For letting him touch her. And we know he's touched her. Touched what doesn't belong to him.

Resisting the urge to let our frustrations out on her body, to punish her for her transgressions, I turn away and scan the space that was once so familiar. A second home.

Memories long forgotten creep forward, causing my monster to thrash with rage inside my chest.

The pallet beneath the stairs catches my eye, and I stride toward it. A dusty pile of threadbare blankets lay atop the wooden slats—once my refuge from Aunt Lisa. From her wrath when I displeased her.

She thought leaving me alone in a suffocating space devoid of light would fix me. Instead, I acquainted myself with the dark, learning to listen. Learning to *be*. It was here I met my monster for the first time. A quiet introduction. A fog seeped in beneath the door until it filled my lungs and embedded itself so deep it'd never come out.

We became one.

Suppose we should've thanked her before we slit her throat in her sleep. If it hadn't been for that venomous bitch, I might never have found the other side of me.

The *real* side of me. Of *us*.

She tried to beat it out of me. Hoped the darkness would chase it away. The dumb bitch. All she did was feed it.

I inhale deeply, the musty scent of the earth and rot coating my tongue.

No. She doesn't own us anymore. Doesn't control us. She can't.

She's fucking dead.

But she left us this house. This legacy of broken glass and blood-soaked lessons. And it's here, in these walls and shadows, where Clara will finally see the truth. Where she'll finally understand.

This is where she'll find herself.

With us.

And then we can go *home*.

Together.

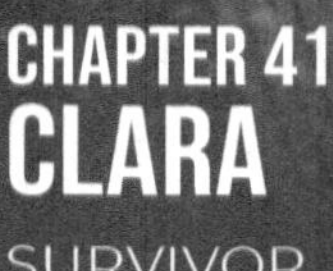

CHAPTER 41
CLARA
SURVIVOR

PAIN.

It's the first sensation I wake up to—a sharp, shooting pain in my neck that feels all too familiar. My brain feels foggy, cloudy, like the feeling you get when you pull an all-nighter and only get an hour of sleep. It takes far too long for me to come to the stark realization that this pain in my neck is one I've felt before.

The night I woke up in that warehouse.

Just as I start to understand the implications, memories from the last few hours play like a movie reel in my head. Maverick leaving for Rochester with his team. Tamara coming over to keep me company. The two of us cooking dinner together. Worrying that I hadn't heard from Mav since he texted about getting the warrant. The doorbell ringing...

I stifle a gasp when I remember opening the front door and seeing *him* standing there.

My heart ricochets when the scent of dirt infiltrates my

senses. It doesn't smell the exact same as when I was trapped in that fucking coffin—there's something else mixed in, rotten wood maybe—but it's close enough that panic grips me. My eyes snap open, causing me to wince as my vision settles on a single bright bulb flickering above me.

I avert my gaze to a dark corner of the ceiling and take stock of my body. My arms feel heavy, disconnected, like they belong to someone else. I flex my fingers—they're stiff and cold but unbound. No rope burns around my wrists. No zip ties cutting into my skin. My hands rest against what feels like packed earth beneath me, cold seeping through my clothes with a bone-deep chill that makes me want to curl into myself.

I wiggle my toes inside my shoes—my feet are also free. The absence of bindings should be reassuring, but instead it feels wrong. Deliberate. Like he wants me to know I could run, even though I have nowhere to go. I don't even know where I am.

My shoulder blades press against the uneven ground, small stones and debris digging into my back through my shirt. When I shift slightly, trying to relieve the pressure points, dirt crumbles and gives way beneath my weight.

I'm still fully clothed—another small mercy that feels more like psychological warfare than kindness.

My legs are straight out in front of me, and when I try to bend my knees, my muscles protest with a deep ache that suggests I've been unconscious for hours. How long have I been down here? Where's Tamara?

Keeping my body still, I slowly turn my head and

survey my surroundings. I'm in a small space—a basement or cellar. The walls appear to be rough stone or concrete, disappearing into deep shadows that the single overhead bulb can't penetrate.

A wooden staircase to my left leads down from above, its rails rickety and worn. Beneath it sits what I initially mistake for a mattress topped with blankets. But when I squint and focus, I make out the distinct outline of wooden slats.

A pallet. A makeshift bed.

The sight fills me with terror, and I tear my gaze away, needing to look at anything else.

The only sound in the room is the steady *buzz, buzz, buzz* of the overhead light. I don't hear anything else. I don't see anyone else.

With that small comfort, I slowly—painstakingly—unfurl my body from the dirt floor. A groan escapes as I sit up, my stiff limbs aching with each movement.

I'm so focused on the effort it takes to sit and steady myself that I nearly miss the shadow rising from the pallet.

"You're awake."

I freeze at the sound of his deep, smooth voice.

Samson prowls closer, the harsh shadows from the bare bulb making his presence even more menacing.

"Where's Tamara? Is she okay? What did you do to her? Where am I?" I fire off the questions in rapid succession, leaving no time for him to answer. My pulse thunders beneath my skin as I glance around the room in a futile search for any way out.

Resignation starts to settle in my bones: the likelihood of escaping this man a second time is nonexistent.

God.

I never wanted to see him again—this man from my nightmares. Never wanted to be alone with him. Never wanted to even *think* about him. And yet here we are.

Samson remains silent, leaving my questions hanging between us like smoke. I can feel his heavy gaze on me—studying, calculating.

Closing my eyes, I take a deep breath and envision Maverick's handsome face, hoping that his presence—even if it's just in my mind—is enough to keep me calm.

"You don't need to worry about Tamara anymore. It's just you and me now, Clar."

I push myself up off the ground, forcing my legs to support me despite their trembling. "There is no you and me." Steeling my spine, I straighten and meet his eyes. I may not be able to escape him again, but that doesn't mean I'll make this easy. I'm a fucking survivor.

He moves with predatory speed, giving me zero time to react as he seizes my shoulder with one hand and grips my throat with the other. "Don't. Say. That." Each syllable drips with veiled menace.

The wild, unhinged look in his eyes paralyzes me. I don't move when he leans in and breathes against my neck. Not even when he trails his nose along my jaw like some kind of animal scenting its prey.

"We've missed you. You're going to be happy with us this time," he whispers against my cheek.

We? Who is we? And who is us? My forehead creases as I narrow my eyes on his face. "Us?"

He doesn't answer. The slight tightening of his hand on my throat is the only indication he heard me.

"You'll be treated better this time, Clar. Just like I told you in my letter. Did you get it? I'll take care of you."

I don't dare pull away, but I can't withhold the disbelieving scoff that falls from my lips. "You kidnapped me. You held me captive. You raped me, then you put me in a coffin and buried me alive. You left me to die. And now you want to 'take care of me?' Make me happy?" I shake my head at the absurdity of it all.

"He was wrong. I shouldn't have listened to him." His voice sounds distant, as if he's speaking to someone else entirely. He doesn't stop trailing his nose along my jaw and neck, his hot breath making my skin crawl.

"Who was wrong? What are you talking about?" My head is still foggy, but I know this confusion isn't from whatever drug he injected me with. He isn't making sense.

Finally, Samson releases his grip and steps back—just slightly. Still too close. With his eyes locked on mine, he lifts a finger and traces the outline of my lips with disturbing tenderness. "I mean, I was wrong. I didn't realize how perfect you were. I should've kept you. I wanted to keep you."

Beneath his breath, I swear I hear him mutter, "I told him to keep you."

"It wasn't supposed to be this way," he continues. "But when we found out you were alive… He wanted to finish it. He doesn't like loose ends. Everything has to be perfect, you know? But then you took over our head, our body. We couldn't stop thinking about you."

"Samson—*James*, whoever you are—you aren't making sense. Who is *we*? What do you mean by *our*? I don't understand."

"Samson," he growls, pressing his face close to mine until I can feel his breath on my lips. "I'm *your* Samson."

CHAPTER 42
MAVERICK
VENDETTA

WE CAN'T FUCKING FIND him.

The mayor wasn't home when we executed the warrant. His house gave us everything we needed to bury him—journals documenting his hunts, a surveillance setup that would make the NSA jealous, and enough evidence to put him away for life. Then he all but vanished.

After meticulously packing up Evans' computers, surveillance equipment, and handwritten journals, we left the rest of the evidence collection to a secondary team. Everything we didn't take would be en route to the Minneapolis field office for processing, but that didn't matter if we couldn't find the son of a bitch.

Cruz and I had raced to the mayor's office downtown, expecting to find him sitting behind his desk since he wasn't at home. We were prepared to slap on the cuffs and march him through the walk of shame. But he wasn't there. His assistant—a nervous man in his fifties who kept fidgeting with his hands—hadn't seen him since he left for our meeting this morning. He kept asking if his boss was in trouble, his voice getting higher with each question we wouldn't answer.

"You're telling me this guy has zero fucking family and friends? There's got to be something we're missing," I'd muttered to Cruz as we stood in Evans' pristine office, scanning the walls for any clue about where he might be.

But there wasn't. No second home or family properties on file. No family photos in his office or home. No known associates outside of work. The sick bastard covered his tracks well. At least on paper.

Now I'm standing in the hallway outside the FBI resident agency's conference room, needing a moment to think without the cacophony of voices and noise. The buzzing fluorescent lights make my eyes ache; they're too bright for this level of exhaustion. I lean heavily against the wall and close my eyes—a temporary reprieve from the harsh white light.

When we met with Evans this morning, he had no idea we were onto him. He left the building under the impression that he'd lead the next press conference. We assumed he'd head back to his office to write the public statement. Where the fuck could he have gone? Did his assistant call him as soon as Cruz and I left?

I swipe a hand down my face and drop my head back, staring blankly through the glass doors of the conference room. The space we've commandeered has been transformed into what Cruz calls our "war room." The long conference table is covered with laptops, case files, and printouts, while multiple phone chargers snake across the surface like electronic ivy. Empty evidence boxes from Evans' house line one wall, their contents now spread across every available surface.

I force myself to take a deep breath and push off the wall, ready as I'll ever be to dive back into the organized chaos.

Arlo and Spencer are hunched over their laptops at the far end of the table, their fingers a blur as they work to crack Evans' multiple hard drives. Lines of code scroll across their screens in green text that might as well be hieroglyphics to me. I can only imagine the amount of evidence we'll find once they break through his encryption.

Cruz sits at a portable table with three RPD task force officers. Two of them are sifting through traffic camera footage, hoping to track the direction Evans fled. The other two are digging deeper into his background, looking for any connection, any place he might be.

Jesse and Evie have claimed one corner of the room, methodically cataloging Evans' journals and uploading crime scene photos to the database. Every few minutes, one of them mutters something under their breath—likely coming across a particularly disturbing entry, if what little I've seen is any indication.

"Holy shit," Jesse says suddenly, his voice laced with disbelief. He's holding one of the earlier journals. "Boss, you need to hear this."

I stride over to where he and Evie are working. Cruz stands and follows close behind.

"He was younger in this one—it's number seven. I can't

pinpoint his age, though," Jesse explains. "He talks about his aunt, Lisa Evans. And fuck. She locked him in the cellar for days at a time. Called it 'correcting his behavior.'"

Evie looks up from the journal she's cataloging, her face pale. "There are pages and pages of this shit, Mav. About how she beat him, kept food from him, left him isolated in complete darkness—things you'd see in a horror movie."

"She was a fucking lunatic," Jesse cuts in. "Psychologically tortured Evans for shit like mistaking the salad fork for the dinner fork. A fucking *fork*, boss."

"Jesus," I mutter, scanning the array of journals spread out on the table.

Jesse grabs another one and flips several pages ahead. "There's more. Journal number twelve. Listen to this: 'Aunt Lisa will never hurt me again. I waited until she was deep in sleep, then I drew the blade across her throat. I watched the blood drain from her body. God, it was fucking liberating. And now the only darkness I'll be in is the one I welcome.'"

"He slit her throat while she slept," Cruz says, his grim voice slicing through the absolute silence the room has fallen into.

"No wonder he's fucked up," I muse, shaking my head. "Let me know if you find anything else in those." I nod to the worn journals before pacing behind the row of chairs. Sitting still isn't an option—not when time is working against us. Not when we can't find him.

"I got something," Riley reports, her fingers flying across her keyboard. Multiple screens display GPS tracking data, cell tower pings, and traffic camera feeds. "His phone went dark four hours ago."

"Wait, what?" I blink hard, rounding the table to stand behind her. *"Four hours?"*

She nods, keeping her eyes locked on the screens. "Last ping was on I-35 northbound between Rochester and Minneapolis. After that, nothing."

"I want eyes on every route between here and Minneapolis," I order. "Traffic cams, highway patrol, anything that moves. And get a BOLO out to every jurisdiction within 400 miles from here." It's fucking 8:45 p.m. If Evans has a four-hour head start, he could be anywhere.

"Already done," Cruz responds, leaning over his laptop.

"Rhodes, Cruz, you might wanna take a look at this." Officer Marquez stands up and walks to the printer, snatching a set of papers from the tray. He meets us halfway and hands them over.

It's a property record printout showing ownership details. But it's the address that catches my attention: a house on the outskirts of Minneapolis.

"What are we looking at, Marquez?" Cruz asks, taking the paper from my hands.

"That's the house the mayor grew up in," Marquez explains, pointing to the address. "It's been sitting empty since he killed his aunt. She might've tortured the shit out of him, but she left him the house in her will."

My pulse quickens at the possibility of a lead. "What are the chances he headed there?"

"Pretty fucking good, I'd say," Cruz mutters, studying

the deed. "Especially since Riley confirmed he left Rochester."

Before I can respond, Cruz's cell phone rings. He fishes it out of his pocket and glances at the caller ID, his forehead creasing as he swipes the screen and brings the phone to his ear.

"This is Detective Cruz."

I'm immediately on alert when his head snaps up, his gaze catching mine. I watch his expression change from focused to something I can't decipher but know I don't like.

"Hold on." Cruz sets the phone on speaker and holds it steady between us. "Repeat that." The look he gives me as he barks the order makes my blood run cold.

"Yes, sir," a deep, unfamiliar voice responds. "This is Officer Williams with the Minneapolis Police Department. We responded to an emergency call at a residence on Cedar Avenue fifteen minutes ago—"

The blood drains from my face, and it takes a herculean effort to remain standing when my knees buckle.

"Who made the call?" I interrupt, unable to keep the panic out of my voice. Because I live on Cedar Avenue. And Tamara and Clara are at the house.

"Tamara Martin. She wouldn't let the ambulance take her to the hospital until I called and spoke with Detective Cruz and a Maverick Rhodes."

"Yeah, that's me," I respond absently, taking the phone from Cruz's hand and bringing it closer. "Is Tamara okay? Is there another woman with her?"

"No, sir. Tamara was alone when we arrived at the scene. She—"

There's a scuffle on the line, a number of raised voices coming through the speaker.

"Ma'am, you need to sit back down." Officer Williams' voice sounds distant, as though he's holding the phone away from his face.

"Is that him? Did you call him? I need to talk to Maverick," a woman's frantic voice sounds in the background. "Give me the phone. *Please* give me the phone."

"Officer Williams," I bark, my eyes filling with unshed tears at Tamara's panicked and pained voice. "Give her the phone."

A moment of silence passes before Tamara's voice comes on the line. "Maverick? Oh my god, is that you?"

"It's me. What happened, Tamara? Where's Clara?" I ask, my voice breaking on her name.

"I couldn't stop him," she whispers. "I couldn't stop him. I'm so sorry."

I feel, more than see, Spencer's approach. His strong hand on my shoulder is enough to choke me, reminding me of the last time he lent me his strength.

"Tamara, it's Cruz." Cruz leans toward the phone, taking over without removing it from my hand. "What happened, sweetheart?"

"Clara and I w-were cooking dinner," Tamara starts, her voice shaking and racked with sobs. "She w-went to answer the d-door. I went to check on her b-because she was t-taking too long. I s-saw him, Jonathan. He had her on the f-floor. I tried to s-stop h-him." She pauses, sounding as though she's on the verge of hyperventilating. In the background, someone tells her to take a breath. "I'm okay, I'm okay," she tells the voice.

"And then what?" Cruz presses.

I can't speak. If it weren't for Spencer, I wouldn't even be standing. My knuckles are white from how hard I'm clutching the phone, and my chest feels like it's caving in.

"H-he knocked m-me out. I was out f-for hours. T-two, I think. I called 911 and m-made the o-officer call you."

"Good," he replies, running a hand through his hair. "You did good, sweetheart. You need to let them take you to the hospital. We're going to get her back, okay? We'll get her back."

Officer Williams takes over the line again, and Cruz orders him to ensure Tamara's safety and put out an alert for James Evans, the mayor of Rochester, Minnesota.

As soon as the call ends, Cruz takes the phone from my trembling hands. "I'm calling the chief. We've got a chopper. We'll take it to Minneapolis. You'll be there in no time."

"We're with you, Rhodes," Spencer adds, squeezing my shoulder. "We'll find her."

All I can do is nod.

That sick motherfucker has my Clara. He took her, and I failed.

I fucking failed.

CHAPTER 43

CLARA

THOUSAND EYES

I'M YOUR SAMSON.

The urge to recoil becomes too powerful to fight when his forehead touches mine. I rear back, my vision sharpened with shock. My Samson? *My Samson?* He's delusional. He has to be. There's no other explanation.

And I know the absolute last thing I should do is provoke him, but God help me—I can't help the words that come out of my mouth.

"You're not my *anything!*"

His head snaps up, and the madness I see in his gaze terrifies me more than anything. The unhinged expression on his face screams at me, telling me I made a mistake.

The blow comes so fast I don't see it coming. White-hot pain radiates from my cheek to my temple as his hand connects with devastating force, whipping my head to the side. My legs give out instantly, and I crumple to the dirt floor.

I barely have time to register what just happened when

I'm forced onto my back. Samson straddles me, his legs bracketing mine as his hands wrap around my throat. I try to breathe, but the air won't get past his grip. My vision swims with black spots, and the metallic taste of blood fills my mouth.

CHAPTER 44
HIM

FUCK. Fuck, fuck, fuck.

Why would she say something like that? Why did she make us do that? We didn't want to hurt her again.

A sound tears from our throat—half anguish, half fury—as we stare down at her still body sprawled in the dirt. Our fingers claw into our scalp, nails digging deep as we yank at our hair until the sting cuts through the chaos in our head. We circle her like a caged animal, our feet wearing a path in the packed earth.

She's wrong. I am *her Samson.* We're *her Samson.*

Now we have to punish her. She has to understand that she's ours, but her behavior can't stand.

Glancing up at the lightbulb, we know just what to do. We unscrew the bulb from the socket, letting the darkness swallow the room whole.

We don't need light to navigate this space. It's our space. We stride to the pallet and sit, prepared to wait for her to wake.

The darkness will fix her.
Just like it fixed us.

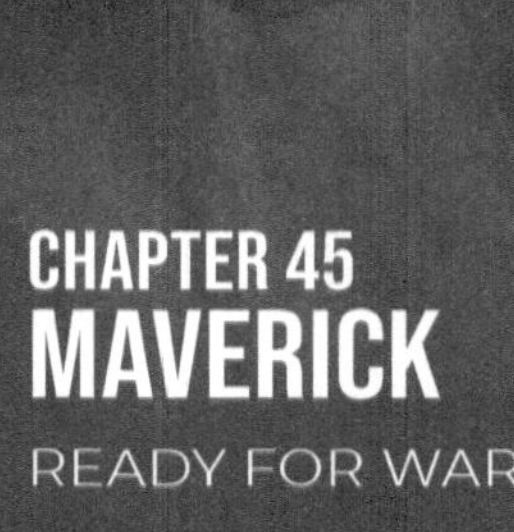

CHAPTER 45

MAVERICK

READY FOR WAR

HELICOPTER BLADES CUT through the night air, the thunder of the engine doing nothing to drown out the chaos in my mind. I stare out the window, lost in the city lights blurring past, my hands clenched so tight my knuckles have gone white.

This is my fucking fault.

I should've known better than to think distance would keep her safe from him. We were hunting a predator who'd been perfecting his craft for years—who'd been hunting Clara with obsessive focus for far too long.

I told Cruz I'd be her protective detail. After Evans left a message for Clara at the FBI rental, I thought moving to my house in Minneapolis would keep her safe. But I should have fucking known. He found her at her apartment. At the rental. He sent her that fucking letter. I should have moved her after that. I should have fucking had agents protecting her around the clock.

Goddamn it. Why did I think I could keep her safe?

I thought I could outsmart him, thought I could play his game. But he's played me this whole time.

He knew where Clara was when he met with us this morning. He had already planned on taking her from me while he was pretending to be the concerned mayor.

God, I was wrong.

I was so fucking wrong.

"ETA three minutes," the pilot's voice crackles through my headset.

Cruz leans forward from the seat behind me. "Mav, you can't blame yourself for this. You know this isn't your fault."

I don't respond. Can't. Because it is my fault. If anything happens to Clara—if that sick bastard hurts her because I failed to keep her safe—I'm done. There's no coming back from that. The job, the team, none of it will matter.

"He would've found her at some point. You know that, right? He wasn't going to stop. This isn't on you," Cruz continues, reaching over to squeeze my shoulder before sitting back.

"Rhodes." Spencer's voice cuts through my spiral, forcing me to turn my head and meet his eyes. "We're going to get her back. You hear me?"

I nod, but his words feel hollow. Evans has had her for hours. *Hours*. And I know what he's capable of. I've seen the crime scenes, witnessed his growing obsession, had nightmares about Clara's time in his captivity. There's no telling what he could be doing to Clara—what he could've already done.

The helicopter begins its descent toward the staging area, a park roughly one mile from the house. Through the window, I can see the controlled chaos below—Minneapolis PD patrol cars with their lights dark, SWAT vehicles positioned strategically, black federal SUVs gleaming under the street lamps, and the FBI command unit prepared to monitor it all. There's even an ambulance parked behind the police vehicles, ready to follow behind.

As soon as we touch down, I'm ripping the headset off and jumping down. Agent Mark Morrison, Minneapolis' tactical unit leader, jogs over, his expression grim.

"What's the situation?" I bark, not bothering with pleasantries.

"House has been under surveillance for forty minutes," Morrison reports, falling into step beside me as we move toward mobile command. "No movement visible from the exterior. Thermal imaging shows two moving heat signatures in the basement level."

Two signatures. That means Clara's alive.

For now.

"Local SWAT is deferring command to our tactical unit. Everyone's ready to roll on your signal," Morrison continues.

"Good. We'll need a silent entry," I say roughly, stopping in front of the command center. The massive mobile unit is essentially a fortress on wheels, its exterior bristling with communication arrays, emergency lights, and storage areas. Just as I open one of the large exterior compartments, Spencer and Cruz approach.

The compartment door swings open with a heavy

thunk, revealing rows of tactical gear and three drawers with firearm lockers. I grab two tactical Kevlar vests and hand them to Spencer and Cruz before taking a third and strapping it on. Opening one of the lockers, I bypass the array of handguns and snag two magazine pouches, securing them to the front plate carrier of the vest. The weight of it is familiar and reassuring.

"Let's move," I order, slamming the storage compartment shut.

"The plan is for the motorcade to roll dark," Morrison says as we walk to one of the black SUVs, Spencer and Cruz following closely behind. "We'll stop three blocks away and walk the rest. My team's already got the house surrounded."

"Neighbors?" Spencer asks, concerned about the families and collateral.

I should be concerned. I should've asked that question myself, especially as the Supervisory Special Agent. I know there's a part of me that is concerned, but it's being overridden by the need to get to Clara.

She's all that matters to me. What does it say about me that I'd sacrifice everyone else for her?

"Aren't many. The neighborhood is fairly spread out—no less than half an acre between properties, some even more than that. And the Evans house has been unoccupied for decades."

The four of us take the lead vehicle with Morrison at the wheel. He keeps the headlights off but flashes them twice to signal the others.

As one, we drive down Prescott Road. Within minutes, the motorcade comes to a stop on a corner street.

The walk to the house feels like it takes hours, though it's less than five minutes. The neighborhood is spread out, just like Morrison said. It would be picture-perfect with large colonial- and Victorian-style homes surrounded by equally large, well-maintained lawns if it weren't for the dilapidated colonial with its dark windows staring back at us like dead eyes. The white paint has long since started to peel, the wood siding more rotted than not. It looks completely abandoned and out of place. No indication of the horrors inside—past or present.

The tactical teams move like shadows between houses, approaching in formation. The night works in our favor, plenty of darkness to match our movements.

"Remember, silent entry," I whisper to Morrison, who has taken point in the stack. "Can't risk alarming the suspect and setting him off. Hostage is our priority."

Something dark and primal recoils inside me at calling Clara a hostage. It makes me want to breach this door and explode inside, setting fire to any and everything until she's in my arms.

But I can't.

Morrison nods and signals the team with his hands. He holds up three fingers, then two, then one. When he holds up his fist, a tactical agent moves to the front door, setting up a door blaster. He clamps it to the door frame, steps to the side, and activates the remote. Within seconds, the door is forced open, and we flow through the house like water.

Local SWAT moves to clear the upper level while Spencer, Cruz, and I join Morrison's tactical unit through the main floor, clearing the dark, dust-covered rooms with silent precision. Living room—clear. Dining room—clear.

We're moving through the kitchen when a scream cuts through the silence—raw, terrified, unmistakably Clara's.

It sounds as though the scream came from the kitchen, but that's impossible because we're in the kitchen. I glance around, my heart racing a hundred miles per minute. I don't see a door. I don't see a fucking entrance to the basement.

It takes me a moment to notice an old, circular latch on the floor. I don't remember moving. One second I'm standing in the kitchen, the next I'm throwing open the hatch and storming down the stairs, taking them three at a time.

The cellar feels like a tomb. Stone walls, low ceiling, the smell of damp earth and something fouler underneath. A single bare bulb casts harsh shadows across the space.

And there, in the center of the room…

I see them.

CHAPTER 46

HIM

DOWNHILL

"PLEASE," she whispers, her dejected voice hoarse from screaming.

Clara doesn't know we're still in the cellar with her. We haven't spoken a word, haven't made a sound. We bet she looks so pretty with tear stains on her face right now. So fucking pretty. Can't wait to see them.

We've lost track of how much time we've sat in the dark, listening to her beg, plead, and scream. She doesn't like the dark like we do. Doesn't find solace in it. The musty air carries the salt of her tears, the fear-sweat that makes our mouth water. Sooner or later, she'll learn to embrace it.

"Turn on the light, turn on the light, turn on the light."

It sounds like a prayer, and we wonder who she's praying to.

"Please, please, *please*." Her voice is getting louder now. She's gone back and forth between an angry little kitten and a sobbing mess.

"Turn on the fucking light, Samson!"

"Well, that wasn't very nice," we say suddenly, causing her to shriek. "That isn't how you ask, Clara. Try again." We reach beside us on the pallet, fingers closing around the knife's handle—cold metal, sharp promise.

"Why are you doing this? Just turn on the goddamn light!"

"Try. Again." We let the silence stretch, counting her ragged breaths in the darkness. One... two... three... The knife feels perfect in our grip.

We hear her shift on the dirt, hear her inhale deeply before she exhales. Makes us wish she were close to us, so she'd breathe us in and we'd breathe *her* in.

"Samson." A broken whisper, but she says our name like a plea. Like now we're the one she's praying to. "Will you... *please* turn the light on? Please, Samson."

"There's my good girl. See how sweet you can be when you try?" We push up from the makeshift bed, tucking the knife behind us into our waistband. It takes no time at all to screw the lightbulb in and turn it on.

We glance down and find Clara with her legs pulled up to her chest, her arms wrapped around them like they'll comfort her.

But only we can comfort her now. And we were right —she's so fucking beautiful when she cries. Her face is streaked with dirt and tears, just like we imagined. Perfect.

"Stand up," we order firmly. The command echoes off the stone walls, bouncing back to us like an amen.

We can tell she wants to refuse, but she's smarter than

that—especially since she woke up from her earlier disobedience in the dark. Her punishment.

She hesitates, but she obeys and stands to face us. Her legs shake, and her entire body stiffens to hold herself up.

We circle her slowly, drinking in every detail—the way her chest rises and falls too fast, the pulse hammering in her throat, the way she tries not to flinch when we move closer. The knife feels heavy at our waist—a reminder of our control.

As soon as she's steady on her feet, we move and pull her in. Fuck, it feels good to have her body pressed against ours again. She's so warm, so alive.

"We missed you so much, Clara," we say, nuzzling her neck. "Missed your smell, your skin. Mm, the way you fit against us."

"No," she pleads, an almost inaudible whisper. "Please don't do this."

"Need to feel you." Our words come out more as a growl than anything else. We trail our nose along her neck and flick our tongue against her ear. "Need to taste you." The salt of her skin… so fucking delicious.

Clara forces her hands between us, placing her palms against our chest in an attempt to push us away. "Samson! No!"

We pause, letting her think she has a chance. Letting hope bloom in her eyes before we crush it. Because we can't have that. We *do* need her, and we're done waiting. Abruptly, we spin her around, banding one arm beneath her breasts and the other across her hip. "Be still for us, Clara. You're only making this harder for yourself."

Her scream is a force to be reckoned with—that's all right. We don't mind. We said we'd be good to her this time around, but that doesn't mean we don't still love hearing her scream for us. The sound bounces off every surface, filling our ears like a symphony.

She thrashes against our body in a futile attempt to escape. Doesn't she realize that makes us want her even more? That she's just making it worse, rubbing herself against our cock? Fuck, we're so hard.

Holding her close with one hand splayed along her ribs, we reach down and unbutton her jeans. We just need them down a little bit—just enough to sink into her. This time is going to be fast and hard. We can't help it; she made us wait too long.

Her pants are below her hip bones when we hear the unmistakable sound of the hatch being thrown open. A sound that doesn't belong in our sanctuary—metal groaning against metal.

Heavy footsteps sound above us, deliberate and purposeful. Who the fuck is that? Who has the fucking audacity to disturb us? No one's supposed to fucking be here. No one's supposed to know where we are.

"We have company, Clar," we whisper in her ear. Pulling our hand from her pants, we reach behind us, retrieve the knife from our waistband, and press the tip to her throat. "Don't move. Don't want you to accidentally hurt yourself. That'd make us very upset."

The footsteps thunder on the wooden steps—so loud the rickety staircase creaks beneath the onslaught.

We keep our gaze fixed on the bottom of the stairs,

waiting to see who dares come in uninvited. Just when the thundering footfalls stop, that motherfucking FBI agent appears, gun pointed directly at us.

Our lips pull back in a snarl. "You're not supposed to be here," we growl. "She's ours! Ours!"

CHAPTER 47
MAVERICK

PARDON ME

THE SIGHT of Clara standing in the middle of the cellar, locked in this sick bastard's arms with a knife pressed against her throat... Fuck, I'll never be able to unsee it.

Evans' lips pull back in a snarl. "You're not supposed to be here," he growls, his voice barely recognizable. "She's ours! Ours!"

Time slows. I can see Clara's chest rising and falling rapidly against him. Can see the bruises forming on her neck, the cut above her left eye, the bruise on her cheek. Her watery eyes meet mine, and the absolute, utter terror in her expression threatens to break me.

I keep my gun trained on them, knowing there's no way I can take the shot—not without hurting her. And this fucker knows it.

"Drop the fucking gun, Rhodes. You know you won't hurt her," he says as he tightens his arm around her torso, causing her to wince and groan.

"I can't do that, Evans," I say, struggling to keep my

voice calm despite the rage thrashing through my body. I can't afford to fuck this up, can't afford for him to press that knife deeper into her skin. I have to stay calm.

Evans' attention snaps to something behind me. His eyes are wild—feral—the mask of civility completely gone. He doesn't even look like the same man I met with this morning.

"Federal agents!" Spencer's voice booms from above as he, Cruz, and Morrison thunder down the stairs. Their pursuit comes to a startling halt when they take in the scene before them.

Clara held against a madman with a knife at her throat. My gun pointed at the two of them with nowhere to shoot.

"Drop your weapons! Don't come any fucking closer," Evans warns, his voice full of a lethality I don't want to test.

"James," I call, drawing his gaze back to me. "Put the knife down, James." Not letting go of the gun, I raise my free hand in a show of acquiescence. With the addition of Spencer, Cruz, and Morrison, there's no telling what Evans will do.

I won't risk it. Won't risk *her*.

"No!" he shouts, tightening his grip on both Clara and the knife. A trickle of blood beads on her skin. "Not James! Samson! Clara's Samson!"

My brows furrow when he calls himself Samson. The realization hits me that he didn't say Clara was *his* when he saw me. He said she was *ours*. Before I can question it further, Clara's eyes catch mine, and I don't like the look in them. She gives me the most minute shake of her head, then places a hand on Evans' arm.

"Samson." Clara's sweet voice sounds hoarse, broken. "Please. Please don't do this," she begs. "I'll go with you."

"The fuck you will," I growl.

There's no fucking way. There isn't a world that exists where I'd let him take her from me.

I won't fucking lose her.

CHAPTER 48
CLARA

EYES ON FIRE

SAMSON SOUNDS WILD, unhinged. Like he's on the verge of breaking down and setting this place on fire all at the same time. The intensity of his voice makes me flinch, sliding the knife further across my skin. A sharp sting follows, and I feel warmth trickle down my neck.

The look on Maverick's face exudes determination, and despite my debilitating fear, I have to do something. I don't know what the fuck I'm going to do, but I know I need to draw Samson's attention away from him. Away from the gun he won't use without risking me.

I close my eyes—the tears falling relentlessly—and harden my resolve. When I open them again, I catch Maverick's gaze. The look he gives me is searching, but I don't have the answer he wants. With the smallest turn of my head, I go for it.

"Samson," I force out, the swelling of my throat coating my voice in gravel. "Please. Please don't do this." I swallow through the pain, then say the words that nearly make my heart stop: "I'll go with you."

Ignoring Maverick's protests, I place my hand on Samson's arm. His hold on me is so tight, it feels as though my ribs are on fire with just that movement.

I feel the moment Samson's attention falls to me—it's in the way his body stiffens against mine, the way his hand holding the knife slackens ever so slightly. His breathing changes, becoming deeper, more controlled.

"Say it again," he demands. He tilts his head down until his lips feather across my ear. His breath is hot against my skin, making my stomach churn.

"I'll go with you, Samson," I repeat, willing myself to force the fear out of my voice. This needs to work.

"We don't believe you." He pretends not to hear Maverick's shouts and reaffirms his grip on the knife. "Why should we believe you?"

"Turn me around," I whisper. "Turn me around so you can see my eyes."

"Sunshine." Maverick sounds as if he's breaking apart. "You're not going with him, do you hear? Look at me!"

I'm unprepared for Samson's strength when he turns me around. I stumble over my feet and nearly fall into him, a pained sound echoing around us. The moment I face him, the blade is back on my throat, forcing my chin to tilt up uncomfortably. His face is inches from mine now, close enough that I can see the madness swimming in his pupils.

Shit. He didn't drop the knife. I needed him to drop the fucking knife.

"No! You don't get to look at her," Samson snarls over my head toward Maverick.

It takes everything I have to withhold a grimace as I raise my hands to Samson's chest. "He can't look at me now, see?" I trace small circles with my fingers and stare into his dark eyes. "Just you." My skin crawls at the contact, but I force myself to keep touching him, to sell the lie.

There's a struggle behind me. Maverick's shouting at Spencer and Cruz to let him go. The sounds of the scuffle —boots scraping against the packed earth, muffled curses —tell me they're physically restraining him.

God, I wish I could see what's happening. I wish I could tell Maverick that I love him.

"Just us?" Samson looks down at me, his brows knitted together. For a moment, something less feral, something almost human, flickers across his features.

I nod, hiding a wince. "I'll go with you," I say again. My voice sounds steadier now, more convincing. I hope.

The knife finally leaves my throat. Just as Samson brushes his lips across mine, I gather every ounce of fucking strength I have and drive my knee between his legs. Right into his fucking dick.

The impact sends a shock up my leg and to my ribs, making me double over, but the satisfaction of his strangled cry makes it worth it.

Fuck. Him.

CHAPTER 49
MAVERICK

LEGENDS NEVER DIE

THE MOMENT EVANS DOUBLES OVER, clutching himself and letting out a strangled scream, I break free from Spencer and Cruz's grip.

"Clara!" I shout, lunging forward as she bends forward in pain, wincing from the impact of her own strike. She attempts to get away from the bastard howling in agony, but she's struggling—unsteady.

"Rhodes, wait—" Spencer calls out, but I'm already moving.

I reach Clara just as Evans starts to straighten up. I wrap my arm around her waist to steady her and pull her behind me in one fluid motion.

"Stay behind me," I order, training my gun on Evans while positioning myself as a shield between them.

I'll gladly give my life for hers if it means this asshole never touches her again.

Evans sways on his feet, still clutching his groin with one hand, but his grip on the knife doesn't waver. His eyes are feral—animalistic—locked on Clara like she's the only thing that exists in this fucking world.

"She's ours!" he roars, taking another unsteady step forward. "Ours!"

"Drop the knife, Evans!" Cruz shouts from my left, his gun aimed at Evans' center mass.

But Evans doesn't seem to hear him. He's beyond reason now, beyond pain. All that seems to matter to him is getting to Clara.

Spencer moves to flank him from the right while Morrison circles behind. They're trying to box him in now that there isn't a knife to Clara's throat. But I can see it in Evans' eyes—he's not going to surrender. He's going to keep coming. He won't stop until someone stops him.

"You're not taking her from us again," Evans gasps, blood trickling from where he must have bitten his tongue. "It's us! No one else! No one!" He screams as he raises the knife and lunges forward with a roar of fury, aiming for the person standing in his way of what he wants. Me.

Gunshots explode through the cellar. Evans' body jerks violently as the bullets tear through him, his manic expression remaining frozen. The knife clatters to the dirt floor as he collapses. His body hits the ground with a sickening thud, blood pooling beneath him and spreading across the packed earth in dark rivulets.

The cellar falls silent except for the ringing in my ears and Clara's ragged breathing behind me.

My gun never leaves Evans' motionless form, finger hovering over the trigger. If he so much as twitches, I'm putting another bullet in him.

"Clear!" Morrison shouts, loud enough to echo off the stone walls and make my ears ring even more.

The wooden staircase trembles as the rest of the SWAT team floods into the cellar. Their tactical gear and weapons sweep the small space, ensuring there are no other threats lurking in the shadows. They must've been waiting at the top of the stairs until given the all clear. I don't even want to think about what would've happened if Evans had seen an entire tactical unit thunder down the steps.

Morrison approaches Evans cautiously, his weapon still drawn, and kicks the knife farther away from the body. After checking for a pulse, he looks up and nods. "Target is down. No pulse."

"Send the medics down!" Cruz calls up the stairs.

"Medic!" Spencer calls out, holstering his weapon and moving toward us. "We need a medic down here!"

I finally lower my gun, my hands shaking with residual adrenaline.

Clara is safe. Evans is dead. It's over.

But when I turn to check on Clara, she's already collapsing against me, her legs giving out as the shock and pain finally overwhelm her battered body.

"Sunshine," I whisper in a cracked voice, catching her before she can fall. "I've got you, sunshine. I've got you." Careful of her injuries, I lean down and press my lips to her forehead. "I'm so fucking sorry, baby. I'm so fucking sorry."

I couldn't protect her, but I wasn't too late to save her.

CHAPTER 50
MAVERICK
FIRE MEETS FATE

I CAN'T STOP STARING at the left side of Clara's face —swollen and discolored, the skin around her eye and cheekbone turning that deep purple-black that'll take weeks to fade. The split in her lower lip has stopped bleeding, but it's still angry and red. Every time I look at her injuries, the rage resurfaces beneath my skin.

The bruises around her throat haunt me the most. Dark finger-shaped marks that make my hands shake every time I look at them.

I was so close to losing her. *So close*. What would have happened if we hadn't gotten there when we did? I don't even want to think about it, but I know the *what-if's* will torment me in my sleep for the rest of my life. Just the thought of any other outcome where Clara isn't safe with me fucks me up.

"Mr. Rhodes, I need you to step back so I can examine the patient properly," Dr. Martinez says for the third time, her voice patient but firm—brooking no argument.

I'm hovering. I know I'm hovering, but I can't seem to make myself move more than a few inches away from Clara's bedside. Every instinct I have is driving me to stay close, to keep her in my sight, to make sure she's safe.

"It's okay," Clara says softly, her voice hoarse and scratchy. She reaches for my hand, wincing slightly at the movement. "I'm okay, Mav. I'm okay."

But she's not okay. She's sitting on the edge of a hospital bed in another fucking hospital gown, looking small and fragile and hurt, and it's my goddamn fault. All of it.

We're not okay.

Dr. Martinez waits until I move back before she continues her examination. She checks Clara's pupils with a penlight, gently probing the swelling around her eye and cheekbone. "Any dizziness? Nausea? Double vision?"

"No," Clara answers, but her eyes never leave mine. It's like she's anchoring herself to me. Or maybe she's anchoring me to her.

"Good. The swelling should go down in a few days. Ice packs and ibuprofen will help. Unfortunately, there's not much we can do about the bruising on your ribs beyond the ibuprofen." Dr. Martinez makes a note in her chart, then clears her throat. "I'd like to keep you overnight for observation, given the head trauma and..." She glances at Clara's throat. "The strangulation. We'll want to watch for any delayed onset complications."

My jaw clenches at the thought of Clara's *strangulation*. It's just another reason I wanted to put more bullets in that bastard. I take a deep breath, keeping my eyes locked on Clara's, keeping myself centered with her presence.

"I want to go home," Clara says quietly.

"Sunshine—" I start.

"I want to go home," she repeats, more firmly this time. "Please."

Dr. Martinez looks between us. "I understand, but given the circumstances—"

"What circumstances?" Clara's voice cracks slightly. "I'm fine. I'm not dizzy, I'm not nauseous. My throat hurts, my ribs ache, my face throbs—all to be expected. *I'm fine.* I just want to go home."

The doctor sighs but nods. "If you insist on leaving, you'll need to sign an AMA form consenting to be discharged against medical advice. And someone needs to stay with you for the next few days to monitor for any changes."

"I'm not leaving her side," I say immediately.

After Dr. Martinez leaves to get the discharge paperwork, the room falls silent except for the steady beep of machines. Clara stares down at her hands, picking at the edge of the blanket.

God, what I wouldn't give to hold her right now. But I'm afraid she wouldn't welcome it, wouldn't welcome *me*.

Five minutes later, a nurse comes in with the AMA and discharge papers. She tells me everything I need to look out for when we get home: delayed swelling of her neck, difficulty breathing... essentially everything that will ensure I won't be sleeping for the next week.

As soon as we get home, Juno bounds up to Clara and nudges her hand.

"Hi, my sweet boy," she says, her voice tender and riddled with exhaustion. With ginger movements, Clara bends down and runs her fingers through his fur, resting her forehead against his and scratching behind his ears. She presses a kiss to the top of his head before standing and heading straight into the bathroom. She surprises me when she asks me to join her without any hesitation, and something loosens in my chest. The idea of leaving her for even a moment is panic-inducing.

In the shower, Clara's practically dead on her feet. I'm careful not to jostle her while I simultaneously clean her body and hold her up. When we're both clean and she's lotioned, I carry her into the bedroom. She doesn't even protest—a clear sign of just how exhausted she is.

I lay Clara down gently on our bed, pulling the covers up to her chin. The soft lamplight catches the worst of her bruises, and I have to force myself to look away before the rage takes hold again. She needs me calm right now.

I climb in beside her, keeping some distance between us despite every instinct screaming at me to pull her close—to hold her the way I did this morning. "Can I hold you?" I ask softly.

"You never have to ask," she whispers, and relief floods through me.

I carefully gather her into my arms, mindful of her ribs. She turns to face me, and for a long moment, she just stares. But she's not really seeing me—her eyes are distant and unfocused.

"I can't sleep until I talk about it," she sighs, sounding weary.

"You don't have to talk about it," I tell her, brushing a strand of dark hair from her face. "Not until you're ready. I'll never rush you."

She's quiet for so long I think she's not going to respond. Then, without looking away from my face, she starts speaking.

"I didn't check the security camera. I didn't even look through the peephole. I just... opened the door, thinking it was the grocery order." Her voice is barely above a whisper, but I can hear the blame she's putting on herself.

"Clara, baby." I cup her uninjured cheek gently. "It's not your fault."

Her eyes fill with tears, but she doesn't acknowledge my statement and continues. "When I opened the door and saw him there... I was terrified. Before I could do anything, he drugged me. Again. I woke up in that cellar. I didn't know where I was, or what happened to Tamara. He said not to worry about—oh god," she cries, pressing her face into my chest. "Tamara... Is she... Is she?"

"She's okay, sunshine. She has a concussion, but she's alive," I answer, my hand stroking her hair.

"Oh, thank god. I need to see her. I need to apologize."

"Apologize for what, Clara? You have nothing to apologize for." My tone is adamant. It kills me that she's blaming herself for this.

"Yes, I do," she says emphatically, pulling back to meet

my eyes. "She got hurt because of me! If she hadn't been there, she would've been just fine!"

I'm silent for a beat before I lean forward and kiss her forehead. "Do you remember what you told me when I blamed myself for Heather's death?" I pause, but I don't let her answer. "You told me that it wasn't my fault. You told me that it was the driver's fault—he hit her and left. Baby, I beat myself up for years, and it wasn't until you that I really believed Heather's death wasn't on me. And this? This isn't on you. It's not your fault that Tamara got hurt. It's *his*. He was never going to stop."

She breaks down in my arms, burying her face in my chest. I say nothing else and simply hold her, my hand moving in slow circles across her back.

Just when I think she's fallen asleep, she snakes her arm across my waist. "In that cellar... he kept referring to himself as *we* and *us*. I couldn't figure it out, but he wasn't... he didn't sound sane." Another lengthy pause. "He kept me in the dark for hours. To punish me because I said he wasn't mine."

She takes a shaky breath and lets it out.

"When you found us..." She trails off, her breathing coming fast and shallow.

"You don't have to—"

"He was going to rape me." The words come out in a rush, like she has to get them out before she loses her nerve. "I tried to get away, but he was too strong. He was trying to... he was trying to..." She can't finish the sentence, her voice breaking completely.

"But he didn't," I say firmly, running a hand down her

arm. "You fought him, Clara. You're a fighter, just like I said you were when I first met you."

"Because you came. If you hadn't—" Tears are falling down her cheeks now.

"I'm so fucking sorry, sunshine." My voice cracks, and I pull her closer, my own eyes burning. "I should've been there. I shouldn't have left you. I should've fucking had a protective detail outside of the house. I failed you, sunshine." The words taste like poison in my mouth, but it's the fucking truth.

The irony isn't lost on me—telling her it's not her fault while I'm suffocating under the weight of my own guilt. But this is different. This is on me. I promised to protect her, gave her my word, and I couldn't fucking deliver. The one thing that mattered most, and I let her down.

CHAPTER 51

CLARA

SPELLS

THE PAIN in Maverick's voice cuts through me deeper than any physical injury I'm carrying. I can feel the guilt radiating off him, the way his entire body has gone rigid against mine. He's spiraling, drowning in self-blame, and I can't let him do this to himself.

Not when he's the reason I'm alive.

"Maverick, no." I shift carefully, schooling my expression despite the pain in my ribs. My hands frame his face, and I tilt his head gently until I'm staring into those tortured espresso eyes. "You didn't fail me. You saved me."

He tries to shake his head, but I hold him firmly. I won't let him drown in his guilt the same way he wouldn't let me drown in mine. "My love. Listen to me—"

"Sunshine, if I had been there—"

"If you had been there, we might both be dead," I say fiercely, surprising myself with the strength in my voice. "You literally just told me that it wasn't my fault that Tamara got hurt. You *just* told me he was never going to stop. You think he would have walked away if you'd answered that door? He would have killed you to get to me, Mav. You know that."

His jaw clenches, and I can see him fighting against my words, against the absolution I'm trying to give him.

"You found me," I breathe, my thumbs brushing across his cheekbones. "*Again*. And when I was in that cellar, when I thought… when I thought I was going to die, I held onto you. The thought of you. My love for you. And you came. Because you always come for me, Maverick."

Tears flow down his cheeks now, and it breaks my heart to see this strong, fierce man—my protector—crumbling beneath the weight of misplaced guilt.

"I should have protected you better," he says, his voice raw.

"You did protect me, my love. You healed me. Made me whole again. You made me stronger." I press my forehead against his. "I'm here, Maverick. I'm alive. I'm in your arms. That's not failure—that's everything."

Maverick doesn't respond. He doesn't deny anything I've said, though he doesn't agree, either. Instead, he captures my lips with his in a tender kiss—one that speaks to me more than his words ever could. I part my lips for him, flicking my tongue against his. His mouth moves slowly, lovingly, before he pulls away and rests his forehead against mine.

"I love you so much, sunshine." A soft kiss to my lips. "So fucking much."

"I love you, too." I inhale deeply, breathing in the scent of him—letting it fill me and center me. Sliding my leg between his, I nestle closer, tangling our limbs together. "Hold me. Don't let me go," I whisper.

His arms band tighter around me. "Never. I'll never let you go."

And despite the nightmare the last twenty-four hours have turned into, I fall asleep knowing two things are true: Maverick will never let me go. And I'm finally, truly *safe*.

CHAPTER 52
CLARA

LAND OF CONFUSION

I'M HOVERING SOMEWHERE between awake and not, a distant, persistent buzzing stirring me from the depths of sleep. I'm cocooned in warmth—Maverick's solid chest pressed against my back, his arm draped possessively across my waist like he's afraid I might disappear if he lets go. Another weight pins me down, heavy and almost too hot on my legs. Juno. He's claimed his spot at the foot of the bed, sprawled across my feet like a furry anchor.

The phone continues to vibrate relentlessly on the nightstand, just out of reach. I try to shift toward it, but Maverick's arm tightens reflexively around me. I wiggle my toes, but Juno doesn't budge an inch.

"Mmph," I mumble, stretching my fingers toward the nightstand. The movement sends a sharp reminder through my ribs, and I suck in a breath.

Maverick stirs behind me, his voice rough with sleep. "Who is it?"

I manage to snag the phone just as it's about to go to

voicemail, squinting at the bright screen. The clock in the corner tells me it's just after seven in the morning, but it's the familiar face filling the screen that makes my heart skip.

"Tamara's FaceTiming," I say, already swiping to answer before Maverick can fully process what I've said.

"Best friend," Tamara exclaims, smiling too brightly for this early in the morning. "Did I wake you?"

"No," I lie.

"Yes," Maverick grumbles at the same time.

"You're such a liar." Tamara laughs, then immediately presses a hand to her forehead and winces. "Ouch, shouldn't have done that."

"How are you feeling?" I ask, brows drawn together in concern as I notice the way Tamara's still holding her head.

The room she's in is semi-dark, the only light stemming from the windows. I catch sight of familiar vertical blinds, clueing me in. Tamara's propped up against stark white pillows, the distinct headboard I know so well supporting her back.

"Wait," I interject just as Tamara opens her mouth to answer. "Are you in the hospital?"

"Yes," she replies sheepishly. "The ambulance brought me here yesterday, and the doctor kept me overnight because I was out for two hours. But he's cleared me to go home, so that's something!" She tries to add a little excitement to her voice toward the end, but I know her so well—she can't fool me.

Something about seeing her hurt and alone in a hospital room cracks my chest wide open.

"I'm glad you get to go home," I sigh. "So how are you feeling? How's your concussion?"

I angle the phone carefully, making sure only my face is visible while I settle back against Maverick's chest. His arm loosens just enough to let me get comfortable, but I can feel his attention sharpen behind me. He's listening to every word, protective even in his drowsy state.

"Well, I mean, I feel like my brain is made of cotton and someone's hitting it with a hammer," she admits. "The headache's better than yesterday, though." Tamara shrugs and purses her lips as though she's debating whether she wants to share the next part. I'm about to press her when she sighs and continues. "I'm not really steady on my feet… I have to hold on to the walls or furniture when I walk." Her voice wavers, and her eyes shine with tears.

Tamara's always been so strong and independent. She never lets her guard down—never lets herself be vulnerable. Having to depend on someone else is something she swore she'd never do, and now she doesn't have a choice. Because she can't freaking walk on her own.

The guilt hits me like a physical blow—I should be there with her. She's there because of Samson, and he was there because of me. It takes significant effort not to fall back into the depths of self-pity, blaming myself for everything she's going through.

"I'm so sorry, Tam." I shift slightly, rubbing my eyes to disperse the welling tears. Maverick's hand comes to rest on my hip. The gentle pressure is comforting, grounding me in this moment instead of letting my mind drift back to yesterday's nightmare.

"You have nothing to be sorry for," Tamara asserts. She shifts against the pillows and studies my face through the screen. "But enough about me! I'll be okay. The doctor said it's normal, and I should be feeling brand spankin' new within a few days. But *you*! You scared the shit out of me. How are you doing? And don't you dare lie to me again."

"Sore," I answer. "My ribs are bruised, so everything hurts. I'll be moving as slow as a damn sloth, but I'm fine."

Tamara stares at me, tears trickling down her cheeks. Her voice cracks when she speaks. "I keep thinking about what happened. I should've stopped him, Clara. I should've—"

"Stop." I feel Maverick's breath warm against my hair as he presses closer, silently offering support. His presence gives me the strength to be strong for her. "You can't think like that, Tam. It wasn't your fault. It's none of our fault. That shit lies with that asshole."

"But I was supposed to protect you," she whispers, swiping the tears from her face. "That's what best friends do. I promised Maverick."

"Don't, Tam. You fought for me—that's all that matters," I say firmly.

"Did they get him?" Her voice is barely audible now.

"They sure did. He's dead." The words come out flat, final. There's no satisfaction in it, just relief that he can never hurt anyone again.

"Well, can't say I'm sad about it. The only thing I'm sad about is that I didn't get to cut off his dick and feed it to him."

I can't help the laugh that bubbles up from my chest,

and I clutch my side when the movement sends a sharp pain through my torso. "Don't make me laugh—it hurts." I breathe through my nose until the pain lessens, then pin her with a look. "I did kick him in the balls, though."

"Yes, girl!" Tamara squeals and straightens, fist pumping the air. "That's what I'm talking about!"

Behind me, Maverick traces soothing, featherlight circles over my ribs. I glance away from Tamara to offer him a grateful smile. "Thank you," I mouth.

She squints at the screen, trying to look past me. "Is that Maverick behind you? Hi, Maverick!"

Maverick chuckles quietly behind me, the rumble vibrating through his chest and into my back. I can practically feel his amusement. "Morning, Tamara. I'm glad you're okay."

"Yeah, me too. I can't wait to bust out of this joint, though. Sleep in my own bed and wear my own damn clothes." She tugs at the hospital gown with obvious distaste.

"Who's picking you up?" I ask. My chest tightens with guilt again. I hate that I can't be there for her the way she was for me when I was in the hospital. "Are you at Minneapolis Regional? We can come get you," I offer without even asking Maverick.

"No," she says—a little too quickly. "You need to rest. You probably shouldn't move around until your ribs heal." She fidgets with the collar of her hospital gown before rushing out, "Besides, Cruz is coming to get me."

"What?" Gingerly, I prop myself up onto an elbow and

bring the phone closer to my face. "Cruz is coming to get you?"

"It's nothing."

"Oh, it's nothing, huh?" I tease, wiggling my eyebrows. "And how exactly did Detective Cruz end up being your personal chauffeur?"

"Shut your mouth, best friend. Don't say—"

A knock at her door interrupts her mid-sentence. She glances somewhere off screen, then looks back at me. "I gotta go, the nurse is here. They won't leave me alone," she stage-whispers.

"Love you!" I call out quickly.

"Love you, too!" Before I can say anything else, the phone goes dead.

I lie back and let the phone drop to my chest with a soft thud, suddenly feeling the weight of everything that's happened. Silence fills the room until Maverick's lips press against my shoulder, soft and warm.

"She's going to be okay, sunshine," he murmurs against my skin.

"I know. It's just… seeing her like that." I close my eyes, leaning into his solid presence. "It should have been me alone in that hospital room."

"Hey." His voice is firm now, and he shifts so he's leaning over me. "Don't do that to yourself. You both survived. That's what matters, remember?"

I nod, but the guilt still sits heavy in my chest. Maverick seems to sense it because he presses another kiss to my shoulder, then another to the curve of my neck.

"How are you really feeling?" he asks softly. "And I want the truth this time."

I take stock of my body—the persistent ache in my ribs, the tender bruising on my face, the way my whole body feels like it's been through a blender. "Like I got hit by a truck," I admit. "But also... better. Being here with you, it helps."

He nuzzles his nose into my neck, and I feel him breathe me in. "Good. Because I'm not going anywhere."

"You have to eventually. You have a team to lead, responsibilities—"

"Clara." The way he says my name stops my protest cold. "Let me worry about that, okay? Right now, all I need to do is take care of you."

Before I can argue, he carefully extracts himself from behind me, mindful of my injuries. Juno lifts his head as the bed shifts, giving Maverick an accusatory look.

"Come on, boy," Maverick says, giving him a gentle nudge. "Time to move."

Juno stretches dramatically but eventually hops down, padding out of the room with his tail swishing. I immediately miss the warmth of both of them.

"I'm going to make you breakfast. What sounds good, sunshine?" Maverick pulls on a t-shirt that does absolutely nothing to hide how good he looks first thing in the morning. His dark hair is completely rumpled, and his trimmed beard is slightly mussed. He smirks when he catches me staring at him.

"Surprise me," I say, settling deeper into the pillows.

"I've got you covered." He leans down to press a gentle

kiss to my forehead, expertly avoiding the bruises on my face. "Rest, baby. I'll be back."

Twenty minutes later, Maverick returns with a tray that makes my mouth water. Toast cut into triangles, fluffy scrambled eggs, and fresh fruit arranged like he's running a five-star hotel. A steaming cup of black coffee, my pain medication, and a glass of water round out my breakfast-in-bed.

"This looks amazing." I struggle to sit up without jarring my ribs, using my elbows to scoot back and take my weight.

"Easy," he murmurs, helping me get situated and adjusting the pillows behind me. "Take your time."

He settles on the edge of the bed, watching as I take a tentative bite of toast.

"Good?"

"Perfect. I could get used to this," I say, using the toast to gesture to the tray. "But where's yours?"

"I ate while I made yours. I can multitask with the best of them," he says, tapping my hand—a familiar command. "Eat. Or I can feed you." The tone of his voice tells me he'd prefer the latter.

I shake my head and smile, then take a bite of eggs. "Yes, sir."

His answering grin is worth every ache in my battered body.

CHAPTER 53

CLARA

WILD LOVE

"HE'S DRIVING me freaking crazy, Ash!" I whisper, my tone full of exasperation. I glance at the closed office door as though Maverick might be listening in from the other side before turning back to the screen. "He's still treating me like I'm going to break."

It's been four freaking weeks. *Four weeks*, and he has been the sweetest, most accommodating man ever. He hasn't left my side, and he's always finding ways to touch me, to hold me, to care for me. I want for nothing—except his *touch*. He refuses to do more than kiss me, and damn if I'm not over it.

Ash chuckles and shakes her head, her eyes gleaming. "Have you told him how you feel?"

"I knew you were going to ask that." I scrunch my nose, then sigh. "I haven't told him that he's driving me crazy, no. I mean, I've gotten frustrated when I tried to push things and he pulled away. You know I have subtitles on my face, Ash—there's no hiding my frustration when that happens.

But then he kisses me and tells me he just wants to make sure I'm fully healed and doesn't want to hurt me. So I let it go… I know I probably shouldn't."

"I think it would be worthwhile to tell him exactly how you're feeling. Don't leave it up to him to guess. If you're ready for more, you need to tell him."

"I know," I concede. "You're right." I shift in the leather chair, grateful that the movement doesn't send pain through my ribs like it did just a week ago; the bruises on my face are barely visible now. I feel like me again. "I'll talk to him."

"Good," she says, a smile etched on her face. "How are you sleeping?"

"I'm sleeping okay. The nightmares aren't as frequent… It's almost like Mav and I take turns having nightmares, but waking up next to each other washes away any lingering fear."

"It's good that you two have each other. It'll help you heal—both of you. And you know I'm here whenever you need me."

"I know. Thank you for that. Being able to check in with you so often has been helpful."

After everything that happened with Samson, I knew I needed more sessions with Ash. We started with twice a week but ended up with daily sessions, and I don't think I'd be where I am mentally if it weren't for her. Maverick's even joined a few of them, and hearing him process his emotions with me—having him *listen* to me during some of my most vulnerable moments—has made me fall in love with him even more. The vulnerability we've shared during those sessions has brought us closer together in every way except the one I desperately need.

"You're doing the work, Clara. I'm just here to help guide you through it," she says softly. "When you talk to Maverick today, remember to be honest and open about how you feel and what you want. Communication is key, especially after what you two have gone through together."

"Yeah, I know. I think he's still carrying his guilt. He's not drowning in it, but it's definitely still there. Mine is, too, I guess, and we both have to work through it. I just... I need him."

"Tell him that, and let me know how the conversation goes tomorrow, okay?"

"I will. Thank you so much, Ash—for everything."

"Have a good rest of your day, Clara. I'll see you tomorrow!" Ash waves and signs off.

Closing the laptop, I lean back in the chair and stare up at the ceiling. I need a minute to just breathe. And to gather my courage.

With a sigh, I stand up and head for the door, smoothing down my oversized shirt—his shirt—as I go. *You got this, Clara.*

I find Maverick at the kitchen counter, the sleeves of his Henley rolled up to his elbows, his back to me as he works. He's taken over cooking most of the meals, and I can't say that I don't enjoy it. I love our little bubble of domesticity and the way he takes care of me. But it's time I took care of him, too.

For a moment, I just watch him, taking in the way his muscles move as he effortlessly wields the butcher knife.

He alternates between chopping what looks to be spinach and stirring something on the stove—onions and garlic? Whatever it is, it smells delicious.

"Mm, smells amazing in here, my love," I say, walking into the kitchen and stopping directly behind him. I circle my arms around his waist and press a kiss to his spine before resting my cheek against him. I automatically glance toward the sliding door, spotting Juno in the backyard through the half open curtains. I'm not surprised that he's sprawled out in his favorite spot, soaking in the sun.

Maverick sets the knife down as soon as he feels me. His hands find mine on his stomach, and he brings one up to kiss the inside of my wrist. "Hey, sunshine," he says, turning in my arms, and that familiar smile—the one that still makes my heart skip a beat—spreads across his face. "How was your session with Ash?"

"Good. Really good, actually." I run my nose along his chest, then peek behind him. "What are you making?"

"Thought I'd try that pasta recipe you bookmarked last week," he says, wrapping his arms around me and drawing me closer.

"The Marry Me Chicken one?" I ask hopefully. I've never had it before, but when I was looking for different pasta recipes, this one had me at sun-dried tomatoes and heavy cream.

"That's the one," he says, amusement lacing his voice.

"I can't wait." I reach up to kiss his chin, then settle my cheek on his chest.

He places a soft kiss on the top of my head. "What is it, sunshine?"

"I miss you," I whisper, locking my arms even tighter around him.

"I'm right here, baby." His fingers trace the path of my spine. It's soothing, comforting—but I need more.

I lean back just enough to meet his gaze. The urge to hide my face is overwhelming, but I need him to see that I'm serious. That I really do need him. "No, I miss *you*. You haven't really touched me since that day… and *I miss you*."

Maverick gently grips my chin between his thumb and forefinger, his brows knitting together. "I miss you, too, sunshine." He leans forward and brushes his soft lips against mine. "I just… I just don't want to risk hurting you."

"You're not going to hurt me," I say firmly, my hands moving to frame his face. "Mav, look at me. Really look at me."

His warm brown eyes search mine, and I can see the war happening behind them—want battling with worry, need fighting against fear.

"I'm not the same bruised and battered Clara from four weeks ago," I continue, my thumbs brushing across his cheekbone. "I'm healing. My ribs don't hurt anymore, the bruises are gone. I'm stronger than I was before, and that's because of you—the way you take care of me—but you're treating me like I'm fragile. I can't stand it."

He closes his eyes and leans into my touch. "Clara—"

"No, let me finish." I take a deep breath, centering myself before continuing. "I need you to hear me. I need you—all of you. Not just your gentle kisses and innocent touches. I need my Maverick back. I need the man who isn't afraid to love me completely, to *show me* he loves me completely."

When he opens his eyes again, I see something shift. The careful control he's been maintaining wavers.

"I'm scared," he admits, his voice full of emotion. "What if I do something, and it—"

"Then I'll tell you," I interrupt. "I promise you, if anything feels wrong, or if I need you to stop, I'll tell you. One breath at a time, remember? But Mav, I'm not made of glass. And this—" I gesture between us, "—this distance you're keeping? I know you have good intentions, but it's hurting me."

His hands tighten on my waist. "God, sunshine, that's not—I want you so much it physically hurts. But then I remember what *he* did to you, what he almost did to you, and I can't—"

"Hey." I pull his face down enough to press my forehead against his. "That wasn't your fault. We've talked about this —together and with Ash. You know it wasn't your fault. It wasn't mine, either. The fault isn't with us, my love. I need you to believe that."

"I know that up here," he taps his temple, "but in here —" he places my hand over his heart, "—it's not as easy."

I can feel his heart racing beneath my palm. "Then let me convince you," I whisper. "Let me show you that I'm okay. That *we're* okay."

The timer on the stove beeps, but neither of us moves to turn it off. The moment hangs between us, fragile and full of possibility.

"The pasta—" he starts.

"Can wait," I finish, reaching behind him to turn off the burner without breaking eye contact. "This is more important."

He searches my face one more time, and I let him see everything—my frustration, my need, my love, my certainty that I'm ready for this.

"Are you sure?" he asks, the question laced with doubt.

"I've never been more sure of anything in my life," I breathe.

Finally—*finally*—I see his resolve crumble. His hands slide up to cradle my face, and when he kisses me this time, it's different. Deeper. Full of the want he's been holding back.

"I love you," he murmurs against my lips. "I love you so fucking much, sunshine."

"Show me," I whisper back, and I feel him smile against my mouth.

"Are you sure you're ready?" he asks one more time, pulling back just enough to look into my eyes.

"Maverick." I hold his gaze, my voice steady and sure. "I'm ready to feel like myself again. I'm ready to feel like us again."

He nods slowly, and I can see the last of his walls crumble down. "Okay," he breathes. "Okay."

Oh, thank god.

I step out of his hold and walk backwards without breaking eye contact. When I hit the kitchen island, I reach for the hem of my shirt and pull it over my head, letting it fall to the floor. My fingers hook into the waistband of my biker shorts, and I watch Maverick's composure break—his lip caught between his teeth, his hands clenched at his sides. He lets out a groan when I slide my shorts and panties down, stepping out of them and kicking them off to the side.

"What are you waiting for, my love?" I challenge, standing there in nothing but a sports bra. By the time I pull it off and add it to the pile of clothes at my feet, he's right there in front of me, cupping my breasts.

"Fuck." His strong fingers pinch and roll my nipples—the feel of his calloused skin on mine an accelerant to the fire burning within me. When I gasp and arch into him, he traces his lips down my chest, taking a nipple into his mouth. He nips and tugs the sensitive flesh with his teeth before lavishing the sharp bite of pain with his tongue. I thread my fingers through his dark hair, drawing him into me while he lathers the same attention to each breast.

Maverick kisses and licks a path up my neck, tracing my jawline until he reaches my mouth. He claims my lips without hesitation, seeking to conquer and devour me whole. Sliding a hand in my hair, he tightens his grip and guides my head exactly where he wants it, deepening the kiss with the slide of his tongue. It's desperate and all-consuming, composed of weeks of pent-up desire and need.

I moan into his mouth when I feel his hand travel past my navel to the apex of my thighs. I'm so desperate for this man, there's no hiding how wet I am. A guttural groan leaves him when his fingers reach my soaked sex, teasing my clit.

"Maverick, *please,*" I beg.

"You're so wet, baby." He licks the seam of my lower lip until I open for him. The moment his tongue slides into my mouth, he thrusts two fingers into me.

I cry out, hooking a leg around his waist, wanting—needing—more. My hands fall from his hair and reach for his sweatpants, diving inside and wrapping around his thick, hard cock.

He thrusts into my hand, a low groan rumbling from his chest. "God, I fucking missed you, baby," he murmurs into my skin.

"I need you," I breathe, my chest heaving. I bury my face in his neck, grazing my teeth against his skin. "Need you now. Need to feel you inside me."

His fingers curve inside me just right, and I ride his hand, my hips matching his rhythm—seeking, chasing. But just when I'm about to shatter around him, he withdraws, drawing sounds of protest from me.

"Fuck, sunshine. When you come, it's going to be around my cock." He brings his fingers to his mouth and sucks them clean. "I never want to forget what you taste like again," he says, his voice deep and rough.

Maverick reaches behind him and rips off his shirt before shoving his sweatpants down. My body is trembling from being brought so close to orgasm, and I squeeze my thighs together when my gaze lands on his weeping cock, needing more friction.

"You need me, baby?" he asks as he grips the backs of my thighs, hoisting me up and setting me on the kitchen island.

Holding his gaze, I lean back on my hands and spread my thighs. "Show me, Maverick."

He wastes no more time and steps between my legs, locking them around his waist. He lines himself up, grips my hips, and drives forward, pulling me down and entering me in one hard stroke.

"Maverick!" I scream. The force of his thrust pushes me up the counter, but he anchors me to him—his hands tight on my hips.

"Goddamn, sunshine," he groans. "Feel me, baby." He strokes a thumb over my clit, not giving me time to adjust before he slides out and thrusts back in—deeper and harder. "Do you feel how much I fucking want you? How much I fucking need you?"

"Yes!" I cry out, digging my fingers into his shoulders. It's all I can do to hold on as he slams into me, stealing the air from my lungs and overwhelming my body with pleasure. "I feel you—you feel so good."

"Look at me," he commands. "Look at what you do to me." He glances down between us, and I follow his gaze to where he disappears into my body. "You stretch around me so fucking beautifully. Take it, baby."

"Please," I beg. I don't even know what I'm begging for —I just know that I need him. I need him everywhere, in every part of me. I'm on the cusp of an intense orgasm, yet somehow I'm desperate for more. My legs tighten around his hips, urging him deeper.

"I got you, baby." Maverick dips his head and nips my neck, forcing me to arch my back. Picking up his pace, he pistons deeper, lifting my hips and slamming me down with each thrust.

My mouth falls open on a silent scream when my orgasm hits me, waves of pleasure crashing into my body as I come around him.

"Fuck yes," he breathes. "Your pussy's squeezing me so tight. That's it, baby." He drops his head onto my shoulder, groaning long and loud, his thrusts slowing to shallow strokes as he comes inside me.

"I love you so much," I whisper, panting and breathless. I run my hands up his arms and thread my fingers through his hair.

Maverick turns his head just enough to kiss my neck and speak into my skin. "I love you, sunshine. But I'm not done with you yet."

Before I have a chance to respond—before his words even register—he captures my nipple in his mouth, teasing the peak with his tongue and teeth.

My moan turns into a hiss when he withdraws. He pulls me from the counter and situates my body, bending me over. My legs tremble as he lines himself up and thrusts in. I curse, the angle making it seem like he's so much bigger.

"Tilt your ass back, baby." Maverick surges deeper, banding his arm beneath my breasts, bringing my back to his chest. "Just like that." His fingers resume their assault on my clit, pinching and soothing, making the sounds coming out of my mouth ones I don't recognize.

I stand on my toes and push back to meet his thrusts, crying his name. The orgasm blindsides me, building so quickly it makes my vision blur. Maverick groans, hissing as he grinds his cock into me. "God, baby. Fuck, fuck, *fuck.*"

He brings his hand up and settles it on my throat, encouraging me to turn my head so he can seal his mouth to mine. "Jesus, Clara. Is this what you needed?" Each word is punctuated by a deep thrust. "You know I'll always give you what you need."

"Maverick! It's too much." My body is trembling, strung out on the pleasure he's giving me. My legs give out, but he takes my weight, bending me at the waist and driving into me in earnest.

"You can take it, sunshine. I'm going to show you at least one more time just how much I fucking love you."

This. This is what we needed. To come together and feel. To connect. To let go.

CHAPTER 54
CLARA

EMPIRE

"YOU'RE THINKING TOO LOUD," Maverick murmurs, his fingers gently combing through my hair. "What's going on in that beautiful head of yours?"

We've been binge-watching an entire series for the last two days—something Maverick's never done before, nor had the time for. But I've been staring blankly at the TV screen for the last ten minutes, using his thigh as a pillow and listening to the familiar clash of swords and battle cries while my mind drifts elsewhere.

I shift slightly, turning to look up at him. "I keep thinking about calling Rosie."

"The nurse from the hospital?"

"Yeah." I bite my lower lip, that familiar knot of anxiety tightening in my stomach. It's been months since I was discharged from the hospital—since Rosie wrote her number on my discharge paperwork, telling me I looked like I needed someone. "I just… what if it's been too long? I didn't want to call her with everything going on, but now that it's over... What if—"

"Sunshine," he interrupts gently, his thumb tracing circles along my temple. "She gave you her number for a reason. She wanted you to call."

"I know, but..." I trail off, letting out a sigh. Rosie reminded me so much of my mom my heart ached, but it was also a balm to my grief. I miss having someone to call when something good happens—or when everything falls apart.

Maverick must see something in my expression because he leans forward slightly. "But what?"

"What if she asks me questions I don't know how to answer? How do I know what I can tell her? I mean, do I share everything?"

"If you don't know how to answer a question, you tell her that. As far as everything else, that's up to you, sunshine. You've been in the news ever since the second press conference. She's bound to have seen the news story. I don't think she's going to judge you for anything, Clara."

I hum, considering this and rolling it around in my mind. He's right—Rosie had been nothing but kind and patient with me during those awful days in the hospital. Still, the uncertainty gnaws at me.

"Maybe I should wait a little longer," I say, even as I'm sitting up, disturbing Juno, who huffs and waits until I'm settled before he lies back down next to me.

"Or maybe you should just call her now, before you talk yourself out of it completely."

I reach for my phone on the coffee table. As soon as I

grab it, Maverick's hands find my hips and pull me toward him. I let out a nervous laugh as I practically tumble onto his lap, then shift to get comfortable, swinging my legs over his so I'm curled against his side. Juno follows suit, curling into my other side.

"Too far," he whispers, pressing a kiss to the side of my head, his arms wrapping securely around me. "Call her."

My phone feels heavy in my hands as I scroll to Rosie's contact. My finger hovers over her name, my heart beating faster with each passing second.

"I'm nervous," I admit.

"I know," he says softly. "But you've got this. And I'm right here."

Juno huffs as though he's in agreement, reminding me he's right here, too.

Taking a deep breath, I hit the call button and bring the phone to my ear. It rings once, twice—and then Rosie's warm voice fills the line.

"Hello?"

"Rosie?" My voice comes out smaller than I intended, but there's no going back now.

***

"You're sure you don't want to come inside?" I twist in my seat, looking at Maverick's handsome face.

Rosie was nothing short of ecstatic when I called, telling me how she had been hoping I'd call her one day. She tried insisting on driving up to Minneapolis to see me, but I managed to convince her to stay put—that I'd drive to Rochester instead.

The drive felt both endless and too short. Maverick's hand rested on my thigh the entire way, anchoring me against the anticipation and nerves that threatened to overwhelm me.

Now we're idling in her driveway, and I'm stalling.

"I'll wait right here, sunshine," he says, leaning over and pressing a soft kiss to my temple. "Take as long as you need."

"But—"

"Clara." He stops me with a finger to my lips. "*Go.* You need this."

Before I can lose my nerve, I'm walking up the stone pathway to the modest ranch-style house, admiring the bamboo wind chimes hanging from her porch. I raise my hand to knock, but I don't even have the opportunity to hesitate because the front door opens, and there she is. She looks just as I remember with her gray hair thrown in a bun on the top of her head, her deep brown eyes warm and kind.

"Oh, my darling girl," Rosie breathes. Suddenly I'm enveloped in arms that smell like jasmine and home cooking—her embrace feels like the safest place in the world.

"Hi, Rosie," I manage, my voice thick with emotion.

"Come, come inside," she says, pulling back to look at me with tears in her eyes. "Let me see you properly."

She guides me past her living room, which feels warm and inviting, filled with family photos, and into the kitchen. The rich aroma of garlic and tomatoes permeate the space, reminding me of growing up, of cooking with my mom. It makes my heart squeeze with longing, and I inhale deeply to keep the tears at bay.

"Sit, sit!" Rosie gestures to the kitchen table before checking on the food. "I made chicken afritada—you look too skinny. Don't worry, I'll feed you, *anak ko*."

I laugh despite my nerves and wipe away the tears at the easy way Rosie called me her child. Blinking back the moisture, I take in the kitchen and soak in its warmth. It's full of life and everything that is Rosie. My gaze lingers on the rice cooker steaming on the counter, a bowl of ripe mangoes and tropical fruit on the island, and a bamboo broom tucked in the corner—it's so familiar that my chest aches with memories.

Clearing my throat, I move around the table and stand against the kitchen island. "What can I do to help, Rosie?"

"Call me Mama, darling," she answers without looking at me, her voice so sure and warm.

At my stunned silence, Rosie turns away from the stock pot, her small hands on her hips. "You're Filipina—I see it in your eyes, the way you move your hands when you talk —I can always tell. And you have the Filipino nose." She nods as she speaks, her accent thicker than it was at the hospital. She's at home—she's comfortable, she's herself. "We call everyone auntie and uncle, you know—everyone family. And you don't need to be blood to be family, my darling."

As I take in everything she's saying, the dam breaks and the tears flow freely. My shoulders shake, the sobs coming from somewhere deep—a place I've locked away since I convinced myself my mom died.

Through my tears, I look at Rosie's kind face and finally understand why she felt so familiar from the moment we met. She reminds me of my mom, and it hurts, but it's more than that. She doesn't hesitate to take me in, to call me family, to *be* my family—there are no conditions, no judgment, just love.

Rosie clucks her tongue and walks over to me, drawing me into the kind of hug a mother gives her daughter. "I don't need to have pushed you out of my vagina to consider you my daughter—to be your mama, you know, *anak ko.*"

I lean into her, unable to hold back the cackle that erupts from my throat. "Oh my god, you didn't just say that!"

"I did, darling," she says matter-of-factly, though her brown eyes are twinkling with mischief. She pulls back but leaves her hands on my arms. "It's true. Now, you help me by telling that handsome man from the hospital to come inside. Why he waiting out there? Tell him come eat. I cooked too much. As far as I'm concerned, you're my daughter, and he's my son-in-law," she pauses, then shrugs, "well, almost."

"Thank you… Mama." It feels odd—comforting but odd—to call Rosie Mama. It doesn't matter that she and I don't know each other well yet. This is how we are—Filipinos. We take in new family all the time. It's been so long since I've been around my own family that I'd forgotten about it. But Rosie's right. Growing up, I'd call my mom's friends *auntie* or *uncle*—that's how they were introduced to me. It's just what we did.

But Rosie isn't Auntie Rosie. She's Mama, and there's no suppressing the smile on my face.

"Thank me by bringing in your handsome man and eating my food," she replies, essentially pushing me toward the door. "Go, go."

Shaking my head, I hustle to the front door and open it just enough to draw Maverick's attention. I wave him inside, the smile on my face so wide it hurts.

He exits the SUV and strides toward me. "What is it, sunshine?"

Once he's within touching distance, I reach for his hand and pull him inside, interlacing our fingers. "She said you have to come eat."

"Oh. Well, that I can do. Lead the way," he says, brushing his lips across my forehead.

We sit with Rosie—Mama—for three hours, though it feels like a handful of minutes. She tells us about her family: how her husband passed away a decade ago, how they'd always wanted a big family but couldn't have one of their own, so she loved on her nieces and nephews instead. All twenty of them. When I tell her about my family and how I had to walk away from them, she takes my hands and holds my gaze.

"Ay, *anak ko*," Rosie whispers, shaking her head sadly. "Parents who choose judgment over love... They forget what family really means. Your mama may have forgotten how to love you properly, but I won't."

When it's time to leave and she insists on packing

enough food for a week, I don't protest. When she makes me promise to call every Sunday, I don't hesitate. When she hugs Maverick goodbye and whispers something in his ear that makes him blush, I don't ask questions.

Later, as we're driving back to Minneapolis, Maverick's hand finds mine. "You're glowing," he says softly. "You look happy, sunshine."

"I am." I bring his hand to my lips and press a kiss to his knuckles. "I am happy, my love."

My heart is full, and I feel… whole. Not because the pain of losing my birth family is gone, but because I've found that family isn't just blood—it's choice.

CHAPTER 55
MAVERICK
ORDINARY

"CHATSWORTH PD REACHED OUT," Riley starts, swiping through her tablet until she finds whatever she's looking for. "Catherine Bennett's family got closure yesterday. We thought she had no next of kin, so it took longer than expected to find them. They were the last of the families to be notified."

"Good," I nod, leaning back in my chair with a sigh. There will always be a part of me that wishes we caught that bastard before he claimed so many women—the regret of failing them is etched into my bones. But Evans is also the reason Clara is in my life, and I would face it all again if it meant having her where she belongs.

With me.

"The press conference went well, too," Evie adds. "Clean wrap-up. Minneapolis and Rochester PD were there. No loose ends."

Spencer's eyes narrow slightly as he studies my face. He knows me too well. He can probably read the tension in my shoulders, the way I'm not quite meeting anyone's gaze directly.

Today is the first day I've been back at work since the night Evans made his play and lost. I took a leave of absence the next morning and haven't spent a day without being near Clara in two months. The heavy feeling of being away from her now—even if it's only been a couple of hours—solidifies my decision.

I clear my throat, gaining the attention of the team gathered around the conference table in my office. My team. "There's something I need to tell you all," I say, my voice steadier than I feel.

The room goes quiet, all their eyes on me. Arlo even closes his laptop.

"I've put in my resignation."

"What?" Evie breathes.

"No way, boss!" Jesse says at the same time.

Spencer just nods slowly. "I was wondering how long it'd take."

"You knew?" Riley demands, turning to Spencer with wide eyes.

"I suspected," Spencer replies, his knowing gaze still on me. "You're sure about this, Mav?"

I run a hand through my hair and swipe my face, feeling the weight of their stares. "I'm sure," I respond with a dip of my chin. "If I miss it that much, I can always reinstate. Or maybe I'll consult, I don't know. But I need to do this— for me. It's time."

Arlo leans forward, pushing his computer away from him. "We're such a good team," he says, his brows knitting together. When Arlo's comfortable, he's comfortable, and it takes him a while to open up and adjust to changes. "And the work we do—"

"I'm not walking away from the work," I interject gently. "Or from you guys. This team," I say, gesturing around the table, "is what made this decision one of the hardest I've ever had to make. This family we've created," I pause, my throat tight, "I hope it extends beyond the badge."

Riley stands abruptly and rounds the table. Before I can react, she pulls me into a fierce hug. "You better not disappear on us, Rhodes."

"Wouldn't dream of it," I murmur, returning her embrace.

One by one, they each say their piece. Evie makes me promise to invite them to the wedding—a comment that makes my heart race with anticipation. Arlo thanks me for bringing him onto the team, for taking a chance on him. Jesse threatens to hunt me down if I don't stay in touch.

Spencer is the last to approach. "You're doing the right thing, brother," he says quietly, reaching out to squeeze my shoulder.

I reach out and clasp his shoulder in return. "Thank you, brother." Spencer has been my rock, my sounding board, for years. I might not walk beside him with my badge after today, but I have no doubt we'll still walk through life together.

After they file out, I sit alone in my office for a few minutes, taking it all in. Then I pull out my phone and type a quick message to Clara.

Maverick

Looking forward to our date tonight, sunshine.

Clara

I can't wait, my love.

At exactly six o'clock, I pull into our driveway and kill the engine. The sight of home—*our* home—makes something warm unfurl in my chest, knowing she's waiting for me inside. But tonight, I don't use my key. Tonight, I knock.

The door swings open, and the breath leaves my lungs in a rush.

Clara stands before me like a vision—her dark hair falling in soft waves just above her shoulders, her full lips tinted a teasing red that makes me want to kiss the lipstick right off. The dark green wrap dress hugs her curves, the V-neck and tied waist making my fingers itch to reach for that bow and…

"Why'd you knock?" she asks, tilting her head with a smile that lights up her entire face. And damn if I don't live for her smiles. "You live here."

I step closer, my hands finding her hips and drawing her against me. I run my nose along her jaw, breathing in the scent of her.

"It's our first real date, sunshine," I murmur against her skin before pressing a kiss to the corner of her mouth. "I wasn't going to do anything else."

I trail my lips down to her exposed collarbone, letting

out a playful growl that makes her laugh. "But we need to go before I change my mind."

The rooftop Italian restaurant in downtown Minneapolis is exactly what I'd hoped for when I made the reservation—intimate, with string lights casting a warm glow over the tables, and the city skyline stretching out beyond us. We're seated at a corner table, close enough that I can rest my hand on her thigh, feel the warmth of her through the soft fabric of her dress.

"This is perfect," Clara says, twirling chicken fettuccine around her fork. The white wine brought a flush to her cheeks, and she looks radiant in the soft light. *Happy*. She looks happy.

"You're perfect," I reply, earning myself an eye roll and a smile.

We eat and talk about everything and nothing—her latest session with Ash, *my* latest session with Ash, Juno's latest destruction of the backyard, and how Tamara left The Pour House to focus on teaching yoga full time. But underneath it all, I can feel the weight of what I need to tell her, what I need to ask her.

"I resigned from the FBI today," I say as she takes a sip of wine.

Her glass pauses halfway to the table, her forehead creasing, her sweet lips turning down. "What?"

"I put in my resignation," I say again, my voice confident. "I'm done, sunshine."

"Mav..." She sets down her glass and turns to face me fully. "Wow. I wasn't expecting that. What are you going to do?"

I shrug, my fingers tracing circles on her thigh. "I'm not sure yet. But I know I want to enjoy more time with you."

When the tiramisu arrives, I slide it closer to me, ignoring Clara's protests. "Let me feed you."

"I can feed myself," she laughs.

"I know you can, sunshine, but where's the fun in that?" I load the spoon with the perfect bite and hold it out to her. "Open, baby."

She huffs but obliges, her lips closing around the spoon, making me shift in my seat. Fuck, what was I thinking? A bit of mascarpone clings to the corner of her mouth, and I swipe it away with my thumb before bringing it to my own lips.

"Mav," she breathes, her pupils blown.

I lean closer, my hand coming up to cup her jaw. "Sunshine, I've been living in the dark for so long." My thumb strokes across her cheekbone as I hold her gaze. "But you... your fight, your fire, your smile... your love... You're my sunshine. You've shown me what it is to live in the light, and I never want to go back."

Tears gather in her eyes, and I know this is the moment. This is what I resigned for, what I've been building toward since the day she came into my life and changed everything.

"Tell me you'll marry me," I whisper.

For a heartbeat, the world stops. The city noise fades, the string lights blur, and there's only Clara. My Clara—

her sharp intake of breath, the tears spilling over, the way her beautiful face transforms with pure joy.

Then she's throwing her arms around me, kissing me with everything she has. "Yes!" she cries against my lips. "Yes. I can't wait to marry you, my love."

I'm about to deepen the kiss when the sound of applause erupts around us. We break apart, both breathless and laughing, to find Spencer, Riley, Arlo, Evie, and Jesse emerging from behind the rooftop bar, huge grins on their faces. Cruz, Tamara, and Rosie follow close behind, Tamara bouncing on her toes with excitement and Rosie wiping tears from her eyes.

"Congratulations!" They all shout, Riley and Tamara's voices leading the charge, and suddenly we're surrounded by our family—our chosen family—all talking at once, pulling us into hugs, celebrating this moment that feels like the beginning of everything.

Clara turns to me, tears still streaming down her face, her smile brighter than all the lights in the city. "Did you plan this?"

"Spencer and Tamara helped," I admit, pulling her close. "I wanted everyone here. Our family."

She kisses me again, soft and sweet and full of promise. "I love you, Maverick Rhodes."

"I love you, too, sunshine. Forever."

This—Clara, this love, this life we're building together... This is worth everything.

EPILOGUE

CLARA

TWO YEARS LATER - DOWNTOWN MINNEAPOLIS

I BREATHE in the intoxicating aroma of fresh coffee, the creamy sweetness of steamed milk, the rich scent of bourbon and vanilla—and my heart swells with pride and disbelief. After everything we've been through, I'm standing in the middle of my dream made real.

The brass bell chimes as the door to Redemption Coffeehouse & Bar opens. I pause mid-wipe and look up from the espresso machine, spotting Mama—still dressed in scrubs—locking the door behind her. I drop the rag and round the counter, meeting her halfway and wrapping her in a tight embrace.

"Mama! I'm so glad you could make it! Did you get enough sleep?" Mama still works the night shift at the Clinic Hospital, and she has the tendency to stay awake all day if she isn't scheduled to work that evening. I worry about her.

"Pah, I can sleep later," she waves dismissively, though her eyes sparkle with pride as she takes in the coffeehouse. "I'm here for my daughter and son-in-law's grand opening." She squeezes me tight and takes my hand. "Look at this place, *anak ko*. It's beautiful. I'm so proud of you."

My throat tightens at her words. Over the last two years, Rosie has truly become my mama. She's filled the hole in my heart that my birth family left behind—not by replacing what was lost, but by showing me what unconditional love actually looks like. Her love comes freely, without judgment, without the need for me to be anyone other than exactly who I am.

"Thank you, Mama. I love you," I whisper, touching my forehead to hers.

"I love you, my darling," she says, bringing our joined hands to her heart. "Now where is my son-in-law?"

"Right here, Mama," Maverick announces, appearing from the back room like he has some sixth sense about when she needs him. He pulls her into his arms and leans down to kiss her cheek. "Do you want coffee? Or you can rest in the office with Juno until the opening," he suggests, already guiding her across the space toward the back, anticipating her exhaustion.

This man. He's essentially adopted her as his mama, too, and watching the way he takes care of her—the way he loves the people I love—still makes my chest tight with emotion.

"Oh, I want to see Juno. I miss my boy," Mama says, her voice laced with exhaustion but pure adoration. When she took me in, she took in Maverick and Juno, too—without question, without hesitation. Juno's more spoiled than ever now because of her, and I wouldn't have it any other way.

I watch them disappear behind the sliding barn doors marked "Employees Only," then move to stand in the center of the room, letting myself really take in what we've built.

The seating is exactly what I envisioned: single armchairs and loveseats strategically placed near the coffee bar, creating intimate nooks where people can curl up with a book or lean in for quiet conversations. Free-standing bookshelves are tucked between the seating areas, filled with every genre imaginable but heavy on the romance novels—because everyone deserves a happy ending, and I want people to believe in them here. Bar tables of various sizes and chairs fill the rest of the space, all positioned for perfect views of the south wall where the raised platform sits ready for live music and poetry nights, the illuminated Redemption logo glowing behind it like a beacon of hope. It's also the perfect spot for Tamara's weekly yoga classes, transforming from performance space to sanctuary with just a few rolled-out mats.

I take a deep breath, letting the earth-toned palette wrap around me—the rich espresso oak hardwood floors, deep brick walls, the exposed ceiling with dark wood beams, the warm golden glow from the hanging bistro lights creating an atmosphere that feels both sophisticated and welcoming. But it's the dark green accent wall that makes my heart sing—my favorite color stretching the entire length of the space, with the mahogany coffee and bar counter spanning its width. The espresso machines, beer taps, and cocktail station aren't just equipment; they're the physical manifestation of dreams I was once too afraid to speak out loud.

And it's all because of Maverick.

After resigning from the FBI, he threw himself into bringing my dream of owning a boozy coffeehouse to life with the same intensity he once brought to solving cases. While I worked at a local coffee shop—learning every aspect of the business from Margaret, the owner, who took me under her wing—Maverick spent his days here, doing everything from negotiating with contractors to taste-testing drink recipes, determined to turn what I'd once called my "impossible pipe dream" into reality.

It didn't take long to settle on a name. Redemption isn't just about second chances—it's about healing, about the daily choice to keep choosing love. To keep choosing to build something beautiful from the broken pieces of what came before. Redemption is about letting go of the guilt and regret that can burrow so deep they prevent you from finding true happiness.

Maverick is my redemption, and I am his. And in three short hours, Redemption Coffeehouse & Bar will open its doors to anyone seeking a little joy, a little hope, a little proof that beautiful things can grow from the darkest places.

The news crew in the corner wraps up their interview with a customer, the reporter's voice carrying over the ambient noise: "Nearly two and a half years ago, Clara Rhodes survived a harrowing ordeal. She channeled her strength into Redemption Coffeehouse & Bar, a unique space that serves as both morning refuge and evening gathering place..."

I lean against a bar stool, listening as the reporter approaches another patron. Hearing my story reduced to sound bites still sends a flutter of anxiety through my chest, but Maverick's timing is perfect—it always is. He appears behind me, sliding his arm around my waist and anchoring me in the present moment. He leans down to kiss my forehead, his voice soft with emotion. "You did it, sunshine."

"We did it, my love. *We* did it," I correct, tilting my head up to meet my husband's eyes. The love I see there—fierce and steady and absolute—still takes my breath away after all this time. He brushes his lips against mine, then rests his chin on top of my head. Together, we watch our world unfold around us.

The most important people in our lives are easy to spot scattered throughout the space we've created. Spencer, Tamara, and Riley cluster around the bar—Spencer adjusting his tie as he chats with the girls, who look like they're already nursing their second espresso martinis of the afternoon. Evie and Jesse huddle near the stage, comparing notes about the playlist—who knew they were so into music? Arlo has claimed one of the armchairs, examining a romance novel with full-blown curiosity. Cruz and Margaret lean against a table covered with coffee samples, discussing the best way to make a cafecito.

When the initial rush dies down and the news crew packs up their equipment, our chosen family naturally gravitates toward the bar. Spencer raises his coffee mug—black coffee, because he's the responsible one even on celebration days—and declares, "I think a toast is in order."

Maverick's arms tighten around my waist, and I feel that familiar surge of overwhelming gratitude for these people who chose to love us through everything.

Mama appears from the back room, Juno trailing behind her like the devoted shadow he's become, and accepts the drink Jesse holds out to her. She clears her throat and raises her wine glass. "To family," she says, her accented voice thick with emotion, "the kind you choose and the kind that chooses you back."

"To family!" we echo, raising our glasses. My eyes burn with happy tears as I look around at these beautiful faces. I would go through everything all over again to be here, in this moment, with them.

"And you all come over Sunday for dinner," Mama adds —not asks, demands, in that way that makes my heart full. "I'm making lumpia."

"We wouldn't miss it, Mama," I say, leaning back into Maverick's warmth as laughter fills our space.

I spent so many years living in an illusion of safety— thinking I was protected when I was really just hiding. Now I know what real safety feels like: Maverick's arms around me, Mama's unconditional love, our chosen family filling the space we built together.

This is redemption.

This is home.

The end.

ACKNOWLEDGMENTS

Holy shit. I did it. I wrote a book! It's something I've always wanted to do but never thought I could. Quite honestly, if it weren't for the example I wrote for my students during our 100-word horror story unit, I don't think this book would exist. The scene where Clara wakes up buried alive was the very first scene I wrote—it came from that 100-word example. When I brought it to my school librarian for feedback—because I wanted to show my students that even adults get feedback on their writing—she said it would make an amazing prologue. And she was right.

So, thank you, Kathryn Leo, for encouraging me to continue the story. For letting me send you chapters and giving me feedback. You have no idea how much I appreciate you, lady!

Chelsey… Thank you for being my sounding board, for talking through the craziness of my serial killer, for reintroducing me to true crime, for giving me constructive feedback—for everything. From the moment I asked if you'd read the first few chapters, you've been my biggest supporter. I couldn't have written this without you. I owe you so many cups of coffee, it's not even funny. Love you, best friend!

ZaBrina… Thank you so much for taking a chance on me and being my personal assistant! I can't tell you just how thankful I am that we've connected—that I have you in my life! You're amazing, and I adore the ever loving crap out of you.

Liz… I'm so happy we found each other! Thank you for being my critique partner, for talking through ideas with me, and for making *Illusion of Safety* better!

To my beta readers, Punam, Ari, Heather, Chelsey, and ZaBrina: *Illusion of Safety* wouldn't be what it is without your feedback. Thank you for supporting me, for helping me make this book the best it can be, and for taking a chance on a newbie author.

To my therapist, Shannon: Thank you for showing me that there is no one way to handle grief. Thank you for encouraging me to use this book—to use Clara—as an outlet, a way to process my emotions. It's been a long journey, and I'm so grateful for you. You're never getting rid of me, #sorrynotsorry.

To my husband: Thank you for putting up with me, for ignoring the fact that I spent hours on the couch typing on my laptop while the laundry piled up and the house was a mess. Okay, all that was happening before I started writing, but still. I love you, husband.

To Tun and J, my father-in-law and stepmother-in-law: Thank you for loving my kids and me unconditionally. Your love is the kind that is eternal and comes with no strings attached. When I think of family, I think of you. I love you both so much.

To my children: You can't read this book, and I don't even want you reading it when you're older, but I hope you know how much I love you. The world can throw whatever it wants at us, and I will always choose you.

PLAYLIST

Each chapter is titled after a song that felt right.

Listen on Spotify

EXTRAS

Visit kingrahamauthor.com for extras:

- Mood boards
- Character art
- Graphics (e.g., victim timelines)
- Recipes (e.g, Filipino chicken adobo)

ABOUT THE AUTHOR

K. Ingraham lives in the Midwest with her husband and three kids. She writes tension-filled, slow burn romantic suspense stories meant to keep you on the edge of your seat. She's a voracious reader, so when she's not writing, she's reading—most likely with a cup of black coffee and her heated blanket!